THE BOOK of LETTERS

To Jasmine Straw,

Enjoy this story of survival and self discovery while following this tale of adventure. May it bring you hours of fun and enjoyment.

MICHAEL SCOTT

Copyright © 2021 Michael Scott
All rights reserved
First Edition

PAGE PUBLISHING, INC.
Conneaut Lake, PA

First originally published by Page Publishing 2021

ISBN 978-1-6624-5248-2 (pbk)
ISBN 978-1-6624-5249-9 (digital)

Printed in the United States of America

To Rick Hanson, for his years of unwavering friendship and encouragement. Also, to my daughter Samantha White for her love and her personality, from which Alice was created.

CHAPTER 1

Never before has so few written words screamed so loudly or so catastrophically changed one's future. I stood there staring at the line that formed the sentence of my fate, as if to confirm its existence or the possibility of some horrible, elaborate joke. It only took a glance at my mother to tell me it was real, and I quickly sat down, my body suddenly feeling numb as my mind raced with questions that my mouth couldn't seem to protest or assemble. Mom quietly sat next to me. I could see tears and anxiety texturing her face as she waiting for my shock to pass. I looked back to the words—what had once been a childhood game, now prophesized a coming horror.

The only word that stumbled out of my mouth was "How?" Mom got up, wiped her tears, and then pulled me up from the chair. She held me tightly in her arms for a few moments, then whispered in my ear, "Let's go for a walk, and I'll tell you everything."

A walk. My mind was whirling, and that was the last thing I wanted "But what I need is—"

Mom quickly stopped me and put her finger to her lips then pointed across the room; I saw what she indicated and knew my life would never be the same after tonight. In the corner of the room, mounted on the wall, just like every building and home, was a SOROS (Social Operations Request Options System). It was there to help us in times of emergencies: for news updates, answers, movies, music, travel passes, and permits. It was there for our benefit, but now with a new clarity, I perceived the true danger of its attentive parasitic ear. The prickle of fear ran across my skin. I had heard the rumors, but till now I had only thought of them as urban folklore to scare kids. Now I wondered. The weight of my apocryphal world was crushing in around me, the small room suddenly seemed suffocating and I felt the overwhelming need for the open air.

We grabbed our coats and headed out into the brisk October night; outside of our building the cold air flooded into my desperate lungs and helped to clear my panic-fogged head a bit. After a few minutes to regain myself and to get past my initial shock, I braced myself with apprehension as I waited for answers that I was beginning to dread. In silence, I followed beside Mom as we walked several foreboding blocks; the streets were nearly abandoned of their usual patronage as most sought warmth from the night cold. The glow of the city lights that once seemed bright no longer held their charm for me, but now it gave me the illusion of a thousand prying eyes staring into the dark. All of them ready and willing to report what I had yet to understand, all because of labels place by the blind face of power.

Could they see my plight, or were they already gathering for the theft of a life that lay ahead? I felt the climbing tide of fear rising again and fought it down; panic wasn't going to help right now. Mom, silent as a crypt, continued to pull my arm forward as she walked beside me, her eyes constantly scanning the area around us like a trapped animal searching for a way out. Aged brick walls reverberated the clicking of our heels on the hard pavement, in my current state, sounding like a drum roll calling for the hangman. Questions began to pour through my mind in rapid-fire motion, each one bringing with it a score of others and building with a crescendo effect.

I pulled back on my arm and in hushed tones snapped, "Mom, enough! My patience is at an end, and I need answers to the bomb you dropped on me back there!"

Mom's back went stiff. When we stopped she looked at me; her eyes I will never forget. They were not the eyes of a woman with a story to tell, but of a terrified mother hiding a secret nightmare that she hoped would never come, yet come it did.

"You're right, honey, and I'm sorry for having to burden you with so much so soon," she finally said softly, and then she scanned

THE BOOK OF LETTERS

the area around us again. Tonight, she looked older and her troubled eyes haunting, in the dim overhead halo of light. Please, let's keep walking as I tell you of how you came into my life and who your mother was."

Seeing my astonishment and confusion at her statement, she took my arm, cleared her throat, and then hesitantly began her tale as we started once more on our late-night journey for answers from the past. I watched loose strands of Mom's auburn hair dance as the breeze tugged at them and her forehead furrow as she recalled some painful memory, causing her to once more go silent. As I waited, we pushed on into the night's growing frigidity, while around us North Portland's skyline etched into the dark horizon with its prodigious arrays of lights splayed as far as you could see. Their normal gaiety was lost to me among my mood of intensifying clouds of paranoia and fear of pending imminent prospects. How far do the eyes of an unseen enemy reach, and who do you trust when compliance brings reward? Mom's soft voice began again, and in hushed tones, she slowly continued on with the account of my abstruse beginnings. The illusion of my fabricated life was destroyed as the details unfolded, only to be replaced with trepidation at the possibility of a daunting new reality, my reality.

Mom, Mary, was in her early twenties when she was given her assignment at the hospital. Her test scores had landed her a nice nursing position complete with advanced training and private housing. It was the opportunity she had worked so hard for, and within a few years, she rose in the ranks to wing charge nurse and earned herself a level of job security at OHSU, now a government-ran university hospital. The same year as her promotion, two other events also took place: she was first granted a child permit, and second, she was approached by Dr. Moipan. He was a young doctor with big ideas who needed an assistant to, as he put it, "help a few folks out."

These folks turned out to be people that, for one reason or another, were stripped of their citizens' rights and health care. Now they were considered invisible and outside the system. When a government gives free health care, it's those in seats of power who control and decide who gets what, and who goes without. The number of people was alarming, but nevertheless it was a problem that the government chose to ignore or view as an urban cleansing. Sickness ran rampant among these forgotten masses, and death, always taking more than it should. Their volunteered help was illegal, but moral convictions drove them to continue their work, so as government resistance grew, they went underground giving treatments in secret and hidden places. It was dangerous, both Mom and Moipan knew that, but they felt that the needs of the many outweighed the potential cost of the few.

Mom slowed our progression, her eyes lost in a past memory, and her breath hanging like ragged clouds in the bite of the night. I could see the strain and pain these phantoms of the past brought to her; it was all a part of her life that had been hidden and I never suspected. Dry fall leaves swirled down the road ahead of us, dancing on the breeze as it carried them along. After a few moments she squeezed my arm, and we continued our strange stroll down through the enigma of her concealed life.

Mom's voice wavered, then gained strength, and went on: "I met your birth mother—Elisabeth or Liz, to those who knew her—one night in a basement where we had set up our clinic. She was as pregnant as I was." Mom grinned as she savored the memory of those days. "Liz was six months along when her child permit was revoked with no explanation. Without the permit, she was denied health care unless she chose to terminate the now illegal pregnancy. Having nowhere else to turn to, she found us, guided by word on the street. She was just a few years younger than me and full of determination to see you come into the world. Liz always had a smile or kind word to those around her. It didn't take long for us to become close friends. We both grew rounder day by day, often giggling at each other's duck waddles and body discomforts as our due dates drew closer."

Mom's voice became strained and tainted with anger. "The problems began when security patrols started intensifying their search for underground clinics and their methods of cracking down hard. Specially trained patrols were sent in to hunt us down and take their revenge out on anyone involved. Some of my friends were caught and taken in the raids. We never learned whether they had been arrested, deported, or killed, they just simply vanished. Dr. Moipan told me to take time off for my safety, being so close to my due date, and then temporarily took on a new assistant to help in my absence."

During the high point of the turmoil and raids, Mom was at home enjoying her time off from the clinic to focus and prepare for the birth of her daughter, whom she decided to name Alice. Two weeks later, the delivery day came, and she was rushed to the hospital. Moipan was the attending doctor on staff when she arrived, and with his assistance, a healthy and beautiful girl was brought into the world. Two days later, Mom and baby Alice headed home to start their new life together. She had barely gotten home with her new daughter when she heard a frantic knocking at the door—it was Liz.

Tears were starting to flow, but Mom was determined to get it all out. "When I opened the door I found Liz standing there, crying as blood soaked the lower parts of her dress. Not knowing what else to do, I quickly called Dr. Moipan and set a meeting point, then wrapped Liz in a long coat and Alice in a blanket then headed out. By the time we got there, Liz had lost a lot of blood and was in bad shape. I was scared for us all. We must have been followed or reported. Either way, they somehow knew where to find us."

Mom couldn't go on; she stood there silently weeping, as the horror of that moment overwhelmed her. I held her and felt her convulse with sobs, as my heart broke for her and the pain she had privately bore all these years. What had happened that brought such unhealed grief to her even after all this time? Slowly the rest of that moment came out in tortured bits and pieces; it wasn't a narrative I wanted to hear.

The parts I could make out between her sobs told the story of a nightmare; only this was worse because it wasn't one you woke up from but lived each day with. Dr. Moipan had met up with Liz, Mom, and Alice, in the back room of an abandoned butcher shop. Mom had been forced to bring Alice despite the danger; there just hadn't been time to get a sitter for her in their race to save Liz. As Alice slept near the door, Mom assisted the doctor with the birth of Liz's daughter. Afterward while Dr. Moipan was working hard to stop the bleeding, the world was split by an explosion. Security

MICHAEL SCOTT

patrols had found them and breached the door with some kind of bomb; for some reason, it didn't go as planned. The oversized blast obliterated the door, sending wood and metal shrapnel in all directions, fire sprouting up among the carnage. Two of their own officers were killed in the discharge, as well as Liz and baby Alice. It was only because they had been shielded by the counter they had used as an operating table that Mom, Moipan, and Liz's baby were spared. During the ensuing chaos, Moipan grabbed me up, while Mom in a state of shock attempted to extract what remains she could find of her precious Alice. Being closest to the door, she had sustained the most damage from detonation. It was Dr. Moipan that tore Mom from her fruitless search through the rising flames of burning rubble. Escaping out a window they fled into the maze of old warehouses, and behind them fire engulfed the building, consuming everything at the scene. What little Mom found of Alice was buried secretly in the dark of night, and then with the help of a veterinarian, Dr. Moipan, and a grieving Mary, I was assimilated into Alice.

As I grew, Dr. Moipan became my pediatrician, and with his help certain medical information was altered, allowing me to occupy Alice's place and with it all the benefits of being a legal. As a legal, I got free education, medical, training, and assignment, but at eighteen I was required to take government placement testing, which also included complete adult physical and blood tests. Dr. Moipan, as a pediatrician, couldn't save me from these tests, and once I was found out it would all be over. Mom paused in her narration of the account, giving me some time to try and absorb the details as well as their significance.

I knew what happened to illegals as did everyone—they were wards of the government who deemed them criminals, as such they were sent to work farms and prisons, or worse. It all depended on which stories you heard or were willing to believe. Either way, it always sounded like hell on earth. This was the future I could expect if something didn't happen soon; my eighteenth birthday was in two weeks. It wasn't much time to change a world that was desirous to punish you for simply being alive or escape it, but it was all the time I had to do the impossible...whatever that might be.

We walked a while in silence like two shadows passing along as lonely specters. I could tell that Mom was emotionally exhausted from recalling the memories she had put away so long ago. Neither of us knew what to say in that moment, lost in our own thoughts as we were. As the concrete passed under our feet, my mind was busy processing all I had been told. In sharp focus was the fact that my life was now on a one-way track to oblivion. All my hopes, plans, and dreams accumulated thus far now died and fell away, like nothing more than leaves drifting with the wind.

Mom turned to me. "Alice, I know this has got to be hard on you or even unbelievable, but it is something that I have tried desperately to protect you from. When you're ready, I have some things from Liz that I have been saving for you. There is even a letter that Liz wrote you just in case she didn't survive the delivery. She also told me of a case that she had hidden. When the patrols were done searching her place, I went in found where she had concealed it in one of the walls of her apartment. It seemed really important to her that you got it. She even called it a tool for salvation. I never understood what she meant by that, but when we get back, if you want, I'll get them for you. It was the last promise I ever made to her."

"Mom, why did you wait so long to tell me?" It was a question that kept nagging at me.

"I was hoping things would change before you ever needed to know, and Liz wanted me to wait till it was safe before I told you about your birth." Mom looked so tired; this was taking a toll on her. "I've tried so many ways to persuade those in power to change the system, but power is a hungry animal that only takes and never gives back. Please don't be mad. I was just trying to protect you the best way I could…better than I did for…"

Her voice trailed off, but I knew she was thinking of her baby, whose name I now carried, and my heart ached for her. She had hidden so much pain over the years just to protect me. How could I fault her for waiting to expose me to this tale of horror? I had no words to say as my heart wept for us both. I pulled her into my arms and looked into her reddened eyes. "I love you, Mom. Always have, and always will."

We hugged each other tight and she softly replied, "Love you, Alice. Always have, and always will."

As I released her, I felt the brush of a warm tear on my cold cheek, but I'll never know if it was hers or mine.

Turning the corner, we headed back toward home; the world for me had now become alien and hostile. The gravity of the situation gripped my mind, while I sought for any possible solutions. What to do, how, why, these unanswered questions clung to me like chains holding me bound. There were so many details I needed to understand and so many blank spots that I wanted to fill in.

"What did Liz look like?" I asked. It seemed a strange question. After all, I didn't even know she existed till tonight.

"You look just like her." Mom glanced at me and smiled. "Sometimes I see her in the things you do, like the way you laugh and are quick with a smile as well as in your strength. She was a great friend, and even though we didn't know each other that long, I still miss her every day."

The last few blocks home were filled with Mom's memories of Liz and her stories of her grandfather and his crazy inventions. He had lived somewhere in the hills of Central Oregon till the government declared everything east of the mountain a nuclear waste zone and forced the people out. We had all learned in school about the war and the bomb that had left the east side of the state a dead zone. Now nothing lived in the radioactive wasteland. Apparently, my great-grandfather disagreed, calling it all a hoax. And within a few days of arriving in Portland, he disappeared, presumably to head back into the toxic environment. Liz said she knew that he went back to his hills, but he was never heard from again. After years passed with no word, she assumed he had died. Then a mysterious case showed up, on the precise day of her fifteenth birthday.

The gloomy exterior of our building came into view, and Mom stopped. She then gave a quick glance to check the area. In low tones, she said, "There is a plan in motion to save you and many others, but I will tell you more about that later. Right now, you have to remember one important thing—when we go in, you have to watch what you say. The wrong word or outburst and we'll be flagged for observation, and that's the last thing we need right now. We can take plenty of walks, and we'll figure it all out together, or we can play the game when we're home. Think you can do this, honey? It's imperative that no one suspects anything, or it's all over for both of us."

I could feel her tensely waiting for my answer; we were both ensnared in this strange drama. I knew it would take work from us both, to survive this, or have any hopes of escape. If we were found out, I would become another unwanted illegal, and Mom would be sent to prison for not reporting me. No one could know! My mouth replied yes to her while my mind screamed, *Do I have a choice?*

Mom looked into my eyes. "Alice, I know right now you're scared, confused, and upset but you can do this. You were raised to be strong, smart, and tough enough to get through this! I know the woman you are becoming, and she is smart, good, and caring. Don't let the evil of this world take that from you! Rise above it, be better than it wants you to be. Get your revenge by surviving, by becoming great where your protagonists fail."

I wish I felt as confident as she did, but fear of an unknown tomorrow hung over me like an overburdened cloud. The knowledge of dark days ahead overshadowed us as we walked reluctantly the last block home. Our home, which was once a place of comfort and security, now left me with a large degree of uncertainty and feelings of vulnerability.

CHAPTER 2

I numbly stood there in the entry of our apartment, my coat feeling impossibly heavy. The warmth of the apartment felt thick in my lungs as it prickled the chill of my face. Home gave me a sense of solitude from the prying eyes of the city but left me conscious of the ever-listening ear that lived in the corner, missing nothing uttered.

Mom said, "Take your coat off, honey, and I'll be right back in a few minutes with some tea to warm up." She then stripped her wraps off and headed into the kitchen. Soon the clinking of cups and teapot sounding out as she worked.

I took my coat off and dropped it, at the moment not caring that it landed on the floor. Flopping down on our worn couch in my usual spot, I used my hands to rub my throbbing head. There was so much to take in, and every time I thought I had a grip on things, the hole just got deeper. It was like a crashing wave that nearly drowns you with panic. I felt sick. Mom's confessions of the night played over and over in my head, and I fought to accept all of it as true; it just all seemed so surreal. My brain felt overworked; there was just so much to figure out if we were going to survive this.

The shrill whistle of the teapot in the background pulled me from my dark thoughts, and in a few moments, Mom appeared with a tray, tea, and even some cookies that she had saved back for special occasions. She must have seen my raised eyebrow at the sight of the cookies because it triggered a response as she seated herself on the couch next to me.

"No time like the present to enjoy the little things in life," she said and, with that, bit into one of the cookies then rolled her eyes in exaggerated delight. Inspired I followed suit and smacked loudly as I ate mine, and it wasn't long before we were both giggling despite ourselves.

I remembered reading somewhere that laughter works as a great medicine; all I knew was that its effects certainly helped our strained nerves that night. After a few more of the cookies, Mom put her finger to her lips, then pointed to the tray and grinned. There on the tray lay the thing that started it all that night, a simple supple string, one that held many memories for me. When I was a young girl, she had taught me the game as she had learned it from her mother, and I remembered the hours of fun we had playing it. Now things were different.

The rules were simple. Once silence was called, you had to ask and answer questions using just the string, and for incentive you got points for right answers and for creative use. I learned to communicate with the game using initials, symbols, simple drawings, or words written in what Mom called cursive. The events of tonight had changed all that. Now it was no longer a simple childhood game, but way to beat this oppressive system and its preying ear. Talking with the string left no evidence of the message when pulled, and while making conversations slow, it also made them untraceable.

I was reaching for the string when I saw Mom pull an old crumpled envelope from her pocket; she handed it to me then used the string to write the word *Read*. When I looked at the name on the worn yellowed surface, I saw that it was addressed to *My Dearest Butterfly*. Realization came as I thought back to every birthday I could remember; each year she had given me a butterfly. Now I knew why. She had done her best to keep Liz in my life without me even knowing, and I admired her for that. It felt odd holding a letter written to me before I was borne by someone I had never met.

"SOROS, play some light jazz." Mom glanced at me and got a nod of approval, then getting up, she added, "I need to get something from my room. You good?"

MICHAEL SCOTT

She watched me till I again nodded, not knowing what to say, then she headed off to her bedroom. In the background music started playing, creating a mellow ambiance in the room, while I closed my eyes for a moment, preparing myself for whatever else I may learn in the next few minutes. After a couple calming breaths, I turned my attention back to the envelope. It had waited so many years to be opened by a girl who would never know the hand that had written to her so long ago. Looking at it again, I saw that signed below *Butterfly* was *Your Mother Elisabeth*. It was the only name she ever used, Mom had told me, and it was her way of trying to protect her parents from her actions. If she had been caught at the clinic or with a child, her parents would have been sent for reeducation while Liz went to prison. Mom wasn't even sure if Elizabeth was even her real name, and in the end, it didn't matter. My hands trembled as I carefully tore open one end of the envelope and shook out a necklace, key, and letter. The glint of shiny metal caught my eye, but my hand followed my heart and picked up the letter. I could feel my pulse quicken as I delicately unfolded its pages and began to expose its long-held secrets.

> Hello Butterfly,
>   Seems funny writing this to you when I can still feel you moving in me and you'll soon join me in this world. However the doctor doesn't seem to think I'm going to be able to make this journey with you, so I'm writing this letter is just in case he's right. It's been such a long time now, that I have dreamt of holding you in my arms and of watching you grow. Even though we have never met face to face, I love you with all my heart. I feel you, I know you, you are my precious little butterfly. I'm so tired and the doctor says I don't have much time if you're going to come into the world but there are things I need to tell you.
>   First, if something does happen to me I have put your care in the hands of my dear friend

THE BOOK OF LETTERS

Mary. I know she will do the best she can for you under the circumstances, and I am truly sorry for the life I have left you. I did the best I could and hopefully in time, when you're ready, Mary will tell you all about me.

Second, is that I don't have much in this world but hopefully you'll get this letter, my necklace, and a case containing a few items including my most prized treasure, a book of letters written by your great-grandfather. The case is more than it seems and so are its contents, the book of letters will explain it all. Just know that everything has a secret and a purpose to it, and each one useful. Look at it all as a possible avenue should life not go as planned, in it you'll find everything needed for the journey ahead. Read the book of letters, he wrote them hoping to help educate me as well as give guidance and possible direction to others.

I wish there was more, follow the necklace and it will lead you in the right direction, toward a safe place you can call home. It is time and I must say goodbye for now, hopefully I will see you soon. I remember your great-grandfather used to tell me, when all hope is lost faith will carry us on. If things go bad, I want you to always remember that and hold on to it. I love you, and I want you to be braver than me. Have faith in something that is true, be strong enough of mind and will to always stand for what is right. Be happy, be free, and know love, real love. These are dark times but somehow, in my heart I know; you will survive and rise above them all.

Love forever, wherever that
may be, your mother,
Elisabeth

I read the letter several times; the words were like echoes of a past I never knew and one I didn't understand. The necklace from the letter lay in my lap, and I picked it up by its gold chain. The small amulet that hung from it was beautiful, and on close inspection, I discovered that the circle in the center was actually a compass. I grinned with sudden understanding as I thought back to the words from the letter: *it will guide you in the right direction.* There were engravings along two sides of it but they were worn and my tired eyes couldn't make them out, I'd have to come back to them later. I put the necklace on in some childlike hope that there might still be some lingering trace of my birth mom's essence or some feeling of connection.

Mom returned with a case in her arms. She smiled when she saw the necklace around my neck and simply said, "Been a long time since I saw that. Do you think you're ready for this as well?"

I numbly nodded and she placed the strangely oblong case on the couch next to me. I ran my hands over its faded fabric cover and wondered what mysteries or treasures it might contain. With the string, I silently asked, *"Do you know what's in it?"*

"Just old stories" was Mom's reply as she swirled the string.

I picked up the key from the letter, and I braced myself for whatever else might be hurtled at me tonight. There's only so much a girl can take at one time, and I was at my limit. The lock was old and untended, making it reluctant to give up its job easily, but give up it finally did. The rusted hinges screeched as it started to open, reminding me of some coffin in an old horror film, and it made the hairs on my arms stand with goose bumps.

"Volume up to thirty-five," I called out, the music rose, and then carefully I finished lifting the case lid. It was a wailing guitar from some golden oldies song out of the 2020s that helped mask the last shrill protest of the hinges. The case seemed unusually long but, other than that, normal. The eccentric collection of items inside, however, was the real surprise. In the middle of its interior was the first thing you noticed—a beautiful instrument but one I had never seen before. I gave Mom a questioning look to which she smiled, then called out to SOROS, "Play mountain dulcimer music."

THE BOOK OF LETTERS

Soon the sounds of bluegrass and tones of a dulcimer filled the room, I liked it. With the sounds of mountain music wafting through the room, we continued our search through the assortment of things in the case. Alongside the dulcimer was one of the biggest books I had ever seen, not that I had actually seen that many. Its cover was handmade and the binding hand stitched, and I knew at once that it must be the book of letters Liz had mentioned in her letter. These days you rarely saw books at all since everything was done via e-files, touch-screen pads, and text messages. Here paper was rationed and expensive, but this paper had a strange unpressed feeling to it, making me wonder if it hadn't been homemade as well. Besides the book and dulcimer we also found a large, wide-mouthed thermos, a hat, an old history book, and a bag of odds and ends that also held two large rattraps.

What an odd assortment of things to inherit from people you never met. The contents were so eclectic, it made me wonder what Liz and my great-grandfather had really been like. Would they have liked who I am? It was a question that I would never know the answer to. As I looked at the odd collection, I remembered Liz saying it was all more than what it appeared to be. She also said that the book would explain it all, so that was where I decided to start.

CHAPTER 3

The book of letters was just that—the letters covered an amazingly wide variety of subjects. From the dates on the pages, it was clear that they had been written over several years and even had complete sketches, how-to pages, maps, and sets of hand-drawn plans. The letters were even divided into sections and listed under such titles as biology, basic electronics, power-generating plants, engineering, trapping, emergence medical treatments, veterinarian notes, principles of survival, chemical components, $E=MC^2$, camouflage, mountain wisdom, logistics of war and peace, talking to animals, and psychology of society—on and on, the myriad of titles went. It was literally a library of condensed information in a somewhat chaotic fashion, with some of the pages even having nearly imperceptible writing that ran around the borders and filled the empty spaces.

Mom and I thumbed through the book, sipping our tea, while the faint sounds of a mountain dulcimer continued to play in the background. It seemed fitting. As my fingers turned the pages, I tried to absorb some of what I was reading, but the cornucopia of information was too much for my weary mind. This book was going to take more time and energy than I had left tonight, so I placed it back into the case and picked up the dulcimer.

It was a simple instrument that had been elegantly designed; its sides were gracefully curved, making the bottom almost twice as wide as its narrow top. The fingerboard was inlayed with different types of wood but was also fretless. There were worn spots on the fingerboard as evidence of having been played a lot as some point in

THE BOOK OF LETTERS

its past. I wondered if it had been Liz's fingers and my hand traced over the worn marks. The patina on the body showed its age as well as the beautifully figured wood. My eyes blurred, and I knew fatigue was setting in hard. What I needed now was sleep, as well as time to process the events of tonight. Everything was placed back into the case; I would look at it all again tomorrow with fresh eyes. As I closed the lid to the case, I spotted the hat, and it called to me. Lifting the lid again, I pulled it out, then as Mom watched I got up and tried the antiquated fedora on.

"Looks good on you, honey," Mom said in observation.

Looking in the mirror, I wondered if Liz had ever worn the hat. There just seemed to be something about it, something that just felt right. As I stood looking at myself, I wondered if the refection looking back was truly what Liz had looked like at seventeen. I decided to keep the hat where it was and locked the case, then I turned my thoughts to bed and sleeping away this bad dream. Was there any slight hope that tomorrow I would wake up from all this? The answer was doubtful at best. Tonight had been filled with insanity, but tomorrow would be a new day with new hopes.

"Get some sleep, honey," Mom said with a hug. "We both have a free day tomorrow, so sleep in and get up late. Then when you're up I'll fix a big breakfast for us."

I felt done in, so I nodded in agreement and headed for my room while Mom had SOROS shut down the music and set alarms. Tired though I was, sleep didn't come easily. My head was still full of unanswered questions. I restlessly stared into the dark and pondered if I would be able to sleep, yet slumber did finally come, and fitfully. The morning sunshine that leaked through my bedroom window woke me, proving once again that morning always comes, no matter how hard you may wish them away. From the vantage point of my pillow, I watched the gray facades of apartment buildings becoming clearer with the rising light. It was a sight that once brought the sense of home, of family, and of neighbors, but now it brought dread and fear because of last night's revelations. It was simply because people didn't know that, in reality, I was actually an illegal, that they accepted me. However, if those same people knew the truth, I would have been reported and sent off to whatever fate the government had in store for me. I rubbed my head, trying to push the thought aside and sat up, my muscles aching from tossing and turning throughout the night, but the smell of pancakes encouraged me.

The cold floor sent my feet into a quick search for my slippers, then finding them, I slipped them on and braced for whatever the day might hold. The brush passed through my dark, shoulder-length hair, catching from time to time on the tangles I had gained from tossing in the night. As I brushed them out, my thoughts continued to rehash last night's bombshell and consider its myriad of consequences. In the mirror I looked at the frightened girl looking back at me; it wasn't a sight that built any confidence. Mom had said I looked just like my birth mother but never said in what ways. As I stood there gazing at my reflection, I wondered if she ever looked as scared and unsure as the girl before me. When all hope is lost faith will carry you on, her letter had said, and I pondered the one question it brought to my mind. What are you going to have faith in, Alice? I asked the figure before me. Right now, for me there was only one answer I could come up with, my mom.

"Breath deep, Alice, you got this," I said as I turned from the mirror. My voice didn't sound very convincing.

Mom's back was to me when I entered the kitchen. Unseen, I stood there watching her as she hummed and swayed to an old hit song that SOROS was playing. Her auburn hair bounced as she danced and flipped pancakes in rhythm to the music. I felt as if I were seeing her for the first time, knowing some of her past helped to revel the real her. She had held so many secrets for so long, and I marveled how I had missed it all. The strength it must have took to do what she did for me, while she privately grieved for a baby she loved but who could never be acknowledged, was unimaginable. I pondered how many other surprises Mom had in the untold layers of her life, then my thoughts were interrupted as Mom caught me watching her, and her face broke out into one of her heartwarming smiles.

"Good morning sleepyhead," she said as she kissed my forehead and pointed me toward the table. I sat down on one of the chairs and felt the warmth of the kitchen almost lulling me back to sleep. It was only the smell of fresh cakes and a grumbling stomach that kept me awake.

"Bet you're hungry this morning," Mom said as she placed a large stack of pancakes on the table in front of me. "Did you sleep well?"

I nodded as I filled my plate with pancakes and added dollop of peach jam, no butter. Butter was so rationed that it was out of most people's price range, but the substitute that was sold was so tasteless and bland we never used it. Mom and I sat there quietly eating, our minds lost in our own thoughts and questions. After breakfast, we lingered over our tea, relaxing before facing the day and what it may bring.

"I wonder what the weather will be like today," Mom suddenly said over her cup.

I looked up at Mom and wondered what she was contemplating, then a moment later from the corner, SOROS replied.

"Today's weather, fair, with a temperature of sixty-two and winds south by southwest at five miles per hour. Chance of precipitation is 20 percent with occasional clouds."

"Why don't we go for a picnic?" Mom asked. "It's probably our last chance to enjoy one more before it gets too cold. We could go to Washington Park."

Washington Park wasn't too far outside of our usual allotted routes, so I knew permits wouldn't be too hard to get even if it did take a while. I could tell from her countenance that she was thinking of more than just a picnic, but she didn't say what it was. I knew it would give us a chance to talk more, so I agreed and we set ourselves to getting ready. Taking our phones into the living room, I placed them on the data-transfer pad next to SOROS. It was a safer method of getting the permits than trusting an open Wi-Fi signal and the hackers that plagued them.

"SOROS, two travel passes and permits for the residents of this apartment, place Washington Park, purpose picnic." After placing the order, I knew it would take some time before we got a reply. It always took time when you deviated from your standard assigned routes. While the order was being processed, I went to dress for the day. As I looked through my closet, I wondered, what do you wear when you're making plans to save your own life?

Tossing aside one outfit after another, it became clear to me that you could never tell what adventures this rabbit trail could lead to, so I stuck to jeans and a pullover shirt, then added a sweater just in case. Picking the necklace up from off the nightstand, I put it again around my neck. The gold was cold to my skin as I felt the amulet settle into place. Somehow, it just felt right, and I knew in that moment I would always wear it. Wearing the necklace was the closest I would ever get to know the feel of my birth mother's embrace. I wondered what kind of a life Liz would have had if she aborted me, and did she regret her decision? It was hard to imagine the sacrifice she made just so I could live, and the love she must have had for me to sacrifice so much. My breath caught as thoughts of Liz and her determination to save me overwhelmed my heart. Tears began to flow as I felt a cascade of love; I was so wanted that not one but two women have given their all that I might have a chance in this life. I made up my mind right then that somehow, someway, I was going to survive this; I would be worth the cost they had paid.

The case drew my attention, and I remembered Liz's comments about how it was all more than it seemed, but what did it mean? It was for a journey or salvation, should things not go as planned, and it was all so cryptic and confusing. I wiped my tears and inspected the case's elongated shape, and while odd, it showed no signs of being anything special. Even the collection of things contained in it showed no evidence of being more than what they appeared to be. What was I missing? What more could there be? The book of letter was supposed to hold all the answers, so while Mom was busy in the kitchen with packing a lunch, I opened the case and pulled out the book. I knew we had time to kill while we waited for SOROS to issue our permits and passes anyway, so I relaxed and kicked back on my bed as I began to delve into the book of letters and its secrets.

With the book on my lap, I randomly turned its yellowed pages, taking time to read bits of the ancient letters here and there. The

THE BOOK OF LETTERS

snippets that I read were small, yet they were starting to give me more of an idea of what my great-grandfather had been like.

March 15

Today I got more done on my generator plant, the main parts were from the old Chevy but with the gasifier in place I should soon have more electricity than I could ever use. I'll try to send you better drawings soon, along with the Savonius wind mill that I was working on last time I wrote.

July 3

Found more Oregon grape today, marked the spot with a tall stack of stones so I can find it this winter. It makes a great medicine as an antibiotic so I always keep an eye out for it.

Sept 27

When you get here Cricket I'll show you the new fish tanks in the greenhouse and even let you catch some of them for dinner. The fish are sure making the garden grow this year, and it looks like it's going to be a bumper crop.

May 8

Your mind is your greatest tool, train it, and use it. Fear is your greatest adversary, unchecked it will control you. Instead, teach yourself to study your fears, and then prepare plans and methods to beat them. Never forget that the greatest tool for survival isn't in what you have; it's in who you are.

These excerpts went on and on, with every page revealing a small glimpse of my great-grandfather. Slowly an image of the man

MICHAEL SCOTT

was emerging through his writing, and I was beginning to understand Liz's fascination with him. Survival isn't in what you have, it's in who you are—that line struck deep with me. I needed to become that person; it was time to rise up and prepare to beat my pending future, not to fall prey to it. I became determined that if this book had the answers to help me in that endeavor, I was going to read every word.

My great-grandfather frequently referred to Liz as Cricket, and it made me smile to think of her as a little girl. I thought of the name Liz had written on my letter, Butterfly, and I liked it. It was a nickname I could live with and one that would always remind me of my true beginnings. My great-grandfather also mentioned his farm outside of some place called Prineville, a town that was almost in the middle of the dead zone. However, I couldn't find the exact location of his farm in any of the letters that I had read so far, only the occasional mentions of the town. I wondered if it was still there, sitting unused, dead, filled with unseen toxic radiation.

Would the land ever heal itself? Only time would tell. Till then we would be forced to live in these cities, cities that were never designed for the masses that now filled them. Cities that now seemed to be breaking down under the strain, with riots that were once unheard of now becoming more common, as were arrests and raids. No one spoke of any of it for fear of being reported, but the signs around us were plain enough. We seemed to have become a people that had grown too accustomed to blindly following our government commands like unarmed sheep, our wills sacrificed on the altar of hoped security. We no longer fought back from our own inevitable but preventable death of freedoms, most now choosing instead to simply accept it as unchangeable.

I put the book back in the case and locked it while pondering all I had read, so much information to sort through, but I knew that the answers I needed would be there—I just needed to find them. The case put away, I put on the old hat and looked at the mirror. The hat was a little too big, so I found some tissue and stuffed the inside band till it fit. There was something about the way it sat slightly cocked on my head and how it gave me a feeling of connection to my origins.

THE BOOK OF LETTERS

I was pleased with the way it looked and the sense of confidence it gave as I tipped its brim further down on my forehead. Keeping it in place, I headed for the living room to see if our requests had gone through yet. Halfway there, I heard the sound of SOTOS's electronic voice sounding out.

"Two travel passes for Washington Park, 4A status, confirmed and delivered. Two travel permits for Washington Park, confirmed and delivered. Curfew is at 10:00 p.m. All passes and permits will be canceled for the day at that time. Have a good day."

I scooped up our phones and joined Mom in the kitchen; food in tow, we headed out the door. Bundled against the morning chill, we went to the bus stop and began our wait in the brisk air; 4A meant our passes were for public bus lines only. Though they were always crowded and late most of the time, it still beat walking miles to the park. When the bus finally arrived, we swiped our phones across the driver's computer screen, pulled our backpacks close, and squeezed into the overheated interior. We were in luck today; the bus was only twenty minutes late and still had some standing room left.

With a groan, the bus pulled out from the stop, and I grabbed the overhead bar to keep from losing my balance as the crowed swayed with the motion. Soon I could see nondescript buildings begin to slide by as we moved along the crowded streets of the city. Mile after mile of government housing could be seen through the dingy windows, each building showing signs of neglect and much-needed repair. The heat from all the bodies pressed into the bus was stifling and even more so encased our jackets, but it was too crowded to even attempt taking them off. I could feel the sweat run down my face and back as I watched for our stop, hoping that it would soon come. When we finally reached the transit center, a large group of passengers got off. Most of them were headed to their assignments working at the shipyards. The buildings no longer dealt with ships and supplies but instead had been converted to large vertical farms that needed incessant care.

It took a steady stream of people to keep the farms running day and night in their attempts to keep up with the constant food demands of the city. All private farming had been stopped because

MICHAEL SCOTT

of current governmental environment laws, making collective farming all that was legal now with all their new restrictions. We were told that it was all for the greater good of the people, but now I questioned it all. My plight had opened my eyes for the first time to the harsh reality of the city and its unyielding rules. Was this world really better for us? Or was it just better and more profitable for those making the rules?

Much to my relief, the park came into view in all her fall glory, and thankfully, there didn't seem to be too many around yet as most people were still waiting till the morning chill was gone and the late day sun fully warmed the fall air. As we stood there getting our bearings, Mom looked toward the east, and I could see her intently studying the wooded area.

"Do you know what is over that direction less than a mile away?" she asked.

All I could see was the autumn-colored trees lining the park, but from the way she looked at me I sensed it was important. My hesitation was answer enough for her.

"The bio farm where you're training, it's not too far past the trees," Mom replied. Then she turned and headed west across the parking lot before continuing, "Did you know that if a person was to walk in a straight line from here toward the sun, you could follow it all the way to the coast. From there, who knows where you could go? After all, anything is possible with a little imagination."

I loved when Mom talked, the sound of her voice and the calmness that it brought. While we walked, she began telling me one of her childhood memories. It was one I had heard many times before but still loved, and that was when a thought came to me.

"Mom," I suddenly interrupted her story. "I've been reading some of the letters from the book. Well, parts of the letters anyway. Did Liz ever tell you why her grandfather called her Cricket? I found a lot of the letters addressed to that name."

Mom looked up and grinned big. "Yes, she did. Apparently, when she was real little she was a bit shy, but she loved to sing. Her grandfather, your great-grandfather, said every time he heard singing he would find her hiding under a bed, behind doors and such, always

THE BOOK OF LETTERS

hiding like a cricket when it sings. That's how she earned the nickname. Liz said that every time your great-grandfather wanted her to sing he would call out to her, chirp little cricket, chirp!"

I couldn't help myself; I giggled and chuckled heartily. Mom soon joined me and added to the sounds of our gaiety. For me it was another picture into the unknown world of my birth mother, Liz. It was an image I liked. I could see her running the hills and singing from her hiding places, and all while wearing the old man's hat. Mom enjoyed the laughter as much as I did; it made life seem almost normal. We located a spot in a patch of grass where the sun had dried off a bit of the dew and spread out our blankets for our picnic lunch.

As I lay back on the blanket, I watched the passing clouds. There weren't many for an October sky, but there were enough to daydream with. Spotting one bear-shaped cloud made me remember something my friend Susan had told me: "You know, they still haven't found the beast of the woods yet."

Susan said it only came out at night, and that was why no one could catch him. She claimed that she was there the first time it broke into the bio farm.

Mom rolled her eyes at the news. "There isn't any beast, honey, just vandals or squirrels built up by wild stories. Susan's going to rot your brain with her crazy rumors; I don't know why you even listen to her."

Susan did enjoy her gossip and enlarging the story line. "Nevertheless, I wouldn't want to be out here after dark. There just seems to be too many weird things happening lately," I replied. We had both heard the reports of the vandalism and rumors of strange sightings in the area but weren't worried as we would be gone long before the sun set. The thought of a beast, real or not, stirred a little fear in me, despite Mom's levity on the subject.

"Besides, we got bigger things to consider than some imaginary beast," Mom said. "We have a lot to consider depending on what you want to do."

I looked at her, flustered, "What I want to do? What choices do I have other than run or be arrested? Nothing else comes to mind unless you have something up your sleeve!"

I knew I couldn't live like a slave for our government's pleasure, but I knew nothing of how to survive outside the city or where I could even go to escape. The cities were watched by cameras and people hoping to gain favorable rewards. In them I knew there simply wasn't a safe place to hide. The woods were unused as special permits were required to even enter them, and few if any were ever given. These days, people were simply required by law to stay within the confines of the cities and for the most part in their registered sections.

Mom pulled me from my dark thoughts. "What if I could get you help, like someone to get you out of here and someplace safe?"

I rolled over and looked at her, a bit startled. Was this another unknown layer of my mom's hidden life?

"What are you trying to tell me, Mom?" I asked, wondering what she knew.

"Alice, what I'm about to tell you may seem harsh or blunt, but we don't have a lot of time before your birthday. Your right, you've only got two choices. However, one of those choices I can help with. In my line of work and because of my past I've made a lot of friends in strange places. Some of those friends have special advantages or skills that could help." Mom's voice was serious. "I have been working with a group, and we have a plan to save you as well as a lot of other people. As a society, we just can't keep going the way we are and ignoring what is happening to us. I won't lose another child to them."

I could see the pain and determination in her face, and I was taken aback by this new influx of information. Not knowing what else to say, we sat there, quietly watching the world go by. It was a world neither of us wanted. I contemplated what she had said. And if there was a way, some small chance to somehow escape all this, I knew I would be a fool not to grab at it. When all hope is lost, faith will carry you on. I thought back to the phrase, and I knew that my hope and faith lay in Mom's plans. Thinking to how the law would react to my sudden disappearance, I knew that Mom would have to go too or suffer the consequences of my actions.

"I'll go if you'll go with me," I finally blurted out. "I can't leave you here. You and I both know they'll come after you once I'm gone.

THE BOOK OF LETTERS

We'll figure this all out together and find a better life somewhere. Please, Mom, I can't lose you."

She hugged me. "I'm planning on being with you every step of the way."

Her words soothed me a bit. I was certain that, working together, we would get through it all. We lingered after our lunch, as we enjoyed the time together talking of this and that, and recalling memories and dreams. Then with the day fading away, we packed up our things and headed back across the park toward the bus stop and our ride home. As we walked Mom added more to my enlightenment, giving me more to think over and consider.

"You should know that there is already a plan in place, and after your birthday, no one will ever have to fear government testing again." Her eyes were stern and showed that she was confident in her statement.

I wondered what this plan was that she alluded to and how many people were involved in carrying it out. I also began to speculate on what role and actions I would be asked to play in all of it. With the last of the sun-warmed air the park was filling up with evening visitors, so Mom wouldn't say much more other than referring to the plan as "Butterfly" and reassuring me it would all work out. With the plan being called Butterfly, I didn't need to wonder why she had chosen to use that name or the date of the event; I just hoped that all her planning and preparation worked out the way she had hoped.

Just before we got to the circle of people that were already waiting for the bus, Mom stopped. "From now on, Alice, you must always be aware of what you're saying and of who is around you. And trust no one, not even your friends. Also, avoid drawing attention to yourself and learn to always watch for escape routes wherever you are in case things go bad. We've only got two weeks to prepare. You've just got to keep it together that long, then we're out of here. The plan is already in motion. I've had eighteen years to set things up, and when it happens, we will disappear in the chaos, unseen and unnoticed before we're even missed."

MICHAEL SCOTT

She looked into my eyes, and I knew the scared girl she saw before her. "Trust me, honey, I won't let them take you from me. We just need to prepare as best we can and as quietly as possible."

The aged bus arrived with its usual groan, and we herded into the worn heap like sheep till there was barely any breathing room left. A few grinding gears later we were headed home, looking like packed sardines in an aquarium as we traveled back through Portland. I was wishing I knew more of the plan but also knew it was probably for the best that I didn't. Living a covert life was new to me. Tomorrow I would have to face the pressures of the world and of keeping my secret hidden; my friends were now potentially dangerous leaks, and besides Mom, I could trust no one.

That night as I lay in bed, once again going through the book of letters, I read the sections on plants that held my attention, and I even recognized some of the plants from my eleventh-year botany classes. I noted the ones that grew in this area and their uses, and then I found some pages on different ways of making fires. On the pages were drawings with names like bow drill, fire plow, fire lens, and dotting the pages were hand-scrawled instruction that wove around and in between the images. I marked the page with plans of memorizing what I could; I knew this could be a lifesaver.

As I went through the pages, I wondered where I would find the answers that I needed about the case and the secrets it contained. Liz had said that it was those very secrets that I would need to help with my journey, but so far I had found nothing. Tomorrow it was back to classes and a training shift at the bio farm, and I would need all my wits about me, so I put the book away and turned out the lights. In the dark I stared off into the abyss of night and queried, where would this journey lead? Deep and unanswerable are the mysteries of unknown tomorrows, and with that thought hanging over me, I felt slumber overtake me. My restless sleep carried me through troubled dreams that played out like a bad B movie, horrifying enough to frighten you but so badly acted out that they left you not knowing whether to laugh or cry.

CHAPTER 4

The alarm saved me from the disturbing images that were corrupting my dreams, and I awoke, my body covered in sweat. Something had been chasing me, something dark and evil, hidden just enough in the shadows that you can't quite make it out but visible enough to let you know it's there. A hot shower washed the sweat off me and helped the dream fade from my mind. "You got this, Alice," I told myself, not sounding too convinced, and while toweling off I could already predict that it was going to be a long day. Mom was already off to an early shift at the hospital, so I was on my own. The day's schedule ran through my head, and I dressed accordingly for it. Looking back at my reflection I double-checked to be sure I hadn't forgotten anything in my current state of mind. I could see that the girl looking back looked nervous and scared, a sure sign to others that something was wrong. Spotting my newly inherited hat, I put it on and pulled it forward to shade my troubled eyes. It didn't really fix the problem, but it helped it a little.

Sitting on my bed, I looked at my clock and saw I had plenty of time before the bus arrived, so I once again opened the book of letters. I had a lot to learn and only a short time to absorb it all in. Would this one book really be able to answer all my questions? The only way to find the answer to that was to just start reading and see what I could find.

"So you got anything on bravery?" I asked the unhearing book as I flipped the pages.

Under the heading of nature, I found a few pages with some really well-done animal sketches and details written about their habits, footprints, and food preferences. It was under the drawing of a mouse standing next to a mountain lion that I saw, in small print, this quote, "Some are brave because they are born with size, while some are driven to bravery by hunger, but some become brave because they have no choice. The field mouse is one of the bravest and toughest animals I know, simply because he has no other choice and no other method with which to face his hostile world."

I knew it was just coincidence that I found the quote, but it still eerily gave me the answer I needed to face my daunting day. Be brave because it's your only choice, fear wasn't an option. If a mouse could do it, so could I, or so I hoped. A glance back at the clock told me it was time to get moving, so I put the book away then grabbed my lunch, coat, and backpack then headed out to catch the bus. During my bus ride, another news report of those arrested overnight came through the overhead speakers, and along with it was listed the rewards that were given to those assisting in their capture by reporting suspicious activities to security-patrol officers. I tried to tune out the government broadcast while at the same time wondering if my name would ever be called over its sound waves.

I passed through my classes in a state of zombience, just going through the motions but with no discernible brain activity; I just couldn't seem to focus on any of my studies. The ringing of the day's last bell brought a relief and an end to my scholastic agony, as well as friends' questions. I was happy and alleviated to finally be heading to my training assignment and away from my classes; there I only had animals to really deal with. My assignment at the bio farm was for training in animal care and nutrition, an assignment that I enjoyed and was doing well at. With my test scores so far, Mom was sure that the government would send me to veterinary school or possibly even medical school—if they didn't find out who I really was, I grimly thought. The farm had been created because of animal-protection laws; the private ownership of most animals and livestock had been revoked and deemed illegal except by special permit. Now all animals

THE BOOK OF LETTERS

were considered government property for the good of the people and animals.

The bio farm had been built where the city zoo once existed, and now the farm animals were raised for their cells. These cells were then grown in lab petri dishes as meat patties, and thousands could be grown from one small needle puncture instead of killing the animal. By doing this the bio-farm labs could fill the city's protein needs using just a few livestock and without breaking the imperious, governmental, animal-protection no-kill laws, which would require another permit with loads of red tape and paperwork. When people are ignorant of their own laws, their lack of understanding will cause those same laws to grow until they dominate them.

Once off the bus, I headed for the main office and today's assignment sheet. As I rounded the corner I spotted my friend Susan in all her blond, Barbie-like excitement waiting for me at the door.

"Wow," Susan said, "rough weekend? Where did you dig up the cool ol' retro?"

"From an old friend," I snapped back. The question unnerved me. "Sorry, didn't sleep much last night."

"Apparently, neither did the watchman," Susan replied excitedly, "the beast is back!"

"Did he see it?" I asked, my curiosity stirred by Susan's obvious excitement.

"No, the beast is too smart for that," Susan replied with a devilish grin. She was certainly enjoying the excitement; she always did.

"Mom says it's just squirrels or something, that's why they can't catch it on camera," I said, more out of hope and with less certainty than I liked.

Susan's look told me she preferred her imaginary beast to the thoughts of squirrels.

"Wouldn't it be exciting if they did find a beast?" Susan burst out. "At least it would liven things up around this dump."

Susan wasn't much of an animal lover, or fond of dirt or hard work or smells. Let's just say that this was the last place she liked being. The smart bet was against her being assigned here after final testing; it was hard not to grin when I saw her customary scrunching of her nose as we entered the building. As we changed into our work outfits, Susan continued to rattle on about the beast and what it could be. I just listened, knowing my input wasn't needed for this conversation. I shoved my clothes in my locker but retrieved my hat before closing the door. I needed all the help I could get, and the hat gave me a sense of confidence.

The assignment chart had me scheduled for feeding in the hog building. Next to me, Susan was throwing her usual tantrum.

"Gross! I got the egg building, sanitation. Those birds are so nasty." Susan's eyes snapped. "I think someone is doing this on purpose. This is the third time this month that I've been sent there."

"Make the best of it, we're only here for a few more weeks," I replied, then waved goodbye and headed to pick up my feed charts.

I told the day-crew leader my assignment, and he handed me the forms. He was a new face, but I wasn't planning on sticking around long enough to make new friends, so I didn't linger to start a conversation or ask his name. Instead, I quickly took the papers and headed for a table. I was just sitting down when he walked up.

"You forgot, last shifts count," he said as he handed me the forms. At my look of confusion, he added, "The name is Kel. Maybe you'd better check your math twice today, you seem a little off." He grinned, winked at me, then strolled on back to a group of waiting trainees.

He had no idea how "off" I really was, and he was right; maybe I had better check it. We took the count sheets and then crunched our nutritional need based on the type of animal and multiplied it by the amount of the gross count, then figured the best feed mix to fill the needs for the day. Once figured, I took it to the day-crew leader, Kel, and he double-checked my figures and approved them.

"Good job." Kel flashed a big smile after reviewing the forms. "Send them in."

His actions, for some reason, left me blushing like an idiot, so I quickly left to send in the feed request and waited in the warehouse while they filled them. When it was loaded, I pulled the heavy cart down the paved path. The hog building was at the back of the farm, so it gave me time to think as I made my way along. Mom had said to start keeping an eye out for possible escape routes, so I scanned the edges of the pathway, noting where the cameras were placed. The bio farm was surrounded by trees; you just had to clear the cameras to get to them, but how? The creaking of the cart wheels sounded out their complaints of being overburdened as I passed down the pathway, but soon my destination came into view, as did the voices of its occupants.

The hogs I was working with today were Kunekunes; they were some my favorite animals. I loved the way their tails would twirl when they got excited and their high-pitched squeals of delight, which were now becoming almost deafening as they caught sight of the food cart.

"Hey, guys, ready for some dinner?" I yelled over the din. The crescendo of noise confirmed that they were, so I got busy dishing it out, taking time with each one, and giving tummy rubs as I went from pen to pen. At the last pen I couldn't find the pig at first, but when I did, I saw that he was in bad shape. The little guy had somehow made a hole in the back wall by pushing on the tin siding, and now he was wedged halfway in and halfway out, too tired to fight any more. Working to dislodge him, I wondered if the night shift was slacking off in their duties because he had obviously been stuck for a while.

I shoved out with my foot against the tin, and as it moved out it widened the hole, allowing the pig the escape he sought. Freed, I checked him over for damages then blew out a big sigh; this meant more paperwork to fill out. The little Kunekune seemed to have fared well, with just some minor abrasions and a couple of light lacerations where the edge of the tin sheet had dug in. Still, they would want a vet check just to be sure, but first I needed maintenance to repair the hole before this guy tried it again. I put the pig into a holding cage for the veterinarian staff, then called the maintenance building and laid out the problem.

"How big is the hole?" the bored voice on the line asked. I had been too busy dealing with the pig to really take note of the hole's dimensions and relayed as much.

MICHAEL SCOTT

"We'll send someone over when they have time. If you could take a look and call back with the extent of the damage, that would help us know what we should bring along." With that, the voice promptly hung up.

Exasperated at the response, I went back to the pen and looked again at the hole. The screws holding the tin in place had pulled through, allowing the tin to flex. Checking to see how far the damage to the tin was, I put my shoulder against it and pushed to see if it would move, and it did. In fact, it gave way, dumping me on the other side of the wall. Standing up, I found myself in a long-abandoned alley formed between the hog building and a retaining wall. The front end had been sided over and back end left open to the brush. That was when I heard a deep growl emerge from the darkness of the closed-off end of the alley, and slowly I turned to face the foreboding noise.

From the shadow-filled depths of the alley emerged the biggest dog I had ever seen, and there I stood blocking its only way out. I had only seen a few dogs in my life, and all those worked with security patrols, but those dogs seemed insignificant and weak compared to what now faced me. As his large feet moved toward me in a stiff-legged walk, I saw his hackles rise and listened to his massive chest keep up a steady, deep rumble. My body froze; I knew there was no way I could make it back through the wall before this gigantic monster tore into me. As he passed through the shadows, I could make out his thick fur, heavily muscled body, and wide face. The sight of his bared teeth caused panic to start climbing up my spine like ice-cold spiders.

My body couldn't seem to make anything respond. I wanted to run, to scream, but all I could do was watch in horror as the dog came closer and closer. When he finally stopped, we were nose to nose, his dark eyes staring intently at me, as if searching my soul. Then as I waited for the worst, he inspected me from head to toe, his hot breath pouring over me. I broke out in a sweat. I had no idea what to do but hope he wouldn't attack. His nose rose to trace my neck then moved to my face, and he suddenly stopped. I saw his nose pulsate at some scent or curiosity. Placing one of his massive

THE BOOK OF LETTERS

paws on my shoulder, he pulled my head forward and turned his full attention to my hat, breathing deeply at some unknown scent that lingered. Suddenly, without warning, he leaped back then started prancing on his front feet and talking in deep mumbles while the rest of him swayed in time with his heavily wagging tail. Before I even saw him move, he jumped and his paws hit me in the chest, sending me sprawling. Alarmed, I quickly scrambled to get up, but the dog was too fast and had already pinned me down. As he crawled higher up, I could feel the weight of his body pressing the air from my lungs. His face now hovering above mine, we looked eye to eye, and it seemed as if time froze. But when I saw his open, tooth-lined mouth dropping toward my face, I knew that for me it would all be over soon.

The long, wet trail of his tongue dragged across my face. At first I thought it was blood, and a whimper escaped me at the thought. When I realized that it wasn't blood, only his drool, my relief left me happy but confused by his actions. What did this dog want from me? Sensing my distress, the dog whined and backed off, enough for me to sit up. He cocked his head at me while he made warbles and whines as if he were trying to ask me questions. His attention, how-ever, was soon distracted when he spotted my hat on the ground; it had fallen off when I got knocked down and now lay on the ground just out of my reach. As he looked back and forth from me to the hat, his intentions became clear, and vicious or not I wasn't going to let him take it.

"You'd better not! That's mine so leave it alone!" I tried to sound scary, but I think the dog laughed as he gave a mumble.

He again made the funny warbled whine and pranced, then after rubbing his face all over the hat he grabbed it up and watched to see what I would do. It was becoming clear this dog just wanted to play, so I grabbed for the hat, but the he was too quick. His tail was wagging like a swinging board and struck me on the leg, making me yelp in pain. The dog instantly stopped, dropped the hat, and sniffed the full length of my leg to be sure I was okay. When satisfied I wasn't damaged, he headed back for the hat. It was then that I remembered the treats I still had left in my pocket from baiting the stuck pig earlier into a crate.

I took some out and placed it on the ground before him, and it only took one sniff to convince him. While he snacked on the tidbits, I grabbed my hat and put it back on my head; it felt good having it safely back in place. Digging out more snacks from my pocket, I handed them to him and panicked when my hand disappeared in his cavernous mouth. He seemed sorry and carefully pulled back his soft lips, my hand now wet with drool but unscathed. His big eyes looked up at me, asking for more, but I was out of treats so I scratched behind his ears instead and from his tail could see he was enjoying it.

My hands rubbed along his sides, feeling the thick muscles under the tangled fur, the swaying of a wagging tail tapping out a rhythm on the hard ground. His head suddenly snapped up off the ground, and his body tensed; something was coming. In one fluid movement he stood up, his tongue flicking my face, and poof—he was gone. It was amazing how fast something so big could disappear.

I got up and was working my way back through the hole when I heard, "You never called back and I was close by, so figured I'd better come check on you myself." It was Jim. "What kind of trouble do you got?"

I hated dealing with Jim. He made my skin crawl; most of the girls just tried to avoid him, but today I wasn't that lucky. For some reason that no one knew, Jim pictured himself a ladies' man. However, in truth, with his slender build, nervous eyes, and narrow face he reminded me most of a ferret. His stories and bragging were constantly getting bigger as he tried to convince people of how tough he thought he was. We all knew they were lies, but most of us just didn't care enough to bother calling him out. Instead, we just laughed at his absurdities when he was out of earshot.

"One of the pigs found a weak spot in the tin and worked it loose," I said then headed for my cart. Turning for the door, I called back over my shoulder, "Screws pulled through the siding, and it just needs to be fastened down."

"Why don't you just hang out while I fix this? Got some news about my security patrol transfer. Just thought, you might like to hear about it." Jim left the invitation hanging in the space between us; I didn't answer. He went on unhindered by the awkward moment, "They agreed that they need more guys like me working security patrols. I told them about my black belt, and they're considering me as a trainer."

My back was to him, and it was a good thing because I couldn't stop the soft laugh that escaped me. I coughed, hoping to cover it. The only way Jim would ever get a black belt of any kind was if he made one. I started to ask what he dyed his belt with, but that just started me giggling again and coughing to hide my amusement.

"Sorry," I said, looking back at Jim. "Dust."

Jim's face showed he wasn't convinced at first, but his ego wouldn't let him stop. "It's going to take tough guys like me to solve some of this city's problems. Given a chance I'll train a squad, and we'll beat any lawbreaker down. Word will get out, and criminals will be too afraid to break any laws."

I looked across the building at him. Seeing me look, he took advantage of the moment to flex his arms in a failed attempt to impress me. The sight left me rather repulsed, so I headed for the door and away from ferret boy.

"I got medical reports and incident reports to fill out and file before I leave, so I need to get going," I said while stepping from the building. As the door closed, I yelled back, "Thanks for fixing the pen, Jimmy!" Then I was gone and free of him.

During the rest of my shift, I kept thinking back to the dog. Should I report him? Mom had said not to draw attention, and I knew reporting the dog would do just that. I knew that if Susan heard about it, she would be sure the world would know about it. Silence seemed prudent for now. The last thing I wanted was people asking me a lot of questions and swarming over this place, trying to catch the Beast of Portland. It wasn't until I was turning in the medical report that I wondered why the dog hadn't eaten the pig. Curiosity steered me to the information desk; the lady there looked up as I approached.

"Hello, can I help you?" she asked.

"This is kind of a silly question, but since the attacks started from the beast, have any of the animals been harmed?" I inquired.

"Attacks?" At first she seemed confused, but then she realized what I was referring to. "Oh, you mean the messes left around here at night."

She laughed then continued, "No, there hasn't been any animal harmed, just dumped trash cans and some busted bags. So who told you it was a beast?"

I blushed. "My friend Susan said it was a beast."

"I kind of figured." She chuckled. "That girl has been in here every day looking for updates. I think your friend is just a little monster crazy."

I couldn't help but agree with her about Susan and was happy to hear the dog hadn't hurt any of the animals; maybe he wasn't as dangerous as he looked. Thinking back to the alley, I wondered at the size and actions of the dog. Where had he come from? How he remained hidden I understood now; he was traveling back and forth through the hidden alleyways between the buildings where there weren't any cameras. How smart was this dog? I wondered. He had run off so I would never know, and it wasn't likely that he would ever come back now that his hiding place had been discovered.

CHAPTER 5

After my shift, the ride home was packed as usual; the mass of bodies could make you claustrophobic sometimes. Everyone on the bus stood or sat in silence while trying to avoid eye contact with anyone; overhead the speakers crackled and whined as another government broadcast droned on. I knew why I was trying not to be noticed, but as I glanced at those around me, I wondered what secrets they themselves hid.

We lived in a dangerous time when you could be reported at any time for any number of things. The information reward program had caused it; too many abused the system either for financial gain or to get rid of those they didn't like. Now no one trusted anyone. They once called this the city of roses, but now from the looks on people's faces, it should be renamed the city of shadows.

They had taught us in school how the future would be better as we worked for the people; I had heard it my whole life but had yet to see it. Each year there were more cutbacks and new rations. The breakdowns in our systems were starting to become undeniable. We all knew the signs and what they meant, but in our fear we stayed silent. I thought back to the dog; strangely, he gave me hope. If a dog that big could move around unseen, then maybe Mom and I really could slip away unnoticed. I needed to know more of Mom's plan.

Home smelled delicious. As I took off my coat and hat, my nose savored the aroma emanating from the kitchen. Lasagna! Mom heard me in the hallway and called out, "Shower first. You only got about twenty minutes left."

MICHAEL SCOTT

"They announced the new shutoff time over the bus radio," I answered back as I headed for my room, then for the shower. They shut the water pumps down to conserve power, but it seemed that every year that time came earlier and earlier. The hot water felt good and helped ease the tension from the day; maybe I was glad Mom waited to tell me. Two weeks like today was going to be a long time.

Now the knowledge of my impending doom was almost like a palatable weight that bore down on me, making me constantly conscious of every word I said and every move I made in public. It would only take one report from the wrong person to end it all for Mom and me. The water clicked off. *Well, at least I rinsed my hair before they shut it off,* I thought and headed to my room to dress.

Pajamas and bathrobe donned, I joined Mom in the living room, dinner dished up and waiting. She was watching a movie I had seen before. I sat down next to her, and she handed me a plate.

"How was your day?" Mom inquired, then quickly added, "ran out of cheese, so I just added more veggies. Not the same but still tasty."

"Okay. Just another school day," I answered as I grabbed a steaming bite, then smiled. "I'm just so worn out from the day. If you don't mind, let's just watch the movie for a while. If that's okay with you."

I caught Mom's eye then held my finger to my lips. Mom grinned with understanding and retrieved the string. The game began again. I told Mom all about the dog, though obviously frightened she held her composure. While the movie played on, I filled Mom in on the rest of the day's events and thoughts that I had considered, like how the dog had moved about unseen. Mom leaned over and kissed me. I knew that my tale of the dog had unnerved her, but she said nothing.

"More tea?" she asked then poured me more without waiting for a reply, her hand still shaking.

Then she took up the string and reminded me of something I had forgotten, our chips. It wasn't just cameras that I had to think of; there was also the citizen chip in my wrist that I needed to deal with. Everyone had one; you had to by law. Most got theirs at birth with a few of the old people getting theirs when they moved the populace west of the mountains. The movie still had about thirty minutes left, so using the string I asked the big question: what's the plan?

Her hand hovered over the string; it was obvious that she was trying to decide where to start. Slowly, with the ever-moving string, she started to fill me in on the group and their plan. First, she told me of how the group formed from the contacts she made as a nurse. The diversity of people involved was what made them so valuable and so hard to track. Using secret codes and signs, they communicated. Delivery drivers, librarians, childcare workers, newspaper boys, anyone that could move throughout the city were used for communications and information. The elderly and less mobile would sit on park benches or by windows around the city, watching and updating the group of changes; they utilized everyone they could.

Mom and the group had first tried by legal means to have the laws changed; they had failed. It seemed the system would not change; they had the power now and would not lose it. A line from my great-grandfather's letters came to my mind: "Those that give up their rights and freedom for security deserve neither." I couldn't remember who said it, but I had to agree with them.

Those before me had done just that, leaving us a world foreign to the idea of a land of the free and home of the brave. We were now a world of the controlled and the fearful, and it seemed like the farther I went down this rabbit hole, the clearer I now saw the world around me. For Mom and me, it wasn't a world we wanted, nor was it one we could easily walk away from, but try we would. The movie ended, but during the rolling credits Mom started laying out bits of the plan. I was shocked at the scope of it.

The government and the city were failing; collective farms were dying, while sickness and crime were on the rise. Draconian laws, rations, and freedom restrictions were being used to quell any thoughts of uprising and to keep ironclad control, but there were signs that their grip was slipping. The people had grown weary of it, but like sheep most continued to go on with their lives, too dumb or lazy to fight against their owners. Those that chose a different way joined the group, and soon a plan was hatched, built upon and named Butterfly.

MICHAEL SCOTT

Mom and I both knew why it had earned that name and the time, October 30, at 3:47 p.m. The time of my birth and the murders of baby Alice and Liz, it seemed fitting. The group had thought it all out and had been planning, watching, and waiting for the right time, but time had now run out. It was now time for action, and things had been set in motion that couldn't be stopped. Do or die, the plan was going forward. and we had no choice but to move with it. Her tale told, we sat there, both not knowing what else to say. Mom finally stood and stretched.

"I'm going to bed, honey. Morning comes real early for me. Early shift again tomorrow," Mom said. Then looking at me, while stifling a yawn: "You good?"

I nodded. "I'll put the dishes in the sink, and then do some reading before bed." Then, hugging her: "Love, you Mom. Always have, always will."

I felt her grip tighten. "Love you, Alice. Always have, always will."

Then she kissed my cheek. "Dream well."

"You do the same," I called back to her as she headed to her room.

As I watched her go, I again was amazed at all she had accomplished without me ever knowing and all the love she had given me. I cleaned up and SOROS, turned off everything, and set the locks, then I headed for my room. I was still wound up from all Mom had told me of the plan. Its scope wasn't just big; it was enormous. The plan not only involved Portland but the other cities as well. The cites of Salem, Albany, Eugene, and other towns along the I-5 corridor clear to Ashland were having their own groups prepare for the day, the day of the Butterfly. Even small towns like Dallas, Independence, and Philomath that housed detentions farms would be part of the fray. Mom was right; it would be chaos.

If all went to plan, slipping out of the city would be doable. The day was set for insanity. On that day the plan was to shut down all testing centers, detention centers, and other facilities. Then flood the streets with protestors crowding the streets like a human wall. It would make it almost impossible for security patrols to give chase.

THE BOOK OF LETTERS

OHSU was where I was scheduled to be given my test, so Mom had laid out our travel plan from there. I closed my eyes and tried to remember all the map details; it was definitely going to be a long hike. This was the wrong time of the year for this kind of a journey, but Mom had friends that we were meeting up with. Once we joined up with them, we would be headed to a safe zone. Mom didn't say where that was, only that it would be safe.

If it weren't for our contacts, I don't know how Mom and I would survive the winter; neither one of us had any outdoor skills. I had eleven days left before the big event, not much time, so I needed to make each one count. I couldn't waste one day on fear or depression, I needed them to prepare for what may lie ahead. In the letters I remembered seeing the page of fire methods and wondered if maybe I should see what else I could find that might help as a backup plan. I pulled the case out again and ran my hand over the worn fabric covering.

What secrets are you hiding? I thought as I opened the case. Once again, its interior gave no hint of it being more than it seemed—an old case full of this and that. The book drew me; it had to have some answers, answers I needed. For two hours I read the book, searching for answers, but not knowing where to look. Aquaponics, improvised explosives, chemical substitutes, booby traps, hunting and tracking, picking locks—there was no end, it seemed, to the subjects. My eyes were tired, and the hour was late. I flipped through the last few pages on locks and found what I had been looking for—or so I hoped.

Under a puzzle box, there was a drawing that closely resembled my case; the more I looked, the more certain I became. As excited as I was, the writing around the image was too small for me to make out with my tired eyes. I marked the page with plans of looking it over in the morning; my brain felt mushy but full of hope over what I had found. Lying there, thoughts of the dog, the mysteries of the case, and the day of the Butterfly invaded my attempts at sleep. I rolled over and pounded my pillow into shape. *One thing at a time, Alice, one thing at a time.*

Finally sleep overtook me, as a kaleidoscope of images from the book washing through my dreams.

CHAPTER 6

Morning once again came too early and uninvited, so I arose to face another day. Mom was already working the early shift, so I rushed through my morning routine, and then I grabbed the book, case, and magnifying glass. With the glass I had a better look at the drawing I had found the night before; I was sure this drawing and my case were the same. The writing, though smeared a bit and small, was readable under the magnification, but what did it mean?

Go forward with the clock, take it back in time, and play a song for understanding.

What did all of that mean? The only other thing was a small arrow pointing at the front of the case, right where the keyhole was on my case. Picking up the case, I looked at the keyhole but saw nothing unusual, just a plain old keyhole. I thought to the words "forward like a clock." That was easy enough to figure out. Inserting the key, I turned it one turn forward, and the clasps popped open. The next line I assumed meant to go backward so I turned the key counterclockwise till it stopped. Still nothing.

The last line, "play a song for understanding," stumped me. I was desperate to figure this out. I knew it was important. Desperate times call for desperate measures, I thought, as I picked up the dulcimer to play a song. There weren't any songs mentioned on the page, and I didn't know how to play this thing anyway, but I was willing to try about anything. There was a built-in box for picks and extra strings, so I opened it for one of the picks. As the lid came up on the box, a hidden compartment at the end of the case clicked open.

THE BOOK OF LETTERS

In the hidden compartment I found an envelope, but a glance at the time told me I needed to head for the bus. The envelope I put in my pocket then closed the compartment and put the case away; I would find time later to read what I had found. That time didn't come till after lunch, and instead of the lunchroom I headed for the library. Finding a disk on dulcimers I sought out a quiet, out-of-the-way corner. Using the viewer's screen for cover, I opened the envelope and what appeared to be three sets of blueprints and one list of items slid out.

Looking quickly around my hidden corner, I opened the first set of blueprints. It was of the case and showed how to break it down to its base components that were hidden in its construction and lining. Great-grandpa was starting to really impress me; this case was indeed a treasure trove of gear. The next page of blueprints was of the dulcimer, and it was as impressive as the case.

According to what I could make out from my quick look, the dulcimer could be reassembled into a repeating bow. Complete with sliding arm, six-shot cylinder, and sights. The bolts came from the case, as did the glue and wax. The last blueprint was of the thermos; it was more than I had suspected. Hidden inside its interior were things needed to convert it into a water still, as well as fishing gear and too other many things to read at the moment.

A noise caught my attention, so I quickly put the papers away; there would be more time later. I was so excited about my find that waiting for my next break was agonizing. My next chance came at the bio farm. Today I was working at the goat barn, and at break time I went behind the building, found a spot, and started reading again in the shade of the brush that had overgrown the unused area.

I was looking over the list that was in the envelope when I heard and felt the warm, damp breath. I knew who it was but couldn't believe that he had been so silent. Lifting my eyes from the list, I looked into his massive face once again, and my breath caught in my throat. His face was covered in white-lined scars; they were like a road map of untold adventures, dangerous times, and lessons learned. He sniffed my hat as he had the day before and looked at me with his sad eyes, and then I felt the thump of something hit my shoe. Looking down, I could see that it was a wrist-thick stick, shiny wet from being covered in drool. The dog stepped back, looked at the stick, and then watched me, waiting. I sat there, not knowing what to do, and wondering about how to get out of this safe. As fierce as he looked, I didn't think he meant me any danger, or at least I hope he didn't.

He stood there prancing and watching while I tried to figure out my next move. Using my foot, I slid the chunk of wood over toward him, and then nearly screamed when he leaped for it. All I saw was a cave of teeth bearing down on me; thankfully, he went straight at the object of his desire instead of my leg. The big guy grabbed up the heavy stick and threw it in the air while twisting in circles. Catching the stick, he brought it over and dropped at my feet again then gave me a wet tongue to the face. As a bearlike sentinel, he stood there watching me and waiting while his tail slowly wagged in anticipation.

I carefully reached for the chunk of wood, while he concentrated on my moving hand and I concentrated on his large teeth. Just as I touched the wet surface, his ears shot up and his head cocked toward the opposite end of the building.

"What is it, boy?" I asked the big guy and got a low growl as my answer.

"Alice, are you out here?" It was Susan calling from the front of the building.

The dog disappeared into the brush; a quick glimpse of his tail as he cleared the old fence was all I saw when Susan came around the corner.

"There you are!" Susan said with relief at finding me. "What are you doing back here?"

When I stood up, I could see the dog tracks around me, so I quickly headed over to Susan before she saw them. "Thought I heard a goat back here," I lied while guiding us back toward the front of the goat building.

Susan, with wide eyes, exclaimed, "What if it had been the beast? You could have been attacked and eaten!"

"You worry too much, Susan. There aren't any terrible beasts out here that I've seen," I replied, trying hard not to smile while

THE BOOK OF LETTERS

imagining what Susan's reactions might be if she were face-to-face with the dog.

Kel, the day-crew leader, had sent Susan down to see if I needed any help. It had been a pretty easy day, and I had already finished with my shift chores, so we decided to call it a day. She helped me gather the tools and empty feed sacks onto the cart, then we headed back to the main building. As we left the goat enclosure, I saw Jim's greasy brown hair sticking out of the shadows and his pervy eyes watching us from where he stood, waiting partially hidden under a group of trees by the trail. I wondered how long he had been standing there and if he had seen the dog. As we passed him, I watched his face and looked for some telling reactions but got nothing except a wolfish leer.

"You girls having fun?" he asked in the wake of our passing. "You want some company? Well, if not, be careful. I heard there's a beast in the woods."

Susan and I gave him a glare. Jim was like a rash you couldn't scratch—irritating!

"I'm here to protect you ladies if you need it," Jim called after us. "I got skills and know how to use them. Ain't no beast that can scare me."

Susan flipped a one-fingered hand gesture back at him as we kept going; the farther we were from this creep, the better. Going into the building, I looked back and saw him still standing there watching us. What was his issue? The day done, we headed for the bus. I scanned the bus stop for signs of Jim, but he wasn't around, thankfully.

"So what do you think of him?" Susan asked. At first, I thought she was asking about Jim and gave her a confused look.

"I'm talking about the new guy," she replied at my look.

"I hadn't really thought about it." Which was true: I had bigger things to think about. Susan, however, wasn't one to let someone else's lack of interest stop her from telling you all about it, so she continued on unhindered.

"His name is Kel, and I've been doing some checking up on him." Susan's eyes sparkled. "He's twenty and single. He even has his own place and lives alone instead of the dormitories."

I could hear the excitement in her voice as she filled me in on all the juicy gossip she had found out. While the overburdened bus bore us toward our homes, she droned on all the way to her stop. By the time we got there, I was sure she was smitten by Kel. I did have to admit that he was a good looking, and maybe at a different time or a different place I could see myself trying to catch his attention. After Susan's stop, my thoughts turned back to the papers in my pocket. I was impatient to study them in more depth. The page of lists I hadn't had much time to look at, but it had seemed to be broken up into categories like first aid, food, and security.

The tone for a public news pulsed over the speakers, then the news anchor's voice crackled on.

"Today, security forces made great headway in fighting a terrorist plot against our way of life and our citizens. Arrests were made when a group of illegals were found stealing from the city's supply warehouse. Several people were shot during the raid, but all were illegals, and no citizens were harmed."

I listened intently, wondering if these were people involved with Butterfly; nothing else was said about it. The broadcast ended with the usual promises of better times and to bring all lawbreakers to justice, the same sermon they preached every day. This time I felt anger and fear over the news; I was now one of those illegals they condemned. I felt fear build in me and wondered if we would be found out before we could make it out of the city.

Turning my mind to the dog, I tuned out the radio and the crush of bodies around me. Where had he come from? He seemed too smart to just be a wild dog, not that I knew anything about wild dogs either. The fact that it seemed like the dog had sought me out today made me even more curious about him and where he had come from.

From his actions today, I realized the big guy was lonely but untrusting. Why he was taking a chance in trusting me I didn't know; maybe I had passed some unknown test of his on that day in the alley. More questions I would probably never have the answers to. Then with a grin, I thought, not unless I learn to speak dog. Despite how bad the dog has scared me each time with his sudden appearances, I was starting to like the big guy.

At home I motioned to Mom that we had a lot to talk over, so we got a quick dinner together, while talking about her work and unimportant stuff. Then we headed for the living room, had SOROS turn on a movie, and brought out the string. I laid the pages I had found in the case on the couch, and then told Mom what they were. She looked them over, and I could see she was as amazed as I had been; her eyes were wide as she went over the pages again.

I picked up the page with the lists and started going through them; there was a lot of things written down. The items on the page were obviously for taking a long trip, but to where wasn't stated; I assumed it would be to the old farm somewhere in dead hills. Not a trip I was planning anytime soon; that would be a fool's path to certain death. However, there were plenty of items listed that could be wise to have, just in case. The thought made me cold. We were going to make it; we had to. I thought back to the mouse from my great-grandfather's letters: we had to be brave; we had no choice.

Mom saw what I was looking at and started reading it as well, and then she tapped my hand to get my attention. She ran her finger down the list. As she did so, she would stop at items then point to herself; these were items that she would cover. The rest of the list we would work on together, at least with the things we could find, but some of the items we would have to do without. Times had changed since the list had been written, and some items had been banned, while others simply weren't made anymore.

"Once we are out of the city, all of this will be worth more than gold," Mom wrote with the string. Knowing what the case and its contents became was a huge help in us preparing for the day of our departure. Thinking of that day, I told Mom about the public announcement on the bus radio, the string laboriously writing the words.

"Only ten days left. Any more details on the plan?" I asked with swirls of the string.

Mom nodded and picked up the string, then started the long task of filling me in. The game worked well, but long conversations took time. You can only write so fast with a string, writing out sentences one word at a time. The details filled in, I felt better about getting out of the city. There was actually a chance we could do this!

Mom had already been granted a day off so she could go to the hospital with me on test day. We were to time our arrival at 3:40 p.m., which gave us five minutes to unload and head into the crowd of other testers. When the chaos started, we would make our way to the woods behind the VA and follow them to Forest Park. There we were to meet up with a group in a northwest section of the park. From there they would guide us to our place of safety; we just had to meet them before midnight.

"So how are you planning to shut down the testing centers?" I asked the string, spelling it out.

Mom's only answer was "Various ways," but that was all she would say about it. She kissed me on my forehead and looked at me with eyes full of love, then whispered in my ear, "Everything will be fine, just stick to the plan."

We put the dishes in the sink; they would have to wait till morning when the water came back on. Back in the living room, we finished our tea and watched the last of the movie. We had missed most of it while talking. We had no idea what the movie was about but didn't care; it wasn't the movie that was keeping us there. I snuggled against Mom and looked around the room; soon this would all be gone. Would the life I was heading for going to be anything like this? This was the only life I had ever known; I had a hard time of imagining what a different life would even be like. Mom ran her fingers through my hair, brushing it absentmindedly lulling me to sleep. Her eyes were scanning the room as well, and I knew Mom had a lot to think about as well.

I was glad we were doing this together. Alone I knew there wasn't a chance, but together we could do anything. We stayed there even after the movie, enjoying the moment and the closeness we felt. Mom was still on the early-morning schedule, so with the hour being late we said our good night, and she headed for bed. I put the list and blueprints back into the envelope, had SOROS turn off everything and set the locks, and then headed for my room.

THE BOOK OF LETTERS

Before bed, I put the envelope back in its secret compartment and read two pages from the book; it was all my tired eyes could take. However, two pages were enough to show me how to make an air gun out of common plumbing parts and show me all the uses of the cattail plant. Not that air guns were legal or that I saw many cattails, but under the circumstances you never knew, and it is always better to be prepared. This book covered so much; I wondered what kind of a man my great-grandfather had been. From his letters I knew he loved my birth mother very much and that when she was old enough, he had wanted her to make the journey to his farm.

CHAPTER 7

The sounds of Oregon rain preceded my morning alarm, setting my mood for the day. It was going to be another day of living a fake life, to fake friends, in a fake world. How was I going to last another ten days? The question irritated me; it made me sound weak. Was I? No, I wasn't weak. Scared, yes, but not weak. I could feel determination building in me. Though my hope was waning, my faith in Mom, the plan, and what I was learning gave me the determination I needed. A look at the clock after the morning rituals told me I still had a little time to wait before leaving, so I flipped open the book of letters again. This time I read up on thermal camouflage and the principles of hiding. It was enough to get my mind working, as well as my imagination conjuring up images of methods suggested that I would like to try. A chime from SOROS told me it was time to go, so I put everything away and braced for the day. At the door I grabbed my hat and looked at the worn brim; it told of many weathered storms.

"Well, brace yourself for another one, old feller," I said to the hat as I shoved it on my head and ran to the bus stop through the pouring rain. The overcrowded bus arrived, and I pressed into the steaming mass of bodies. This was something I wouldn't miss, I thought, as the bus started moving through the deluge of water. Another day of classes; they would soon mean nothing to me in my new life. It was like riding a merry-go-round that you couldn't get off; the whole thing made me queasy and anxious.

At lunchtime I took the dulcimer disk back to the library. After seeing the blueprint for the repeating bow, I didn't see any sense in

THE BOOK OF LETTERS

learning to play the instrument. While there I decided to check out some old news feeds about Central Oregon and the event, finding the feeds and queuing those up brought to life the horror of what happened. The images of the destruction the bomb had caused was shocking; the pictures of the thousands that died I would never forget. These days most people referred to that day as the pulse because of the flash from the nuclear detonation.

Why would my great-grandfather want to go back to that? There was no way for anyone to survive what these news feeds described. The last news piece concluded with a bit on the rebuilding and populating Portland, the blocking the highways leading east, and the establishment of the new state and federal government. The loss of farmland had led to the vertical farms we now used in the city, but it was misconstrued animal-protection laws that led to the bio farm. So much had changed so quickly after the pulse that new laws and government housing had to be established. When the chip was introduced, security methods had to be put in place just to keep people from uprising.

How times had changed. Nowadays most were compliant sheep that wouldn't even raise a whimper, let alone an uprising. There were enough, though; after all, the day of the Butterfly was approaching. I smiled; soon this city would know there are at least a few brave souls that are willing to stand against the stranglehold of a fascist government.

Leaving the library, I passed through the rest of my classes and headed to the bio farm. I was halfway through my shift down at the goat enclosure when there was a call for me to come to the main office. Before I left for the office, I went to the back of the building and left the remains of a sandwich I had snuck down in my pocket. The dog wasn't there, but I was pretty sure he would find it; the memory of his big face brought a grin. The big guy was growing on me, even if his size still brought a tinge of fear.

At the main office, Kel met me and guided me to a cubicle. He wanted to go over my report from the pig incident. We went over my medical report and compared it with the vet's report. He was happy with what he saw, nodding his head from time to time as he read.

"Ever think of being a vet or vet tec?" Kel asked when he looked up from the reports.

I was flattered and could feel a blush coming on, so I quickly replied, trying to cover it. "I was thinking of trying to be a nurse like my mom." When I saw Kel grinning at me, I felt like the room was getting to warm, and my blush continued to rise. "But I do enjoy working with the animals."

"Well, keep it in mind," he replied. "I think you would make a good candidate for continued studies." He then reached for the maintenance report and looked it over. After a couple minutes he apparently found what he was looking for in the report. "Here it is, the maintenance guy's report. Jim said that when he was doing repair on the tin, he found what he thought was animal tracks and scrape marks in the dirt. Do you know anything about them?" His eyes studied my face as he slid me a pad that had a picture of the tracks on its screen.

I looked down at the screen and shrugged. "I'm sure the scrape marks were probably from me falling through the wall. It's in my report."

"Yes, I remember reading that, but what about the other tracks? Did you see anything big enough to make these tracks?" His eyes watched me intently while waiting for my answer.

I thought quickly, and then I did something that I hated to do. I pulled the blonde card out, batted my eyes, and said meekly, "If I saw something big enough to make tracks like that, everyone would know from my screams."

I saw the laughter in his eyes before it burst aloud from him, as he wiped tears from his eyes. He replied, "Good answer, that's the one going in my report." Then he chuckled some more. I wasn't sure if he was laughing 'cause he knew I was lying or because he really thought I would scream like that. The thought was kind of irritating to me. Either he was accepting of liars, or he really did think I was that girly.

"Not that I scream that easily," I said in my defense, only to see Kel start laughing again. I wanted to punch him. How dare he laugh at me!

THE BOOK OF LETTERS

"Are we done?" I snapped, getting up to leave.

Through his chuckles, he said, "Yes, yes we are. Sorry, didn't mean any offense. You're free to go, and thank you for talking with me, Alice."

He shook my hand and I left, ready to get out of that overly hot room and away from his watchful blue eyes. By the end of my shift, I was ready to get out of there and to the solitude of home. I was racing out the front door when I ran into Jim and Susan.

"You see those wicked pictures I got of the beast's tracks?" Jim's voice was full of its usual arrogance. "I was telling Susan about them, and now that I know what we're looking for, I'll be able track it down." His bravado at full tide, he added, "I can track a lizard over a dry rock, and I'm going to get that beast. Just you watch and see!"

Susan and I looked at each other and burst out laughing, then took off for the bus, leaving Jim glaring at our backs. The bus had only gone a few miles when Susan asked, "So did you see the beast?"

"If I had seen the beast, don't you think I would have told you already?" I answered to her questioning glances. "Jim is just a narcissist that likes the sound of his own fantasy world."

Susan giggled in agreement, and then she rattled on about a new transfer that she met at the poultry barn. Finally, her stop came, and I was free to my own thoughts again. I wondered if Jim was going to be a problem; that was the last thing I needed right now. Somehow, I needed to find a way to avoid him before any more problems could start or any more questions were asked.

When I got home, the note on the refrigerator said Mom had gone out to pick up groceries, since it was the third Tuesday of the month. Fresh rations were brought in on those days; that also meant crowded stores. Security patrols were always out in force on those days because of riots over shortages and disputed accounts. I worried about Mom in those crowds, but all I could do was wait and hope for her to return safely.

I put on the teapot and opened a can of vegetable soup for dinner. Mom always said that rainy days were soup days, and she was right. As the soup and water heated, I retrieved the book of letters from my room and began to flip through its pages to distract me

MICHAEL SCOTT

from my worries over Mom. It was at that moment that a realization came to me; through all my reading I had skipped the very first page and never read it. So turning to the beginning, I began to read.

> To my beloved Cricket,
>
> I am so sorry about my quick departure; if only your parents would listen to me you all could have come with me. My prayers are that you will survive this new world, this false world. Your only 8 years old but I have taught you a lot in those years and I hope you remember it all. When you're old enough to understand all that is going on you can follow the necklace home if you so choose. Till then I will continue to work on all of the things I've told you about, soon my dream will be a working reality and a home again to you if you choose to make the journey. Never forget, when all hope is lost faith will carry you on. May you know the truth and have the courage to follow it, till then survive.
>
> I look forward to someday hearing you chirp for me again and watching you run the hills. Somehow I will send you proof and help you find a way, should you want it. I love you and will miss you every day, grow up strong, grow in love, and may grace always walk with you.
>
> Love forever and a day,
>
> Gp

I looked at the letter and could tell from its worn and smudged surface that Liz had read it many times. I turned the heat down on the soup and water then turned to the second page of the book. From the heading I guessed that this was the letter that came with the case on Liz's fifteenth birthday. From its appearance, it had been read as much as the first. I thought of Liz and wondered about what kind of

THE BOOK OF LETTERS

a girl she had been. What had he taught her? I was sure it was things from the book, things that I too needed to now know.

Happy birthday Cricket,

Been a long time but getting mail out has gotten to be almost impossible, I hope this finds you doing well and in good health. If all has gone to plan this should arrive in time for your fifteenth birthday, though I'm not there, my heart is with you all. I hope you like your gifts and in time understand their true nature; they are made to help you if ever needed. The book is all the letters I've written but couldn't get to you; there are a lot of drawings of the projects I've finally gotten built up here and working. The aquaponics system is functioning wonderfully and the greenhouses are producing bumper crops this year.

I found a couple of stray dogs in town last week and brought them home for company. Don't know where they came from, town was abandoned years ago, but they were nearly starved to death. They got full tummies now though, it's been nice having them around and they seem content to stay with me. I think you would like them; you and dogs always seem to connected somehow.

I also sent you proof like I said I would and as you grow older it will all make sense, the choice afterward is yours. Never forget, when all hope is lost faith will carry you forward, just be sure of what you put your faith in. I miss hearing you chirp for me and hope someday I'll hear you again. In time if you fancy a journey, use the necklace and gifts to help you along the way. I'll be here, free from a tyrannical government and their agenda. Bring those of like mind so we can teach them a better way of life, one of truth not the lies the schools are now teaching. Sorry, I get upset when I see what this country has become but this isn't the time. Today is your birthday so celebrate, have fun, and eat too much cake! Live, love, and grow in kindness, in time I will see you again.

Love you, Cricket

Gp

P.S. Blow a candle out for me

I was still looking the letters over, when Mom came home ladened with her tote bags. I quickly went to help. Her haggard looks turned to a smile when she smelled the hot soup waiting; she looked like she needed warming up. Mom stripped off her wet coat while I started putting the groceries away, and she told me about her day, shopping, and the shortages at the store. I noticed that she had bought more canned goods than normal and gave Mom a questioning look.

"Later" was all she said about it. "We'll put the rest away after we eat and I warm up a bit."

We grabbed bowls of soup and cups of tea then headed to our usual spots on the couch. Once we were sitting, I could see that Mom was waiting to hear about my day as well, so I told her about school and the scholastic test preps we were doing. I told her about Kel and him laughing at me, and thinking about it irritated me all over again.

Mom noticed and grinned. "So what do you think of him, when he's not laughing?"

I knew what she was asking and blushed; that was answer enough for Mom. She giggled and then told SOROS to pull up a movie selection. Tonight, Mom chose a classic, *The Call of the Wild* with Harrison Ford, one of my favorites. Like the nights before we talked using the string, while the movie covered our noises. I told Mom about Jim and the photos of the dog's prints, and we both agreed that staying clear of Jim was the best course of action. The last thing either of us needed was attention or too many questions being asked. It was only a little over a week left before Butterfly.

THE BOOK OF LETTERS

Mom told me that she had a backup plan just in case; the cans were for emergency caches. She then pulled out an old map and showed me our planned route. It passed several promising sites, one of them being right behind the bio farm. I thought of the faint trail I had seen the dog use through the brush; surely, I could find a place to hide things in all that overgrowth. We would cache only a few items at a time to avoid any suspicion. After all this was just a backup in case something went wrong with our contacts.

Mom then grabbed her purse and pulled out things she had procured from work. There were gauze rolls, Band-Aids, four pain-killers, and a tube of antibiotic cream. It was a beginning, but I was worried that Mom might get caught and told her so. *Please be careful,* I wrote. She smiled, then replied, *I am,* with a twirl of the string.

Seeing the small pile of our supplies seemed to bring clarity to the reality of our situation—we were really doing this! The fact that Mom was planning cache sites and gathering supplies made me won-der how sure she felt about the plan. Was there something about the plan she hadn't told me yet? I hoped that as the day of the Butterfly came, the rest of the plan details would be revealed.

I sat there with Mom, enjoying the closeness, knowing soon there would be no guaranties of moments like this. Mom's slight snore told me she had gone to sleep, so I covered her with a blanket and put everything away for the night. SOROS performed its duties as I headed for my room. Just a few more pages before bed, I thought to myself. This time with the book of letters back in the case, I picked up the history book.

The more I read of the book, the more confused I got. This wasn't what I had learned in school. There were some similarities, but the facts disagreed entirely in a lot of places. I looked inside the cover to find the printing date—it was 2018. That would be fifteen, almost sixteen years before the Pulse, yet it wasn't what they taught now. Why would you change history, I wondered, and which was right? Was the school lying, or was this book a hoax? That was the big question.

I found a chapter on something called the Bill of Rights and the Constitution. If this book were true, why would people let others

63

take all their rights away? The book was making me question a lot of things I had been taught. I guess that's why they burned all the books deemed wrong by the government. Even having this book was now considered a crime, and now I knew why.

I locked the history book back into the case; this was one book I wouldn't leave lying out. I thought back to what I had read and wondered how people could let my world happen. Why would they let it happen? My head was torn by what I was learning versus what I was taught. A quote from the history came to my mind,

> "Those who would give up essential liberty, to purchase a little temporary safety, deserve neither liberty nor safety," Benjamin Franklin once said.

That night, as I lay there in the dark waiting for sleep's embrace, bits from the library news feed and from the history book sparred back and forth. A picture was starting to form for me, one of chaos and of profound implications. After the war, people wanted protection and safety. Sadly, they were willing to give anything for it.

Somehow, I was running in the woods. I couldn't remember how long it had been, only that they were right behind me, and if I was caught with the contraband, it was prison time. I stooped quickly and hid the history book under a bush then took off again into the dark. The sound of their pounding feet told me they were gaining and that they would be over taking me at any moment. Suddenly, out of the night, I felt a hand grab me and a scream rise in my chest as I braced to take on my captor.

CHAPTER 8

"Alice, wake up! You're having a bad dream, honey!" Mom's voice pulled me from the nightmare.

My eyes opened to her smiling face. "Good morning, sunshine. Looks like you were having some bad dreams. You okay?"

I sat up rubbing my eyes, trying to wipe away the visions I'd seen, and though the dream faded it left a thread of uneasiness in me. The smell of pancakes was in the air, so I quickly got ready for the day. Mom always made pancakes when she was working the late shift. That way she got to cook at least one meal for me. Soon I was plopped down in front of a nice stack of cakes. This made morning better, I thought, as the first mouthful went in.

Full of pancakes and bundled, I headed for the door and another day.

"Don't forget your lunch!" Mom called out, then appeared with it.

The bag was heavier than normal, and a peek inside revealed two extra cans of food with my lunch. Mom looked at me questioningly, and I nodded that I understood. With a kiss on the cheek, I headed for the bus, only nine days left. It wasn't much time, but it would have to be enough. After all, it was all we had.

I went through my day like a shadow there, but not in any tangible way. The bus ride to the bio farm was again a relief. At school people had been noticing that I wasn't acting normal, and unanswered inquiries were beginning to become more earnest. It was just little things, but they were drawing attention. Thankfully, most just blamed it on the pressures of the upcoming scholastic tests. At the bio farm I started the last leg of my day, today at the pig building. While I changed into my work outfit, I slid the cans and a peanut butter sandwich into my purse.

Then I caught Susan watching me with a frown, and I wondered if she knew.

"If you keep eating like that you'll soon be as big as the pigs you're working with," Susan said in a worried tone, then stepped closer. "I used to have an eating problem too, so if you need to talk, I'm here for you."

I laughed, and then replied, "I just couldn't decide what sounded good for break time, so I brought a few choices."

Susan didn't look convinced, but then she spotted Kel, and I knew her mind had switched to a new subject. I was good with that. Kel was still the acting day-crew leader, so he handed us our forms to fill out. Susan practically drooled over Kel's arm, and then proceeded to embarrass herself by trying to flirt with him. Much to Susan's frustration, Kel seemed not to notice.

I was about an hour into my shift when he came by the pig building; he was making his rounds and checking on everyone.

Kel's voice startled me as I hadn't seen him come in. "Looks like these guys like you."

"They just respond to kindness and a calm nature," I replied as I gave a tummy scratch to a sow and got a grunt of satisfaction from the pig.

"I guess they do!" he said with a laugh.

We talked for a while as I continued to feed the pigs, mostly about the animals, which I was happy to do. His good looks and piercing blue eye were getting to me, and I kept hearing myself make stupid comments.

"Yep, those pigs sure eat like hogs." I couldn't believe such stupidity was coming out of my mouth. *Get a grip, Alice!* I thought as my face reddened.

Kel was watching me with a big grin, which didn't seem to help the situation or stem the tide of blushing that was washing over me.

"Well, I guess I had better finish my rounds," Kel said suddenly and much to my relief. Then he stepped real close to me, and my

THE BOOK OF LETTERS

heart started pounding feeling him so near. He leaned over close to my ear and whispered, "If you're interested, there a little trail behind this building, nice place to take a walk on your break time." He smiled then added, "Just keep it secret, or everyone will be using it."

With a grin still on his face and a quick wave, he headed out the door, leaving me to wonder why he had told me of the trail. I was no longer the trusting sort; I didn't have that luxury anymore. With so few days left, it was no time to get careless and caught. Still, more out of curiosity than anything else, at break time, I looked for the trail Kel had suggested.

There were no cameras behind the building and near the alleyway where I had met the dog. I did indeed find a trail into the woods. At the head of the trail was a dog's paw print, and from the size of it I could guess whose. Another quick glance around and then I slipped into the brush. The trail was dim and overgrown with rhododendrons, ferns, and Oregon grape but still visible and passable. I didn't go too far. I had forgotten my phone and wasn't sure how long it would be before someone noticed I was gone. I didn't need any more questions being asked.

I looked back to see if I was being followed and once sure I took the risk to head a little further into the woods. As I quickly passed along, I tried to remember markers, bent trees, rock formations, anything that would help when it came to finding my cache of goods. An old, wind-downed cedar gave me the place I was looking for, and I darted to it. Locating a rotted-out hollow space in the trunk of the tree, I cached my two cans—not much, but it was a beginning. As I crawled out of the tree, I found a now familiar face watching me from the brush.

"Hey, boy, I got something for you," I said as I pulled out the sandwich and tossed half of it to him.

He snatched it out of the air and seemed to swallow it whole.

"You eat like those hogs in the barn," I commented to him, and then thought, why not, beats calling him dog. "Should I call you Hog?"

The dog's tail started to sway; I took it as a yes. "You want more, Hog?" Then I tossed newly named Hog the other half of the sandwich, not needing to wait for an answer. Hog then picked up a stick and brought it to me. His intentions were clear.

"No, buddy, not today. I got to get back so no time for play." Hog seemed to understand, and as I briskly made my way back to the pig building, he accompanied me. I felt an understanding and connection to Hog; together we were two misfits in a world that didn't want us. Just before the trail ended, I gave Hog a good scratching then watched him fade back into the woods as silently as a ghost. I left the woods, wiped out my tracks, and headed back to the pigs.

When I opened the door, I found Jim with my phone in his hand, and with him was another maintenance worker named Wayne.

"Where have you been?" Jim asked with a tone of acquisition. "Came down here to see if you needed any help, and this was all I could find."

Acting relieved, I replied, "There it is, thought I left it in the bathroom." Then I reached up and grabbed my phone from him. "Thanks for finding it."

Wayne headed for the door, but Jim wasn't satisfied. "You never did answer me." His eyes were cold and suspicious.

I was getting mad. Who did he think he was? I snapped back at him, "Are you going to start following me to the bathroom to be sure I go? What I do and where I go is none of your business! Now leave me alone!"

Jim and I stood there. A battle of wills was at full war now, and I was giving glare for glare. It was Wayne that broke the stalemate. "What are we even doing here, dude? We were sent out to change lights in the goat enclosure."

"We ain't doing nothing!" Jim spat back. "Just wanted to see if she needed any help!"

"Well, I think she made it pretty clear she doesn't," he replied back to his raging partner.

Jim turned his glare on Wayne, but he didn't seem bothered by it too much.

"Get mad. I don't care," Wayne spouted off. "I just want to get my work done so I can go home. That all right with you?" And with that he headed back out the door.

THE BOOK OF LETTERS

Jim, still smoldering, stomped out to catch up with his work partner. I could still hear them arguing as they continued on toward the goat enclosure and soon out of earshot. Jim was becoming a real problem and someone to be really wary of. I took a deep breath and tried to let some of the tension go, and then I went back to the task of finishing my day.

As Susan and I headed to the bus stop, I again saw Jim standing in the shadow of the trees, watching us; his snakelike eyes chilled me. By the time I stepped off the bus, I was ready for a hot bath and some solitude from the world. Mom was working the late shift, which meant I had the tub to myself for a couple hours, and I could use them. The tub filled as I stripped off my clothes, and soon I was sliding into it blessed warmth. Slowly the knots of the day surrendered to the soothing water, and I relaxed.

An hour later I was in my closet, thinking of what to take on the trip and what to leave. I looked at my backpack and thought of everything I needed to put in it. I was only going to be taking bare essentials, which meant leaving most of my clothes. Mom had said to keep it light for the long hike and in case we needed to run, so two sets of jeans and winter shirts were laid aside to pack later. Donning my PJs, I headed to the kitchen to fix dinner before Mom got home; she would be tired and hungry after her swing shift.

While I pulled out everything needed for our meal, I considered ways of putting a shoulder strap or sling on my case to make it easier to carry. We had a lot to carry, and anything that made it easier would be a blessing. As dinner simmered on the stove, I laid out what supplies we had been able to collect on the table. There was a sewing kit, some first aid supplies, garbage bags, and numerous other small items. My backpack was going to be full of food, clothing, and whatever else I could fit into it without overtaxing it. I would also have the case and its contents, and then I thought of my coat.

With pockets sewed on the inside of my coat, I would be able to add extra items. I just had to remember to keep the weight down and distribute the weight, or I would be moving like a slug. Better to stay light and maneuverable than too heavy and get caught. I thought over what I wanted to take and what I could cut from my list—there wasn't much. The case, though long, wasn't really heavy. The book was a different story, but as heavy as it was, I knew I couldn't leave it behind. I did find a few things that I could do without and mentally removed them from my packing list.

Looking at the clock, I noticed that Mom was later than usual. I tried her phone but only got her voice mail. That wasn't too unusual when she was working; she often turned off the ringer while she was with patients. I tried not to worry, but under the circumstances it wasn't easy. Turning dinner down to low so it wouldn't burn, I started in on my coat and figuring where to put the new pockets.

Mom was three hours late by the time she came through the door, and to avoid thinking about the time I had stayed busy sewing almost all of the pockets into the lining of my coat. She looked exhausted, so I sent her to the living room while I gathered her dinner and a hot cup of tea to warm her up.

"Sorry I'm so late, the hospital was swamped today. Some new bug outbreak from what the doctors are saying," Mom said as she cradled her cup and looked at her obviously overcooked dinner. Almost four hours in a warm oven had done it no favors: the black bean patty and gravy had congealed into one solid lump. Mom started laughing when she attempted to cut into the coagulated mass; I couldn't help giggling a bit myself. In the end Mom settled for a peanut butter and jelly for dinner, not my best night of cooking.

As she ate, we talked a little about the day, then she emptied her purse and showed me her gleanings from the day. A few more bandages, a couple of Mylar blankets, superglue, and a few more painkillers. It was quite a haul, and the addition of the blankets was huge! With them we had a way to sneak by thermal drones as well as stay warm if we needed.

The hour already being late, we didn't stay up long, but headed to bed after Mom finished her sandwich. I read a couple pages from the book of letters as was becoming my habit, so many subjects to choose from. Slowly fading into my dreamland, I left the cares of the world behind and entered the world of slumber. When morning came, there would only be eight days left. It seemed too long to wait and yet too short to get everything ready.

CHAPTER 9

The week ended without incident, except that the sickness that was filling the hospitals was emptying the workforce. Being shorthanded at the bio farm meant that I had been assigned to the pig building and goat building until further notice. It was more work but gave me an opportunity to keep caching cans and to spend time with Hog. A page from my great-grandfather's letters had been on reading and talking with dogs, and if he was right, Hog and I were bonding. It made me wonder if he would leave with me, given the opportunity; it was something to consider.

Soon Sunday was on us, and Mom had made plans for us to go to a strip mall that was within our designated area, so we wouldn't need to bother getting permits or passes. We enjoyed the day window-shopping, and then stopped and bought a five-pound bag of sugar. I couldn't believe Mom would spend so much of her rations account on something so frivolous, but I kept my mouth shut. Saying nothing about it, she slipped the sugar into her shopping bag, and with no explanation we continued on, my curiosity unanswered. A short while later, we stopped at a small tea shop, a cozy place we had visited many times before. It was a nice, quiet place with only a few tables, and full of wonderful scents and good tea. When Mrs. McDaniel saw us she rushed to the door to greet us, her wide form threading past the tables. It had been a while since we had been in, and her excitement over our visit was apparent. Everyone that was a friend to Mrs. McDaniel just called her Theo, and if you didn't know better, you would think everyone was her friend. After hugs we shed our coats and bags, then sat at down at one of the tables while Theo went to kitchen to fetch a pot of tea.

"It's been such a long time!" exclaimed Theo on her return. "I hope you like the tea I selected, it was one you mentioned last time you were here."

The tea was indeed delicious, and Theo beamed when we told her so—she took great pride in her tea. I saw Mom look around the shop; we were the only patrons at the moment.

"Why don't you guys stay for lunch? It will be my treat," Theo said to Mom, then looked at me and added, "I even have some of that lemon cake you like."

I loved Theo's lemon cake. She was quite the pastry chef, and anything she made you didn't want to turn down. The way Mom and Theo exchanged looks, I knew something was happening but couldn't figure out what. Mom agreed to stay for lunch, and we got down to chatting over tea. Most of the conversation was normal, run-of-the-mill stuff like the weather, work, school, and such. There were a couple times though that I wondered what we were really talking about.

"I can't wait for spring flowers and butterflies," Theo said at one point. "Think they'll be here on time this year?"

Mom eyes grinned a bit, "They'll be here on time and in full force this year."

"Good to hear to hear," Theo replied. "I know a lot of others that are looking forward to seeing that."

Mom started another odd thread of conversation. "I saw all the starlings hanging out in the tree outside, any of them fly in here?"

Theo laughed. "Oh from time to time, probably have one fly in while were eating lunch."

Their conversation was starting to make my head ache from confusion, yet I knew it wasn't just the random talk it appeared to be. We were on our second pot of tea when another customer walked in, and Theo went over to greet the man. After she had served him tea, she headed to the kitchen for our lunch. On a serving cart, Theo brought out our meal and placed our dishes on the table. It all smelled wonderful.

THE BOOK OF LETTERS

Out of the corner of my eye I saw Theo slip Mom's bag with the sugar under the cart, hidden under the cloth draped over it. Then she went over to the man served him and then went back into the kitchen. When I glanced back over at the man, I noticed his shopping bag was missing too, and my curiosity was growing. Theo joined us again but said nothing about the missing bags.

Soon lunch was finished, and we started our third pot of tea. I sat, waiting, trying to figure out what was going on. After a little bit Theo went to fetch our desserts, and again returned with the cart. She served us our dishes and slyly slid Mom's bag back into its spot. Then she repeated the process with the unknown man. Mom caught me watching Theo, then patted my hand and smiled to let me know not to worry.

Theo, finished with serving, sat at the table with us again, all of us just enjoying the time together.

"I bet you I can point north without looking or knowing where I am," Theo said with a mischievous grin.

"This I got to see," I replied. "So what's the trick."

Theo chuckled as she took a glass of water and placed it front of her. Then she tore off a thumbnail-sized piece of paper and gently placed it on the water. From her apron, she took a needle and carefully laid it on the floating paper. Some unseen force made the needle and paper turn and point north; she turned the glass but the needle kept moving to point north. My face must have shown my amazement, so Theo explained.

"The needle is magnetized, so when you let it float, its polarity always makes it line up with north and south," she enlightened me. Plucking the needle from the glass, she handed it to me. "You keep it, every kid needs to know a trick or two."

I put the needle in my bag and thanked her; this could indeed be very useful. I saw the man look in his shopping bag then take it up, tell Theo thank you, and head off into his day. We lingered a little longer; all of us knowing that after Friday we may never see each other again. Theo and Mom cried a little when we said our goodbyes. They had been friends along time, and after watching today's sleight of hand with the shopping bags, I wondered how many secrets they shared.

Mom kept the shopping bag clutched tight to her all the way home, so I couldn't see what she had in it. What had I witnessed at the tea shop? Soon Mom and I were extracting ourselves from the packed bus and headed up the stairs to our apartment. I for one was relieved to be home and, once unburdened, flopped down on the couch. Mom went to her room with the bag, and then returned with her hands behind her back and a smile on her face.

"I wanted to get you something for your birthday," Mom said softly, "just a little something."

She then pointed to SOROS to remind me and with the other hand passed me a pair of hiking boots. These were almost brand-new! So this is what was happening at the tea shop; it was an exchange place for underground trading. How had I missed that with all the years we had been going there?

"Thank you, Mom, I love them." I made sure not to say what it was, didn't want SOROS to check current purchases; my boots wouldn't be on the list.

I tried them on and was pleased with the way they fit. I could cover a lot of miles in these, and I may have to. With a sitcom on the television, Mom and I just lounged on the couch, relishing the moment of peace. Tomorrow scholastic testing began, not that my scores would matter after Friday. A chuckle escaped me, then with the string I wrote to Mom, "I forgot to study for the test, I've been too busy focusing on Butterfly. Hope I don't flunk!"

Mom wrote back, "At least you were doing something practical."

Then she gave me a wink. We both got a good laugh out of it; I've always cherished moments like these. Mom had always been my best friend, and I couldn't imagine life without her. Hopefully, I never would. I snuggled tighter against her, and we stayed there till the hour grew late.

At my bedroom door I hugged her with all my might. "Good night, Mom, love you. Always have, always will."

THE BOOK OF LETTERS

"Good night, honey. Love you too, always have, always will." Mom kissed me on the forehead and placed her hand over my heart. "I will always be with you."

This was the last week and one of long, drawn-out tests. One test after another till your brain was numb, and you weren't sure if you were even answering the right questions. It was the same boring drudgery each day; my only reprieve from it all was time at the bio farm. I was still working with the goats and pigs, which I enjoyed, and it gave me time to stash more cans at my cache site and see Hog.

Our preps at home were finished, and we had almost completed packing—all was going to plan. Well, it was until Thursday, which was the day things started to fall apart.

CHAPTER 10

This being my last day before my physical testing and Butterfly, I brought as many cans as I could hide in my bag along with me to the bio farm to cache away. As soon as break time came, I checked my surroundings and headed for my cache. Hog met me as I shoved cans into the tree, and I tossed him a sandwich from my pocket. Hog and I played for a few minutes then we headed toward the hog building like we had done so often lately.

As we got close, Hog suddenly stopped and dropped to the ground. I followed his actions, not knowing what he had seen. Then the mystery was solved as I saw a figure start down my trail directly toward us; it was Jim. I didn't know what to do. I lay there trying to figure a way out of this, but it was Hog who made the first move and saved me from a confrontation. When Jim was about thirty feet from us, Hog suddenly stood up and advanced, his growl growing louder with each step and his teeth exposed in all their glory. I watched Jim as Hog came into his view. Despite Jim's brave talk and my predicament, I was enjoying the effect Hog was having on him. Jim froze in place at the sight of Hog, but the big guy continued to advance till there were only inches between him and Jim's now uncontrollably shaking body. Like an explosion, without warning, Hog let loose a bark directly into Jim's face then stood there teeth bared and a deep growl growing from his thick chest.

I was pleasantly delighted when I saw the front of Jim's pants unmistakably darken; Hog was having fun now. He stood on his hind legs, making him taller than Jim and looked down on him while

THE BOOK OF LETTERS

his massive chest kept rumbling and sharp teeth kept snapping. It was too much for Jim; he finally seemed to regain control of his terrified body and took off out of the woods. I could hear him screaming something as he made his way up the trail and past the pig building, but I was laughing too hard to make it out. Hog ran back to me, his tail wagging and proud of what he had done.

"What a good boy!" I said in praise, Hog pranced and twisted at the compliment. I gave him a quick scratch behind the ear then raced to get back to the pigs before anyone else showed up, while Hog faded back into the woods. This was the last thing I needed on the day before Butterfly! Why couldn't Jim just leave me alone! The memory of cocky Jim peeing himself helped temper my anger and panic. After all, you got to love seeing braggarts being exposed for what they really are. In Jim's case, he proved he was simply the liar and a coward we all suspected, as well as being a pain in my butt.

It wasn't long before I heard Kel and Jim coming through the door. Jim was still wearing his wet pants, which made me giggle a little despite the situation. He was still yelling about the bear that had tried to kill him, and as expected his story wasn't even close to what had actually happened. Jim hadn't seen me in the woods, only Hog, so Jim built his story to soothe his ego. I nearly burst out laughing when he told Kel about how he had driven the bear off before running to get help.

Before I could stop myself, I innocently asked, "What happened to your pants, Jim?"

Both of the guys looked down at Jim's pants, and I caught a slight twinkle in Kel's eyes. Jim glared back at me; I could see the wheels turning in his head, wondering if I had seen what had really happened. I just looked back wide-eyed and innocent.

"I must have fallen in something wet when I was fighting off the bear," Jim snapped back.

"That's something I'm still trying to figure out about your story," Kel said as he gave Jim a hard look. "You keep saying you fought off some bear, but the only thing dirty on you is your pants."

"Are you calling me a liar?" Jim fired back. "Maybe you should ask her where she was when the attack happened. She wasn't here, I know because I checked."

"Please, one line of questioning at a time," Kel said. "Why don't you show me where this attack happened, so I can get some pictures for my report." He then looked at me. "I'll be back to ask you a few questions afterward."

Kel and Jim headed for the woods, and I rushed to finish my work before they got back. I was loading the work cart with empty feed sacks and tools when Kel returned but without Jim in tow.

Kel watched me for a moment before he spoke, and I could see he was trying to make up his mind as to what to do. "Did you ask Jim to come down here to check on you?"

"No, that just isn't something I would do. That guy makes my skin crawl!" My voice was icy over the question.

Kel chuckled. "Don't get upset with me, just had to ask. I haven't met a gal here who didn't feel the same way about Jim. Not that he would believe it."

Kel's comment made me relax a little. I got the feeling he didn't care too much for Jim either. I looked at Kel; I was going to miss him even if I didn't know him that well. What would he think of me if he knew I was an illegal? I wondered.

"Listen," Kel said, "I don't want to be filling out forms and doing investigations, and I don't think you want that either. I see a way out of it if you'll back me up."

He looked to see if I was agreeable, and with a nod from me he continued, "My report is going to say that I suspect Jim of drinking on the job and showing signs of intoxication. It will also include incidents of harassment that have been reported, believed to have been caused by suspected drinking."

I wasn't sure why Kel was doing this, but I wanted to kiss him for it, and then blushed at the thought. Butterfly was less than twenty-four hours away, and I wanted nothing to complicate things.

"Thank you" was all I could think to say.

"I never have liked that guy, too full of ego while empty on brains," Kel replied. "Guys like that have always irritated me; they

THE BOOK OF LETTERS

always believe their own lies and fantasies." Kel's voice softened. "So tomorrow is your last test. Have any plans for after?"

I didn't know what to say, so blurted out, "Who knows where the wind may carry us."

Kel nodded in agreement. "Well, I was just curious if you would like to go out sometime?"

Talk about bad timing. Was this really happening now? I couldn't believe my luck today. Kel watched me as I tried to come up with a coherent answer.

"I would love to, but right now I'm pretty busy with placement and all. Maybe we can do it another time," I finally replied.

Kel smiled. "Then can I look forward to one when you have some free time?"

I thought, what harm can it do? Then I said, "When I'm done with everything that's going on now, then sure, I'll go out with you."

"Sounds like a date then. And I'm going to hold you to it." He flashed me another smile. "I've got to go write this report up, so I'll catch up with you later." With that he headed back to the main office, leaving me alone to try and calm my nerves.

I didn't see Jim when I returned the work cart or at the bus stop and was thankful for it. Susan was happy today was her last day at the bio farm, and she talked incessantly about all the possibilities she saw in her future. She had some big dreams, though most involved finding a rich husband. At her stop, we hugged tight and said our goodbyes. I would miss her, as odd as she was.

As the Portland skyline passed by the bus windows, memories of the life I would soon leave washed over me. All I had ever known would soon be nothing more than shadows of my past. Tomorrow the wait would be over, and a new life would start. Hopefully it was going to be a good one. I thought over my checklist again; it was hard packing for something you had never done before.

At home, I found the apartment empty and a note on the fridge. Mom had left on some errand and would be home later. On the kitchen counter lay the beginnings of dinner preparations. Putting my things away, I went to finishing dinner. The note hadn't said when she would be back or where she had gone. As the veggies sautéed, I seasoned the protein patties and watched out the window for Mom.

It wasn't like Mom to leave without letting me know where she was going and after the day I had already had, dread started to weigh on me. I had SOROS pull up the daily news. There had been another round of security raids, with suspected terrorists being arrested or shot.

"A prominent member of OHSU's medical staff was also taken in." SOROS immediately had my full attention. "Dr. Moipan was taken in a raid in the Hollywood District, along with one attending nurse whose name has yet to be released. Security patrols also say they have made great headway into underground activities." I told SOROS to change to music; I had heard enough to heighten my fears to new levels. Had Mom been the nurse? The smell of veggies burning snapped me back to focusing on the moment; I put the smoking pan in the sink before any alarms went off and doused it.

I had to think, if Mom had been taken in the raid, what was I supposed to do? Once they knew her name, they would come for me. I looked out the window. Mom's chip would tell them all they need to know once they scanned her at the station. If they were coming, it wouldn't be long. What would I do if they did come? Mom had said stick to the plan, but this was one of those parts we hadn't discussed yet.

I don't know how long I stood there watching out that window, waiting. Waiting for Mom or security patrols, whichever came first. Thankfully, it was Mom. The sun was almost gone when I saw her hurrying down the sidewalk, headed for home. I was so relieved that tears were flowing by the time Mom made it into the apartment.

Still crying, I helped Mom with her coat, but she wouldn't let me take her bags; those she put it her room. I grabbed the string and met Mom in the kitchen where the smell of smoke still lingered. Mom saw the burned pan in the sink then looked at what I was writing on the table.

"Where were you?" I asked with flips of the string. "I thought you had been taken in a raid."

THE BOOK OF LETTERS

Mom could see that I was scared. She hugged me again, then picked up the string and told me what had happened. She had just left the hospital when she heard the news; it was a courier that informed her of a few changes that had been made to fill the needs that the raids had caused. When I asked her about the bags, she got sketchy on the details, other than to say she was dropping them off tomorrow. I was just glad to have her home and safe, so I didn't press her. We were so close to our escape; we couldn't afford any mistakes now.

The rest of the evening, we worked on packing our bags and pockets with our various items till we were satisfied and certain of our preparations. When we left tomorrow, there would be no coming back. We would either be free of this life or prisoners of the state. Tonight as we lay in our beds, we chased after the peace of sleep, but on this night we found it highly allusive.

CHAPTER 11

Morning greeted me with the sounds of Mom singing and the wonderful aromas of cooking. The sky looked angry but no rain so far. Hopefully, it would just pass over. I got up and headed for a shower. Who knows when I might get another one? I dressed and put on my new boots. Today they were going to prove their worth. In the kitchen it looked like Mom had cooked everything in the cabinets.

"Good morning!" Mom said when she saw me. She noticed my glances at all the food. "Didn't know what to fix for breakfast, so I fixed a little of everything." She looked at all the food again. "I may have gone a little overboard." We looked at each other over the ladened table and then burst out laughing.

Everything tasted wonderful, and we sat there eating and talking like old times. These were the moments I would always treasure; I wondered morosely how many more we would have. I pushed the thought away, Today was a day to stay focused on the positive, not the possible negatives. We lingered there not knowing what else to do while waiting for our appointed time to leave, then we went over the plan again.

We arrived at the hospital and blended into the crowd of testers. When the chaos of Butterfly started, we disappeared from the crowd and head toward the VA and on to Washington Park. From there we headed to my cache tree and then turned and headed to meet our contact in Forest Park by midnight. I closed my eyes and visualized the map; I didn't want to forget anything in the chaos. We had one shot at this; there wouldn't be any second chances.

THE BOOK OF LETTERS

Today we would get the rare treat of riding in a taxi instead of a bus, one of the perks for testers. Soon enough our time of departure came. Mom and I grabbed our gear then braced for what was about to come. Our taxi arrived and, once loaded, skirted us off toward the hospital. While we passed through the city, I kept silently repeating the plan to myself, my nerves on edge. Mom's words kept echoing in my head: stick to the plan, stick to the plan.

The driver tried to make light talk with Mom as he drove, while I remained silent, trapped by my own thoughts and fears. The driver said nothing about it, but I could tell he noticed. We had passed the college and were just crossing the Sixth Street overpass when we ran into our first snag. Traffic was at a standstill. Mom checked her watch for the umpteenth time, and again the driver noticed.

Reaching for his phone, he called his dispatch. I held my breath, wondering what he was doing. He caught me watching him and smiled at me while he talked. Hanging up, he informed us that the holdup was because of a security-patrol inspection but that we should start moving soon. Mom checked her watch again. I gripped Mom's hand; I could feel the stress building in both of us as the minutes slowly ticked by. A wave of relief came over me when we started moving again. We only had a short time left before Butterfly would start across the city.

The hospital came into view and, with it, new concerns. The crowds we were expecting, the ones that were always here on testing day, were nowhere to be seen. Instead, there was only an inspection point that had been set up a few yards from the front door of the building and with it four armed security-patrol officers. My breath caught in my throat. I saw the driver look back in his mirror at us. He had to know something was wrong because he was looking around the empty entrance as well.

"This is good right here," Mom said to the driver, and he pulled to the curb a few yards from the guards.

We got out of the cab, and the driver got our bags out of the trunk. As we gathered our things, I heard the driver ask Mom, "Is everything okay, ladies?"

Mom and I froze. What could we say? Mom looked at the driver for a moment, and then took a chance.

"Not really but we are out of time and options," Mom said, her voice strained and full of fear.

The driver looked over at the guards then back at us standing there with our bags. He knew as well as we did that no one needed that many bags for testing. He got back into his cab and rolled down the window.

"Ladies, don't you worry one bit. From what I hear it's going to be a beautiful day. We might even see a butterfly or two," he said with a big smile then looked at his watch. "You two might want to get moving."

Mom grabbed the man's hand and shoved a fistful of her best jewelry into it. "Thank you so much!"

We turned and started toward the inspection desk and the guards. At any minute, Butterfly would start. I glanced down at my phone—it was three forty-four.

"Please place your bags on the table for inspection," ordered the first guard, while the other three started to box us in; we were in trouble. From behind us the sounds of a revving engine distracted two of the guards and as they looked for its source, I heard the screams of tires erupt from where the taxi had been sitting. Turning, I could see the driver was bearing down on us and gaining speed, the sounds of his horn reverberating off the walls of the building and parkade. We dived out of the way then, gaining our feet, took off running as the car scattered the guards and splintered the table.

I had taken off toward the VA like we had planned, but when I looked back I saw that Mom had veered off and was now running for the entrance to the hospital. I turned and started to head toward her, but one of the guards grabbed my backpack and yanked me backward, tearing the pack off my shoulder and nearly pulling me off my feet. I swung back at the guard with my can-filled purse and caught him full force in the chest, knocking him sprawling. The impact caused the purse to burst, sending cans in all directions. I took at quick look around for Mom and found her still running for the entrance.

THE BOOK OF LETTERS

She had just passed through the doors when I saw three of the guards take her down. As she disappeared beneath the wave of bodies, there suddenly came a flash followed by a deafening explosion. Its impact sent a wall of glass and concrete shrapnel into the roadway like a shotgun blast, chewing up everything in its path. I was blown backward by the force of the shockwave and slammed to the ground. My ears were deafened while my head rang, leaving me confused and in a state of panic over what had just happened. My brain started screaming: "Get up and run, Alice, run!" I saw the guard that I had knocked down was still lying on the road but now heavily bleeding; he had been caught in the wave of flying debris and was now dead or dying. I looked back to where Mom had been taken down, and I knew she was dead. The front three floors of the building had been obliterated; no one could have survived in the carnage. The sounds of other explosions were now beginning to sound out across the city of Portland; Butterfly, was in full flight.

I quickly gained my feet and headed toward the VA. Stick to the plan, Mom had said, and having no other options I did just that. Crazy thoughts that Mom may have made it out the back of the hospital spurred me on; I just had to stick to the plan. I couldn't go fast as my leg started to scream and on refection realized I was bleeding, and the pain in my leg was building. Looking down I could see a large shard of glass protruding from my calf; I knew this wasn't good. I found a hidden spot in an unkept hedge, and pulled the dagger like piece of glass out.

Blood poured from the wound, and I quickly added pressure to the gash, hoping to slow the flow, but I was going to need to close it up before I could go anywhere or bleed to death. Mom had the big first aid kit in her bags, and mine had been in my backpack. I went to the pockets inside my coat and found the extra gauze I had put there, and after a few more minutes of digging I found the small tube of superglue that was stored away as well. I tore my pants open a bit more to get a good look at the wound—it looked bad.

Wiping away as much blood as possible, I then put a strip of the glue just above the open incision and set one edge of the gauze on it and let it adhere. Then gritting my teeth, I gripped the gauze and pulled the wound closed, and then glued the gauze down to that side. Once the glue was holding, I wrapped my leg with my scarf. I couldn't stay here; I had to get to my cache. I had lost my backpack, phone, purse, and everything they contained. I took assessment of what I still had; it amounted to my case and its contents and whatever I had in my pockets, but no food or water.

The clouds that had seemed angry this morning now took their vengeance out on the city; it didn't take long for its cold fingers to soak through my clothes. My wounded leg and the pouring rain made travel miserable and slow as I worked to keep out of sight. I kept telling myself to just keep moving, step by agonizing step, as I headed for Washington Park and hopefully my cache and safety. I could hear drones buzzing overhead, searching, and I wondered if they were looking for me.

My leg was like a dead weight, and as I continued on, I could feel blood begin to soak my sock. I needed to stop again but didn't know where. A few blocks later, I found a space between a heat pump and house that seemed empty. I check my wound again. The gauze was holding, but all this walking was not helping, and blood was continuing to seep through the bandaging. I rewrapped my leg tighter with the scarf; I rested and wondered how much time had already passed.

Between my bad leg and the drones that kept passing by, I had spent more time hiding than traveling. Now the daylight was fading, and the overcast skies weren't helping. I still had time before midnight came; somehow, I would make it, I had to. The pain from my leg was torture, but I had to keep moving. If I sat anywhere too long, I knew they would find me. There was my chip to think of. If one of those drones got close enough, it might pick up its signal.

I could hear the wail of sirens as fire trucks and security patrols rushed down Patton road and passed me while I remained hidden in the brush along the road's edge. Once it was clear, I made my hobbled dash to the other side and continued on toward Highway 26; my cache was almost within reach. I wondered if Hog would be there to meet me or if all the noise had driven him off; hopefully it hadn't. From the back fence of a cul-de-sac, I watched the highway;

THE BOOK OF LETTERS

it was aglow with flashing lights from scores of security patrols and emergency vehicles. I sat there hidden and not sure what to do; once again I waited as I tried to figure out some way across.

The sun faded into night, and the city grew shockingly dark. Butterfly had not only attacked state and federal buildings, but had also taken out their vengeance on bridges and power stations, effectively shutting the electrical grid as well as causing travel problems. The clouds helped add to the depth of the gloom by blocking out the moonlight, making the night now seem impossibly black. Though the darkness and rain helped hide me, it also added to my growing list of problems as well as complicating my travel. I had no idea how far I walked along the brush line of the highway, but somehow in the inky blackness of the night, I found a culvert that ran under the highway and crawled through it to the other side.

I rested there in the colorless abyss of the culvert: cold, wet, hungry, frightened, and in pain. My head was foggy either from the pain and fatigue or from the hypothermia being brought on by my rain-soaked clothes. I didn't know or care which it was. Tears started flowing; I knew Mom was gone. I didn't want to believe it, but I knew what I had seen. Sobs started to rack my body. Why did she do it? Had this been part of the plan the whole time? I couldn't accept that, not that I had any choice.

"Get a grip, Alice! You got to get moving!" I could hear my mother's voice yelling at me. I tried to call back to her and then woke up. I didn't know if I passed out or fell asleep, but I was awake now and struggling to get my rebelling limbs moving. My cold body was reluctant to function; yet somehow, I started forward again toward the bio farm. I could see a glow from ahead, and I wondered what it was. My slowed senses finally confirmed my new fears; the bio farm seemed to be on fire. Even from a distance I could see the building flames and the flashing of lights from the fire trucks and security-patrol cars. As I got closer, I could see the place swarming with personnel. This was going to make getting to my cache difficult, but I needed the food and items stashed there, so difficult or not I had to make a try.

Hobbling forward again, I worked my way through the choked woods, branches slapping at me from the darkness as I worked my way through the leaden brush. I used the glow of the fire to orientate myself as I traveled on. I had to hurry; no one needed to tell me that my body wasn't going to keep going on like this much longer. I needed food, warmth, and rest, and I was going to need them soon. My heart sank as I got approached the area of my cache. I could see flashlights fluttering through the woods around my tree and its goods. As I drew closer, I could make out voices calling out as they searched the woods in front of me, one of the voices I knew too well.

"I'm telling you, I know she hid things out here!" It was Jim's voice.

"Well, we been out here for almost an hour and haven't found anything or seen anyone. As for me I'm done with standing in the rain." I didn't know the voice, but from the authority it held, I was guessing a security-patrol officer.

I could see two other moving lights further back, which told me there were at least two other security officers as well and no way to get past them. Then I heard a crashing in the woods of something big moving off to my right. Whatever it was, it was moving fast and hard. A moment later there was a scream of pain, then shouting and gunshots followed by more yelling from the other officers. Someone cried out, "Man down!" Patrols from all directions ran toward the call, some trying to help the wounded while others roamed into the woods around the scene, trying to chase down what had attacked. Jim continued to guard my tree, undeterred by what was happening in the dark around him. I was starting to really hate this guy.

I heard the growl before I knew Hog had slipped past the patrols and returned back to the cache. The night was too dark for me to see clearly, but the sound of Jim screaming and Hog snarling was enough to tell me that Jim was being dealt with. While Hog kept him busy, I quickly moved to my tree and reached in—it was empty. Someone had taken everything; my mind raced for options and found none. Jim's screams had turned to pleading and guttural crying; it wasn't long before the sounds of Jim's torment brought the crashing noises of returning officers headed our way.

THE BOOK OF LETTERS

"Hog, we got to get out of here now!" I called to Hog, and he materialized out of the night next to me. We turned to what I hoped was northwest and headed toward the planned meeting point. I knew I didn't have much longer or much strength left, but fear of being left behind pushed me on. I couldn't stop shivering now and my leg, now stiffened and unbending, dragged along, and then I fell. I don't remember falling; I only remember the feeling of cold mud on my face.

We had only gone a short way further when I fell again. My strength was played out, and now panic was starting to rise in me. I had to make it, and one way or another I would—there were no options. Hog loomed over me, whining; we both knew I was in bad shape. Each time I fell, getting up became harder and harder, but I knew somehow I had to make it or die trying, so I kept fighting. There was still some part of me that believed that I was going to make it out of this alive, but that light was fading quickly.

Overhead I could hear the sounds of another approaching helicopter; I had to keep moving before they found me. Down and on the ground again, my head felt thick and my thoughts came slow. Animal-like, I fought and clawed myself up till I was once again standing. My legs were weak, and I felt sick as I stood there shaking uncontrollably, my head swimming. I looked up into the rain and tried to give a roar of defiance, but I couldn't even muster up a whimper. As the rain continued to pour over us, Hog moved along side of me, and I gripped his fur to help steady myself.

I knew my grip wouldn't last long, so taking my belt off, I wrapped it around Hog's neck and then tied it around my wrist. Letting Hog take the lead, we started forward as I stumbled along beside him. I no longer knew what direction we were traveling in, but it didn't seem to matter anymore. Hog led on through the wet black world, and at times it seemed like we were swimming through some horrific, inescapable nightmare. In my numbed state, I could feel myself dying. The cold, loss of blood, and the loss of Mom had all taken its toll. I knew the end was looming near, and even death called my name into the night. I woke up to the feeling of wet grass and mud. Apparently I had fallen again; Hog was pulling on my arm that he was tied to and whining. This time my body refused to even respond; I woke up again as I was being dragged along the ground by Hog's massive bulk.

So this will be how I die. I will see you soon, Mom, sorry I couldn't stick to the plan. My body spasmed as it instinctively fought off the calming warmth of death. Hog pulled again and whined; I tried one last time but was barely able to even raise my head. I tried to free Hog but couldn't undo the knots that bound us together

My thick tongue slurred my words. "Sorry, boy, I can't do it." I felt cold and eternal embrace of death passing over me, and this time welcomed it, but as I did a voice whispered into the night.

"Charlie, is that you?" They were the last words I heard in this cold, black, odious world.

CHAPTER 12

The sound of rustling leaves overhead and a voice told me I wasn't dead, but my head throbbed like a worn-out drum. The voices that were whispering I couldn't put together, except it sounded like an argument.

"Listen, Charlie, I know you're hungry but you can go out and catch something," one voice said. It seemed I had heard it before, but I couldn't remember where.

From the other side of me came a mumble that I couldn't make out; my sluggish head wasn't helping. Slowly I opened my eyes in the dim light and looked up at a metallic ceiling over the leaf bed I was lying in. My mouth was dry and pasty; trying to get up, I rolled to my side and yelped in pain.

"Someone has finally decided to wake up, it sounds like," said the voice, followed by another mumble, "give her some time, Charlie, before you start mauling her." Again, this was followed by more mumbling: "I know you're worried, but give her a few minutes to get her bearings."

The voices seemed close to me. "How are you feeling, Alice?" one of them asked.

The voice knew my name! Painfully, I turned my head enough to see the bearers of the mysterious voices, and through the filtering light I could make out Kel's tall, athletic form and Hog's large, hairy bulk. At the sight of them I nearly started to cry; it seemed like a miracle. Kel got up and moved to my side; lifting a bottle of water, he held it to my lips. Taking a long drink of the water cooled my parched throat and broke the illusion that this was just a dream. My head was still foggy, but I tried to access the situation; I had no idea where I was, what had happened, or how Kel had found me. Or for that matter why he was even here.

He saw my confusion and started filling the pieces. "First off, no, you're not dead. And yes, you came pretty close. You had Charlie, and I worried for the last few days."

A few days! We had to get moving before they found us. I started to try sitting up in panic, but Kel pushed me back down. "They'll find us!" was all I could say.

"Relax, they won't find us," he said, and then pointed to his arm, then mine. We had matching bandages on our forearms. He then added, "While you were passed out, I went ahead and removed your chip. I left our chips where I found you, and then I carried you to where we are now. It's a place Charlie knew, about two miles west from there. I added the Mylar overhead to camouflage our thermal signatures and to help keep you warm."

I started to relax. There were so many more questions I wanted to ask, but my strength was again fading fast. Kel had opened a can of peaches; I sucked on one of the slices, letting the juice run down my throat. Slowly Kel fed them to me one slice at a time, then darkness washed over me again, and I slept. My dreams were chaotic and jumbled; a profusion images were thrown at me but nothing coherent or understandable.

I woke in a panic. How long had we been here? Painfully, I forced my body to try to sit up; my sore muscles protested but complied. Hog was sleeping next to me, keeping me warm, and he stirred then stretched at my movements. The big guy had to sniff me over first; once I got his approval or at least a lick to the face, I was allowed to sit up all the way. My head was clearer today, thankfully, and I started taking assessment of my situation. My leg had been rebandaged and though stiff wasn't as painful as it was on the night of my escape.

I could see numerous empty food cans piled off to one side of the shelter and wondered how long we had been here. I looked around and found my case setting next to where Hog had been sleep-

THE BOOK OF LETTERS

ing, along with my hat, coat, and boots. From the looks of the hat, Hog had been using it for a pillow, so I straightened it out and set it on the case. I heard movement from the other end of the den, and I knew that Kel was now awake as well.

"Good morning, you're looking better," Kel said as he tried to smooth his tangled waves of hair.

"How long have we been here?" I asked, my voice still a bit hoarse.

Kel handed me a bottle of water then answered, "This is our fourth day. For a while there you had me pretty scared."

I couldn't believe it; I had been sleeping for almost three full days! I was never going to find my contacts now; I needed to come up with a plan. How much did Kel know? And I found myself asking again, why was he even here? The questions were starting to pile up, and I needed some answers, so I could figure out what to do. Kel could see my confusion as I was trying to put it all together, so he took pity on me and helped fill in the blanks.

He handed me a can of food. "Here, eat this while I try to explain. Well, at least all of the parts I know."

Kel had been a part of Butterfly and, unknown to me, was actually the contact we had been planning to meet. It was him that had planted the bombs at the bio-farm labs; afterward he headed to my cache and gathered it all with the intent of meeting us along the way. He had found my tracks days before and traced them back to my tree, so he grabbed the cache on his way out to our meeting point. When we didn't show up, he came looking for us, worried that something had gone wrong.

"That's when Charlie found me, and I found you," Kel said, once I had been brought up to the current events.

"Who's Charlie?" I asked. I hadn't seen anyone else, only heard the mumbles.

"That's Charlie," he said, pointing to Hog.

I laughed as it all became clear. "That's not his name."

Kel gave me a look. "Then what is it, since you know him so well."

"It's Hog," I replied.

93

It was Kel's turn to laugh. "Who names a dog Hog? It's not like Charlie answers to any name anyway."

"Come here, Hog," I said softly. Hog got up, then walked over to me, and gave my face a swipe of his tongue.

"Well, I'll be" was all Kel could think to say. "I met Charlie—I mean, Hog—about three months ago. He had a face full of infected quills. While he was too weak to fight back, I pulled them out and doctored him best I could. Even though I saved his life, he still isn't too trusting. I thought I was going to lose my arm just trying to get your case and coat off you. Oh, and I would be careful picking that hat up, he's pretty fond of it."

I laughed again and defiantly picked up the hat and put it on. Hog got up, came over to me, and sniffed at the hat on my head. Then he flopped down next to me, and I gave him a good scratching behind his ear. I was sure that he had saved my life during that terrible night, and for that I would always be grateful. Hog turned his face to mine and gave me another flick of his tongue; I was falling in love with this big guy.

Kel chuckled. "He's just a big cuddle bear with you." Then he suddenly burst into muffled laughter. "I just had a memory of Jim and his pants after meeting Hog. If he only knew that you were here petting his bear."

His laughter was contagious, and I must admit the thought of Jim's pants was pretty funny. After a bit, Hog got up, stretched, and headed outside to hunt. As I watched him go, I realized that this was his world, one he understood well, and I would be wise to learn from him. One of the pages in the book of letters talked about learning from how animals live and emulating them. In typical fashion, my great-grandfather had simply wrote, "The wilderness is an animal's home, and it is always best to learn from the locals."

After he had gone, I looked back to Kel and tried to tell him about what had ensued at the hospital and with Mom. "It all happened so fast. One moment she was running, then the next—"

Kel stopped me. "I know, Alice, you don't have to go back through it." To my questioning eyes, he added, "You were talking a lot while you were unconscious. I'm sorry, she didn't make it."

THE BOOK OF LETTERS

I hoped I hadn't said anything to embarrassing, but I didn't think Kel was the kind of guy to mention those kinds of things. We sat there silently while I composed myself. So much had happened and so quickly, that it was all hard to take. After a bit, Kel filled me in on what our current plan was and our situation. We had a lot of miles to cover before we could consider ourselves safe, and those miles where now spotted with security patrols and drones looking for escapees from the city as well as from detention centers, reeducation containments, and work camps.

Kel told me that on the day of the Butterfly, the resistance had bombed every holding and detention center, transit centers, data centers, hospitals, bridges, power stations, cell towers, and fuel depots. They were attempting to free as many people as they could while shutting down enough of the city's needed systems to keep most of the patrol units too busy to pursue the escapees. It would have worked too had security forces not tortured out enough info to warrant posting extra patrols. Now they were out in force with every available officer trying to round up or shoot down any and all escapees. We needed a new plan.

"First things first," Kel started. "How is your leg doing? We got a lot of traveling to do, think you can do it?"

I flexed my leg and felt the stab of pain. "Think you could make me a walking stick? I think it would help a lot."

Kel nodded. "You stay here and I'll go find one. If you're up to it I want to leave tonight. We'll have a partial moon to light our way, it should make traveling a little easier." He then crawled out of the den and headed out on his search for a makeshift crutch for me to use.

I pulled my coat and case over to me and started assessing what I had left. It wasn't much, but I would have to learn how to make do. The case had stayed watertight, so everything inside had thankfully stayed dry. I thought back to the blueprints I had found in the case. I just needed time and a place to put all the pieces of the case and dulcimer together. Once assembled the bow and items the case contained could be the difference between dying and making it to safety.

I didn't have a mirror with me, so I had no idea what condition my hair and face were in. I used my fingers to unknot my hair as much as possible, and then I wiped myself down as best I could with the damp sleeve of my coat. With the magnetized needle and some thread, I stitched up the tear in my jeans the best I could. They were the only ones I had left, so it was best to do whatever I could to keep them intact.

Kel returned with Hog and a branch he had found that had a fork in it. With it he soon fashioned a rough crutch for me. He noticed that I had moved the case, and in his eyes I could see his quiet curiosity. I wasn't sure how much I should tell Kel about its contents or why I felt it needed to be kept secret, but I was reluctant to answer to many question about it.

"So what are you packing in that thing?" Kel inquired. "I only ask because it seems a bit heavy, and Hog here nearly ate me when I took it off you."

Hog rolled his big sad eyes as he looked at me, and then laid his head on my lap.

"Oh brother!" Kel interjected as he watched Hog's innocent act. "Go ahead and act like a pussycat now, you know what you did."

I laughed a little over the actions of my big furry guard; he sure had an effect on people. I tried to decide how much to tell Kel. I had no reason not to trust him, but with my world in upheaval, I just didn't want to trust anyone too quickly.

"This was a gift left to me by my biological mother. It was made by my great-grandfather," I replied, then taking a huge leap of faith, I opened the case and pulled out the book of letters.

Kel gave a slow whistle when he saw the book. "No wonder that case was so heavy!"

"These were all letters written by my great-grandfather to my birth mother," I said as I handed him the book. "He said that its information would be helpful in times like these."

Kel gently thumbed through the pages, stopping now and then as articles caught his attention. After a while he handed the book back, and I put it away.

"How can one guy know so much?" Kel asked while he watched me lock the case. "How much of that book have you read?"

THE BOOK OF LETTERS

"Not much. I haven't had it that long," I answered. Then, looking at him, I added, "There's more, but we would need time for that. There are things hidden inside the case, but they need to be assembled."

Kel nodded. I could see that he was thinking of the road ahead. A moment later he glanced back at me and said, "I know a place where we can make some plans and figure things out. It's going to take some quick traveling, though. Are you up to heading out tonight?"

I hurt, but I also knew we needed to be moving before we were discovered here by some lucky patrol, so I gritted my teeth and nodded yes. As we waited for nightfall, we finished the last of our canned food. I gave Hog some of mine as a treat, then tossed him the empty can and saw his big tail thump in delight while his tongue sought out any possible remaining bits of flavor. It wasn't long before it was time to go, and we headed into the night and our personal flight across an active war zone.

Kel took the lead and I hobbled along behind him. Hog, meanwhile, skirted the woods to the side of us. The dim glow of the moon gave the night a ghoulish feel as we worked our way toward the northwest part of Forest Park. Our progress was slow because of my clumsiness trying to walk with only one crutch and one good leg. In time, though, we made it through the park, stopping twice to wait under the Mylar blanket as drones flew over and once for a passing patrol squad.

We were nearing midnight when Kel stopped. My leg was killing me, but I tried hard to hide it. I knew Kel was worried about how slow we were going, but he also knew it was as fast as I could muster. He stared off into the night, his face dim in the moonlight—it was a mask of concentration. Suddenly Kel stood up and helped me to my feet.

"Get on my back," Kel said as he slung his backpack across his chest.

"You can't carry me!" I protested.

Kel leaned in close to me. "Listen, we have about half a mile to go before we get to Newberry Road. Once we get across that, we're out of the park and heading to a place I know, where we can rest up."

He looked worried and continued, "The problem is we're running out of time, so please let me just carry you for a bit. If you could indulge me at least till we're past the road and the patrols, I would appreciate it. Besides, it's not like you could weigh a lot, little as you are." He chuckled.

I hated to admit it, but he was right about our time problem, so reluctantly I climbed onto his back. I knew that with me and our gear he was packing a heavy load, but he never complained, and in a short time we soon saw the road. Seeing Hog drop flat, Kel and I hit the ground as well, not sure of what he sensed. It was only a moment before we spotted the patrol vehicles then watched as they passed us, the harsh glare of their spotlights searching both sides of Newberry Road.

We laid there frozen, too afraid to breath as their lights danced around us. As they continued on, their lights faded, but our fear didn't. If they caught us here, it would all be over, and Mom's death would be meaningless. As the patrols reached a bend in the road, Hog hopped up, and Kel followed suit while grabbing my arm.

"We got to go now!" Kel's voice was urgent.

He hoisted me onto his back and jogged to the road; the patrol lights were almost gone, so we started across. About halfway to the other side of Newberry, we knew we were in trouble. The flash of brake lights was our first warning, and then the sirens started blaring as the patrols started turning back. Kel, spurred into action, started running, and I was surprised at how quick he could move, even with all he was packing. We crashed into the brush on the other side just as the lights started back toward us. That was when we heard the first pulsating thumps of gunfire.

CHAPTER 19

It was the screams that made us look back from the darkness of the brush; it was a scene I will never forget. In the harsh glare of headlights, the security patrols were gunning down people, young and old, as they ran, fleeing for the hopeful safety of the woods. Some scattered as they tried to escape their fate, while others just stopped and clung to each other, waiting for it all to end. We didn't know who they were, but their prison-orange jumpsuits told us enough—they were from reeducation centers and work camps. The officers stood on the hood of their cars to get better views and continue to randomly shoot anything that moved. As bodies fell in the field or on the road, I could hear the shooters give a cheer. The road and the open area that ran along it were soon littered with bodies of the dead, and the piercing cries of the dying. I felt sick and looked away from the surreal carnage; all I wanted now was to get as far from here as we possibly could.

"We got to go," Kel whispered as the patrols continued their slaughter, the sound of the screams now fading but the resonance of them still pounding in my ears, forever embedded in my memory. I could feel the hot flood of tears flow as Kel carried me deeper into the woods and away from the horror playing out behind us. I didn't know where he was taking me, nor did I care, as long as it was a way from the ghastly scene. All I could think of was the people that now lay dead behind us, and the haunting sound of the officers' laughter and cheers amid the sea of abattoir terror. How many would have to die for just one soul to know freedom? Would I know the cold of death or the hope of freedom when the sun rose? Only tomorrow knew the answer.

The cold and fear prickled my skin, regardless of my coat, and I began to shake uncontrollably. Kel just gripped my legs tighter and kept moving. He pushed on, forcing our way through the dark undergrowth, too afraid of what was behind us stop. I felt the slap of branches and the brush snatch at my clothes like bony fingers. I buried my face against his back, trying to pull myself together. Kel suddenly came to a halt and set me down on a mound of ferns; Hog circled around us about thirty or forty yards out, and then returned when he was satisfied with the parameter. Kel motioned to us to stay put, and then moved closer to us so we could hear his whispers.

"We have to cross Cornelius Pass Road, and there's a way under it somewhere near here. I just have to find the marker. Wait here with Hog, and I'll be right back." And with that Kel slipped away into the darkness of the horrific night.

I clung to Hog, my finger holding tight to his thick fur, while my ears strained to hear any sounds of pursuit from the depths of the blackness around me. The sonorous cascade of the gunfire and sirens had faded out behind us, and now the night was silent, leaving an ominous feeling clinging to the damp, dark forest like impending doom. The phantoms of shadows and apparitions of childhood monsters seemed to dance in the night around me, and I trembled as my ears strained for the sounds of Kel's returning boots. Hog's thick tongue licked at my tears and cooed a soft warble, trying to calm me, then his ears went up at the sounds of an approach; and I felt him tense, then relax, at the sight of Kel's wide-shouldered form heading toward us.

"A little ways from here I found the culvert that runs under the road," Kel said softly. "How are you doing?"

I didn't know what to say; the world was self-destructing around us, and he wanted to know how I was doing. Kel's face was close enough that I could clearly see concern etched his face in the dim moonlight, and I felt his hand slip into mine. As he pulled me upright, his arms wrapped around my shoulders, holding me, as if they were trying to impart some of their strength to me. I stood there

THE BOOK OF LETTERS

try to pull back the flood of tears, and slowly regained my composure. I must be strong; I must not surrender to my fears and emotions. There would be time for mourning later, but we had to survive the nightmare we were now in first.

"I'll be fine," I finally said, then choked back a sob as I added, "better than those back there."

"Alice, we are going to make it!" Kel said and from his tone I knew he believed it. His arms tightened, pulling me closer to him. "I know you're hurt and you're scared. Who wouldn't be? But don't give up yet. If you can handle a few more miles, we'll be able to hole up for a while. You just got to hang in a bit longer. Can you do that?"

I nodded, and he headed toward the road. I limped along behind as Hog walked beside me, helping to steady my clumsy passage on through the night. Kel's ghostlike form drifted in and out from a mosaic of foliage, as we tried to match his pace. The road came into sight, and we kept to the brush that ran along the east side. A few yards later, Kel pointed to a worn and leaning sign that had the fading word *Folkenberg* on it. I had never heard of the place and wondered if it were a town. Just past it we found a drainage culvert that ran under the road. Kel checked for any coming vehicles, then waved us into the inky blackness, with Hog taking the lead.

Crawling along, my heart would jump every time my hand landed on something I couldn't identify or the sound of a passing vehicle as it roared overhead. My mind raced with thoughts of rats, spiders, and—worse—snakes in the tomblike confinement. I was still unable to see the end of the pipe, and fears of being trapped began to rise. Panic was starting to take a firm grip on me by the time we reached the other side of Cornelius Pass Road, and I tumbled from the pipe like a drowning animal fighting for air. Kel didn't wait for me to recover but grabbed me by the collar of my coat and dragged me into the concealment of the woods while Hog watched our back trail. I don't know how he did it, but Kel put me on his back again, and then he staggered on, heading for the promised hideout.

We continued west and were soon crossing open farmland, leaving us feeling exposed and unprotected, making our nerves raw and on edge as we watched for any signs of patrols. Kel hurried me through several fences and across irrigation ditches half full of ice-cold water and mud; I could tell our time was short by the sense of urgency in his voice as he coaxed me on and the brightening color of the transforming eastern horizon. A partially collapsed house loomed to our left, and Kel veered in its direction then around one side and on to the remains of a barn. Behind that we found a jumbled cluster of rusting vehicles and scrap metal abandoned and in various stages of being reclaimed by the mud that seemed to be sucking it all into its uncertain depths.

Kel located a leaning, dilapidated van that sat wedged among the rusting pile. While I waited, he ran to it and headed toward the back doors. Then finding the handle and secret release, he opened the ancient door and waved me over. The interior was dark and the smell faintly moldy, but it was empty and dry, so we quickly climbed in and closed the door. I stayed close to the door, unsure of what I might find in the inky gloom. Kel bumped around in the depths till he found what he was looking for, and at the sound of a click, a small overhead light came on. The van interior was covered with old worn carpet from some untold era and looked to be stocked with a few supplies on shelves and blacked-out windows; Kel saw my look of curiosity and surprise.

"Not everyone agrees with the way things are being run," Kel said with a smile. "There's an active underground resistance made up of people from all walks of life. They keep places like this, stocking them with whatever they can spare to help us move about unseen. In one of my dad's old books, I think they would describe this as the new underground railroad of sorts."

On one of the shelves, we found a box of unmarked cans of food and a small alcohol stove. I had seen one before, described in one of the letters from the book. The letter called it a penny stove. They were made from two cans and a strip of cotton then filled with denatured alcohol or certain types of liquor. Kel filled the stove and lit it, then with its blue flames, he started to heat up cans of what turned out to be baked beans. While I stored our gear out of the way, I noted a kind of mat lying off to one side to be used as a bed. I wondered how many times people like us had used this hidden harbor, and how long would we be doing the same. The combination of body heat and cooking quickly warmed the van, and with the warmth and food, I started to relax, allowing sleepiness to come over me. It wasn't long before I curled with Hog on the mat and soon after, I fell into a fitful sleep.

I woke up with a start when I realized that Hog was gone. At first, I couldn't remember where I was, and then seeing Kel looking over a map jarred my memory and calmed my fears.

"Good afternoon," he said with a smile. "Feeling better?"

Nodding, I reached down to rub my stiff leg, then feeling the wounded area I knew that sleep must have hit me hard, because without me waking up, it had been rebandaged. I gave Kel a questioning glance, and he pointed to a box marked with a white cross. "Found that in one of the boxes, it turned out to be a well-kept first aid kit. I didn't wake you because I just figured it would be easier for you to sleep through it, if you could. It's looking better, and it's stopped bleeding. I think it's going to be fine as long as we don't push it too hard."

I nodded in understanding, my head still feeling thick and a little groggy from sleep. Rubbing my face, I wondered if I looked as beat as I felt. He handed me a plastic canteen of water and half a sleeve of crackers he had found in the food supplies. At this point I wasn't picky where they came from and took them. The water felt good going down; the previous night of running had left me dehydrated and hungry. Thirst appeased, I started in on the crackers. They were soon followed by a can of split pea soup; he then surprised me with a jar of home-canned peaches. Eating them, their sweet taste reminded me of a better time and a better place. Kel soon followed suit and dug in, knowing we might go a long time before there was more.

"We'll stay here until dark, and if you're up to it we'll move on." Kel's eyes searched mine, trying to discern my feelings. "There's a group that is hiding out west of here. The plan was to join them there. Depending on how things went, they should still be there for another week, more or less. If we can make it there before they break up, they are sure to get us out."

"I'll make it," I replied, and then asked, "how did you get pulled into this?" It was a question I had wondered about several times. He had seemed like the other "normal" people back at the bio farm; now he was running for his life, with me holding him back.

Kel ran his fingers through his hair and sighed. "Long story but if you really want to know, I guess we got time to kill while waiting." He paused a moment as his thoughts went back in time, then deciding where to begin, looked at me and started into his tale. It wasn't pretty or elegant, nor one that I would have believed before. The horror of Newberry Road opened my eyes to the true evil of government control, given power by the very people that they now controlled.

"My dad was a high school teacher in South Salem High, and he did well at first. Then he found the books. Mom and I never knew where the books came from, and only saw them long enough to know that they were books that were banned and illegal. When we asked, he refused to tell us about the books, saying he didn't want to get us involved. His teaching started to falter after that. When it came to some of his lessons he stopped repeating the government program and replaced them with teaching from his hidden sources.

"Questions started being asked, and then without warning, we were raided. It was in the middle of the night when the troopers kicked in the front door and then hit us with flash-bangs, leaving us momentarily deaf and blind while they handcuffed us. We watched as they ransacked the apartment and burned the books with all our belongings in view of the other residents, so we would be shunned if we ever came back. My parents were then sent to a reeducation center, while I was sent to a training school for boys. It wasn't as nice a place as it sounds, but then again, prisons never are." Kel stopped for a moment at the painful memories.

"Dad died three months later at the center. The doctor said it was a heart attack, but I've never believed that. Dad had never had heart trouble and rarely even got sick, and we were never allowed to see the body. Mom finished her courses and was released two years later, and I was sent back to join her. My mother was only a former shadow of herself, her mind destroyed by whatever trauma she had endured at their hands. It wasn't long before I lost her as well, and in

THE BOOK OF LETTERS

the end I think it was a blessing. I was three days from turning sixteen when she passed, and I was sent to spend my last two years back at a training school, this time working with animals.

"After that I was assigned to the bio farm, and soon after, I was contacted through various messengers of a resistance group that had known my father. Through them, some of my father's old students had found me, and soon I joined them in their plans to free those held captive by this government. I wanted a crack at getting back at those that had killed my parents. Then project Butterfly came into play, and I jumped on board." Kel's face was hard as thoughts of his parents and those who had brought about their deaths danced through his memories.

I reached out and touched his arm. "I'm sorry, Kel." It was all I could say as the weight of loss overtook me. We were both orphans in this world, and we knew too well the bitterness of death. Now it was driving us to fight for life. From his pocket he took out a folded piece of paper and handed it to me.

"This was the last message I received. It arrived about three weeks ago," Kel said, as I took the tattered note.

The message was short, but my mom's handwriting was unmistakable. It simply said, "Save Alice. She is Butterfly." I felt the tears start again as the loss of her once more poured over me. All I had left now were memories and a hollow pain.

"I don't know how much you know of what your Mom was doing, but it was big and involved a lot of people. We were each given a job, which we kept to ourselves. On some of the jobs that were deemed critical, they placed backup protocols, just in case. At first I didn't understand the full meaning of the message, but I do now—you were born an illegal."

My eyes flared wide in shock, and I didn't know what to say. How could he even know? I felt the rise of panic and hoped he couldn't see it, but from his look I knew he had.

"It's okay, Alice. I'm sorry, I didn't mean to scare you," Kel quickly said. "I just figured it out when I pulled your chip out. It was a chip normally used for animals. They're not regulated like the ones used in a hospital. I'd heard stories that a few doctors had used them to hide a few kids in the system. I just hadn't believed it was possible till I saw yours. Then I remembered the birth date on your bio-farm file and who your mother was. That's when it all made sense."

A scratch on the door made us both jump and startle us out of our conversation, and gave me time to think. It was just Hog wanting back in, and I was glad to see him, but not so much for the dead rabbit in his mouth. He had caught himself dinner and was ready to eat, so he plopped down in the corner and started digging in. I tried to ignore the ghastly sight of his meal and the sounds of crunching bones, while Kel chuckled at my squeamishness.

I remembered something he had said about the books his father had found and dug into my case for the history book.

Handing the book to Kel, I asked, "Were any of your dad's books like this one?"

Looking at the book, his eyes brightened. "Where did you get this?" he asked.

"Then what it says is real?" I inquired. "It was one of the things I found in my case."

Kel's hand ran gently over the book cover, like he was greeting an old friend anew. He flipped through the pages, and then turned to me. "It's real, that's why they were banned. It's a truth they don't want you to know, because if people knew the truth they would rebel. So you've read some of it?"

"A bit," I replied, "it's certainly not what they teach in school."

Kel continued to flip through the pages, obviously looking for something. After a few minutes, he found what he was looking for and handed the open book back to me. "Here's why these books were banned."

I looked at the page; it was the beginning of a chapter on the American Constitution and Bill of Rights.

I looked them over as Kel continued, "If people actually understood what was in our Constitution, there would be a civil war, and they knew that. If you change a country's history, you change the way people see themselves. When you take away their victories, their heroes, their morals, their understanding of how they grew as a culture, you leave them to be willing sheep without the will or knowledge to fight back. Then you throw in a mocked-up pandemic or a catastrophe with a sprinkling of worldwide hysteria and let fear bring compliance from the masses. Hold them long enough in that fear, and your rules becomes their new salvation, while leading them to offer up their wills on the altar of the government in hopes of buying safety. It's that lack of will, which allows those in power to maintain a false sense of control."

I thought back to the quote I had found in the book of letters: "Those who give up essential liberty, to purchase a little temporary safety, deserve neither liberty nor safety." It had been written by one of the same men who had signed the Constitution, Benjamin Franklin. The thought that people would be so willing to give all these rights away was baffling at best. How could have people let this happen? Looking at the book made me wonder about everything I had ever been taught in school. Was it all lies? Was my whole education simply the product of propaganda?

Putting the book away, I thought of what Kel had told me. I didn't really know him, but with all that we had been through together, I knew I could trust him. After all, he had saved my life and carried me through miles of hostile woods and farmlands, and all the while knowing the truth about me.

I turned back to Kel. "You asked me why this case was so important, and you deserve to know." Pulling the case closer to me, I opened the secret compartment and handed him the envelope. As Kel looked over the pages, I continued, "The case was made by my great-grandfather, and as you can see from the blueprints, it was made like a hidden puzzle to be taken apart and later reassembled into weapons and tools we will need. He made it for my birth mother, Liz, to be used to get to his farm somewhere over in the dead zone."

"These are amazing!" Kel exclaimed as he continued to study the papers. "These things will definitely help. Now we just need to find a place to put it all together." Kel tipped his head back and thought. And then, snapping his fingers, he said, "I just remembered a place I was told about, and it's on the way too. I've never been there, but I was told about an old abandoned cabin about a mile east of a place they use to call Sky Ranch, marked with tall fir trees. Do you think your leg will hold up to four miles?"

I gave him a hard look, trying to look tougher than I felt. "Made it this far, didn't we? I'm not about to give up now. Like you said earlier, I want a chance to get back at them." Then with gritted teeth, I added, "They got a lot to pay for, but right now, just staying alive is revenge enough."

Kel nodded in agreement then handed back the pages and started looking through boxes, setting aside a few supplies to help with our journey. I wasn't looking forward to another long, painful night but I felt driven; we had to find that cabin. Once there I would be able to finally put my great-grandfather's creations to use, like he had planned so many years ago. Well, almost: we were heading northwest instead of east and hopefully to freedom, not toward the certain death that now lay to the east of the mountains.

I looked over at Hog, who was now softly snoring. I could see his big paws once again holding my hat under his head. I wonder what Mom would have thought of my big friend or of Kel. If she knew how they had saved me, I'm sure she would have loved them. I curled up against the warmth of Hog's body and napped while I still had time, resting for the coming hardship. Kel packed the extra supplies he found into his pack. Besides food and bandages, he had also managed to find another Mylar blanket. The added blanket would help with the thermal drones and, with the weather getting colder, add another layer of warmth.

CHAPTER 14

It wasn't long before darkness once again began to descend, marking the time of our departure. At Kel's prompting I got up and prepared for the hike ahead. He then handed me an old metal crutch he had uncovered in the van. We loaded up and headed into the night, the moon low on the horizon. Using the new crutch, along with the old one, I was able to travel a little steadier and a bit quicker, so we moved along at a good pace. We skirted the open fields, preferring the relative safety of the shadows cast by the woods and brush along the crisscrossing ravines.

In the light of a thumbnail moon, we crossed a gravel road and a couple of fairly large paved ones as well. Each time we did, my heart would beat like a hammer in my chest till we were safely on the other side. Kel would look back from time to time to check my progress, but each time I waved him on despite the growing pain in my leg, we had to get there. Hog stayed close to me, and it gave me comfort knowing he was watching out for me. As the light of morning approached, Kel hid us in a clump of trees, and I was happy for the break.

"Alice, I need to scout around and see if I can find that cabin. I know we're close but that's all. You wait here and rest your leg. I'll be back as soon as I find it," Kel said in hushed tones. And then, as he turned to leave, he added, "Keep her safe, Hog."

Hog replied with a thump of his tail, and then moved closer to me. Kel scanned the area, then sprinted across an open field between the wooded areas, then faded into the wide diversity of shadows and shapes that made up the forest on the other side. The two of us stayed huddled together against the frosty air; each day would be getting colder now with the coming winter. We had to meet up with the group ahead if we were going to make it through the coming cold. I couldn't imagine survive for long without them. Neither Kel nor I knew when they would be leaving, only that it might be within the next week or so. Our only other option relied on one hope, and that was of them having a group large enough to leave a trail that was easy for us to find and follow, but one hidden enough that the patrols wouldn't track them down.

My eyes had starting to grow heavy, when I saw Hog's head pop up, alerting me to someone's approach; a quick look from our hiding spot thankfully told me it was Kel. He stood in a cluster of birch not far from where we were, while he scanned the open area between us. When he was sure it was clear, he waved us over, and Hog and I crossed the open space quickly and rejoined Kel among the white trunks and undergrowth on the other side.

"I found it," he said, as I crouched down into the brush next to him. "It's about a quarter mile from here and well hidden. You guys ready?"

He got a nod from me and a chest grumble from Hog. Turning northwest, we headed for the cabin. Traveling in the daytime was always risky, but we didn't have far to go. And as early as it was, there wasn't much chance of anyone being around. Thirty minutes later we came to a coppice of firs and pines choked with dense undergrowth that concealed the remains of what appeared to be part of an old building, both seemingly now long forgotten. We soon were climbing through a window in the good end of the partially collapsed cabin, the smells of decaying wood and years of unuse greeting my nose. In some bygone era, a windstorm had dropped a tree across the front half of the cabin, crushing it but leaving the back mostly unharmed and buried in its expansive branches. Over time the latticework of dead limbs filled in with blackberry vines and falling forest foliage, leaving the cabin well camouflaged and hard to find.

Even in this condition, people had used this place before us, but from the looks of things it hadn't seen a wayfaring soul in years.

THE BOOK OF LETTERS

There was a sleeping bench along one of the paper-peeling wall and on it the questionable remains of an age-stained, queen-size mattress. The leaves and grass sticking out from one of the mattress corners made me wonder what all had slept on it, or called its interior home. In the opposite corner was a makeshift table, and by the broken window sat a tin-can rocket stove, all in a space that was less than eight feet by twelve. The quarters were tight, but the place was dry and easy to warm up during the cold nights—it would do just fine for our needs.

As dirty as the mattress was, my exhaustion was greater than my repulsion, so I convinced myself that it would be safe next to Hog. He had already taken his place on the mattress, and in his typical fashion, he hadn't wasted any time getting comfortable. Lying on his side, next to the wall, he stretched his long body out full length, which caused his nose to hang off on one end while his hind feet dangled off the other. His dilemma brought a chuckle from me as I spread out the tarp alongside him and climbed onto the bed; snuggling against his warm body, it wasn't long till my eyes grew heavy with sleep.

A few moments later, I felt Kel as he began to slide onto the bed next to me; he was greeted by a growl from Hog. Kel froze in place when Hog's head rose and his lips curled back as he snapped his teeth to display his displeasure. Their eyes locked, and neither moved a muscle. From the palpable tension, I knew that both were trying to decide what course of action to take. For the first time since knowing him, I actually saw Kel looking frightened and unsure of what to do. Inside I chuckled at the revelation of his venerability, but verbally I admonished Hog to break the standoff. "Quiet, boy, he has nowhere else to sleep. He'll be good, or I'll let you eat him for breakfast."

With that, Hog relinquished his threat and lay down again, but only after another deep chest growl in disagreement. Then spying my hat, he pulled it under his chin and promptly fell asleep on it, turning his mumbles into snores. When Kel turned his attention toward me, he caught me grinning back at him. He then gave me a mock scowl while I unsuccessfully tried to stifle a giggle.

"That wasn't nearly as funny from my point of view," he whispered at me, not wanting to wake Hog. "I almost pulled a Jim and filled my shorts!" Kel added with a smile and a chuckle of relief, and then cautiously he moved onto the bed, but this time with his back against me. It felt strange at first, feeling his body so close and pressed against me, but in truth, I was growing to like it. Slumber found us safe, warm, hidden, and soon with any luck on our way to hopeful freedom.

*****

"Run!" Mom's screams tore at my senses as I felt myself being pulled down by unseen hands as they tore at my pack. "Run!" Again, terror flooded her shrieks and split open the world around me. I clawed at the air, fighting for my life, while my legs desperately kicked out at my unseen enemy as they tried to pull me down. Breaking free, I leaped up and started to run. Then hearing the shrill, ululating cries again, I looked back and froze at the sight of Mom's form vaporizing into a thunderous ball of light.

The flash blinded me, and then I felt the wall of pressure and flying glass slamming me once again to the ground. My ears were ringing, and the world spun as I gasped for the air that had been knocked out of me, while a fiery pain began to consume my leg. The scattered bodies of the guards lay around me, some presumably dead, while others cried out in their plight. I started crawling away from them and toward what was left of the hospital entrance. I had to find my mom and pull her from the rubble. My head was pounding as my ears rang. Dully, I could hear that someone was screaming. The screaming grew in volume and suffering, and the pain and torture of it tore at my heart. And then I suddenly realized that it was coming from me. Out of the abyss of my horror a voice pulled at me, like a siren in a storm, calling to me, and in desperation I turned to it seeking refuge from this apparition that now held me. I swam from my dark dream and toward the sounds of the voice as it called to me

"Alice, please wake up!" As I opened my tear-filled eyes I saw Kel's concerned face and heard his comforting voice. "It's okay, you're

THE BOOK OF LETTERS

safe. It was just a bad dream. Hog and I are here with you. You're okay, Alice."

I could feel his frightened hand stroke at my sweat-soaked hair as I fought off the clinging tendril of my nightmare. Pulled from my dark dream, I was soon awake enough to remember where I was, and that I was in a safe place. When I finally sat up, Kel handed we some water to drink, while Hog's worried mumbling continued till his sniffing confirmed that I was okay. I didn't know how long we had been sleeping, but from the light filtering through the window, I knew it was well past midday.

"Are you okay?" Kel asked. "You had me a bit worried."

"I'm sorry," I replied, "bad dreams. I don't really want to talk about it right now."

Kel smiled and rubbed his jaw. "Well, you sure can kick when you're dreaming. I don't know who you were mad at, but you gave them a beating." His humor won me over and cast away the last of my dark memories, and turned my thoughts to better uses.

"Well, since we're all awake, let's see what we can do about some breakfast," Kel said as he rolled off the bed and went to see what he could dig out of his pack.

Hog got up and stretched, then mumbled something to me and headed out the window. Kel and I often laughed at his attempts to talk, although at times, you would swear you knew exactly what he was trying to say. We both knew what we had come here for, so while Kel opened some cans of food, I grabbed up the envelope of blueprints. We didn't have a lot of time, and we knew we only had one shot at this. While we ate we studied the plans until we were sure of what we needed to be done. When we were through eating, I emptied the case of my things, and then laid it empty on the table along with the dulcimer.

Starting with the case, we removed its interior and lining first as per the instructions, then dissembled all the remaining parts from the wooded body. Releasing the lining, we found under it the makings of a crystal radio, paracord, fishing line and hooks, a lightweight nylon tarp, a gill net, a sheet of tin prescored to fold into a pot, maps, several knives, metal arrowheads, and a variety of various small items

I didn't know the use of at the moment. We disassembled the pieces of the case, and everything was saved; we knew everything had a use. Even the varnishlike finish was scraped off and saved. Later it would be added to water and softened to be used as glue for reassembly.

Then we moved on to the dulcimer. Its beauty and craftsmanship caused me to hesitate as I admired my great-grandfather's handiwork, but I knew its true purpose hidden within. We started with removing the strings, followed by the neck and fret board and the dismounted body. As the parts were laid out on the table, Kel would whistle now and then at his amazement over this piece or that. Soon all the parts were spread and staged across the table; I looked at the vast array of labeled fragments and knew we were finally ready to start assembly.

The glue scrapings we put in to one of the empty cans and a bit of water added, and then it was put over a candle to heat up. The bow would be our first endeavor, and while the glue heated, we studied the plans again, trying to commit them to memory. We only had one chance at getting these things right and couldn't afford mistakes; we had no spare parts or time to make them. We needed to be on the move again soon if we had any chance of finding the group ahead, and we still had a long ways to go. Stirring the hot glue confirmed that it was ready, and taking a deep breath, we began.

Kel and I worked together throughout the day and late into the night by candlelight. Piece by piece, we resurrected my great-grandfather's designs, spellbound by each creation as they came together. Completed first was the repeating bow: it had a forty-five-pound recurve bow with a sliding rail that caught the string when pushed forward. Then pulling the rail back, you drew the bowstring with it, and a short arrow would load into firing position out of a six-shot rotating cylinder built into side of the rail. The rail also had sights and a trigger to help with accuracy. I couldn't wait to try it out, but right now we had more to assemble.

We worked for two days and late nights, stopping only when we had to, and slowly before our eyes, everything came together. While we were busy, Hog came and went as he wanted to hunt or explore, and from the rats and rabbits he caught, I was sure he was

THE BOOK OF LETTERS

eating good. It got me to thinking of a page in the book of letters; it covered traps and snares. Pulling out the book, I found the page of sketches. Kel joined me and studied it as well. The drawings covered several styles of traps and snares, and I also noticed that several used a setup called a toggle trigger. Looking at the setup, I quickly realized that some of the earlier misunderstood pieces found in the case were simply hardwood toggles that just needed the lines added.

Our remaining supply of canned food wasn't going to last much longer, so we were going to need another source, one readily available. We found the answer in the book of letters; page after page covered what we would need to know for trapping, fishing, and finding wild edible plants. While we waited for glue to dry, Kel and I used the time to absorb as much of the information as we could. On the last day, I wrapped the book in our new tarp and stuffed it into my makeshift pack. Come nightfall we were going to head out again. Time was running short, and we needed to catch up with the group before they left, if they hadn't already.

CHAPTER 15

The time spent resting my leg had helped, and I was able to move with a little less pain, hopefully with more speed too. We still had quite a ways to go and only a few days to cover it all, but we were determined to do it. As the sunlight faded into the west, we loaded the last of our gear and prepared for what lay ahead. This time with our newly gained tools, gear, and knowledge, we were better equipped to face whatever may come. The contents and pieces from the case and dulcimer had given us an impressive list of items, and I knew that now we now had a real fighting chance in our own survival.

We had gained a repeating bow with thirty short arrows, a wooden-bodied telescope, several knives, a bucksaw, two water bags, a water distiller, fishing gear, gill net, a metal pot, ferro rod, magnesium rod, wax paper, foil, cotton batting, wax and wicks, cordage, knife sharpener, crystal radio, nylon tarp, a stuffed sack blanket, rattraps, snares, sewing gear, several maps, waterproof matches, and more letters. It was astonishing how much had been built into my great-grandfather's designs, and how much thought had been put into it. He had truly planned for a long journey; silently I thanked him for having the foresight to build and prepare something that would give others a chance at survival.

Kel looked up at the thickening, overcast sky, "As long as those clouds don't block out the stars, I can keep us going in the right direction. This is that last place I know of other than our meeting point somewhere west of here, next to a stream called Lost Creek and north of High Butte."

THE BOOK OF LETTERS

I suddenly slapped my forehead. "With everything going on I completely forgot I had this!" Then, pulling on the chain of my necklace, I extracted the amulet Liz had left to me from under my shirt. "It's a compass," I said as I handed it to him.

Kel looked it over, then chuckled. "I guess it's better late than never. Thank you, this is going to help a lot!"

With it, Kel got his bearings, and we headed in to the night, this time with the compass instead of the stars guiding us west. Kel took the lead again but now armed with the bow at the ready, while I continued to hobble along behind on crutches, and Hog patrolled our flanks. If we pushed hard, we could reach our meeting point in eight days, which meant we were going to be later than planned. We didn't know if the group would still be there, and I knew both of us were having doubts, but we still had to take the chance that somehow they would be. The nocturnal chill caused our breath to hang in the air as we traveled on through the towering timber, their silent dark mystic vestiges casting shadows over our passage.

At Skyline Road, we paused in the break along its side, and waited as a convoy of security patrols passed, heading south back to Portland. Then we continued on till we had gone about another four miles. There we found a small grotto to hole up in, close to McKay Creek. We threw the Mylar blanket and nylon tarp over us, and we slept throughout the day, then took off again in the cover of night. Our world became one of dark, monotonous travel and finding safe, hidden harbors to sleep. It wasn't long before the nights and days blurred together.

Only the names on the map and the terrain changed as we followed its guidance, while mile after mile fell behind us. Our march carried us past places with names like Bald Mountain, Cummings Creek, Carlson Creek, Giveout Mountain, and the north fork of Salmonberry River. We were pushing but usually only averaged five or six miles a day, my leg still hindering our speed. When we finally arrived at a branch of the Salmonberry River, Kel informed me, to my great relief, that we were only a day's travel from our meeting point. The cans of food hadn't lasted long, and if we were to go much farther, we would need something to eat. We didn't know what we were going to find when we got to Lost Creek, so we decided to use the day to restock our supplies from what we could find in the area. We caught a couple of hours' sleep while waiting for the light of morning. Then as the glow built in the east, the three of us braced for the day ahead.

In the early twilight of morning, I set out some fishing lines that I baited with lures, having nothing else. Next, I strung a few spring snares and deadfalls, and set the rattraps close to a hole that showed signs of recent activity. Hoping for luck, I headed back. Kel had taken the bow and headed north to see what he might find. I knew he had his hopes set on venison steaks. Before heading out, we had set our plan to meet back at our hideout no later than noon and be on the trail again come dark, then gathering the trapping and fishing gear as we passed them. Hog heard the distant buzz of a drone overhead and alerted me with a low bark. We quickly slid deeper under the canopy of trees, and then I pulled the Mylar over us as we waited till it passed overhead. All clear, we headed back to see if Kel had returned yet. The drone had left me agitated and nervous over our safety.

Hours crept by, and I grew impatient over Kel's remaining absence, so Hog and I again slipped back into the brush and headed to the traps and lines to see if fortune had favored us. On the fishing lines, I surprisingly caught three small trout, and in one of the rattraps I caught a ground squirrel. The snares and deadfalls were empty. It wasn't much, but it was a start. Gathering my gear, I then headed back to the creek to prep my catch. The fish and squirrel I cleaned then wrapped in wax paper saved from the case; eating would have to wait as I didn't dare start a fire for fear of the smoke being seen in the daylight. I put up the tarp, as well as gathered ferns and leaves to make a bed. When done, I tried to nap, but tired as I was my mind couldn't stop worrying about Kel. Sitting there, I scanned as far as I could see with the telescope, my concerns continued to rise as I watched the sun began its western descent. Hog could tell I was worried and stayed close to me, forgoing his usual hunting to keep me protected, and I was thankful for his company.

As sunset settled lower and lower, I began to fear the worst. I had heard the sounds of distant drones throughout the day and was

THE BOOK OF LETTERS

frightened by what it could mean. My brain said I needed to plan for the worst, but at the thought my heart broke and I burst into tears. I had lost so much already, and now I faced being lost and alone in this foreign terrain. How much more could I bear? Soon the last of the sunlight faded, leaving Hog and me alone in a dark and hostile world. I only had a rough idea of where the group ahead was located, and without Kel, it would be a crapshoot to even find them. I knew I was in trouble if he didn't return, but at the moment my mind was blank of alternative options, so I turned my attentions to other immediate tasks.

In the last of the lingering twilight, I gathered and stacked stones into a small semicircular wall, to hide the light of my fire. I found dry, fallen branches and broke them up, then set them to the side to use as needed. Using the finest of the twigs, I built a small pile, and then over top of it I used pencil-sized sticks to form a sort of teepee. Once ready, I carefully struck one of the matches, and then held my breath when a breeze nearly snuffed it out. The small flame recovered when I shielded it with my hand, then gently placing it in the pile of small twigs, I felt relief as I watched it catch and build.

Careful to keep the fire as low as possible, I went about cooking my catch while my heart continued to hope for the best and my brain went back to trying to figure some backup strategy in case hope didn't win. Using the new folded tin pot, I heated some water and added rose hips I had found earlier while checking the fishing lines. The fish tasted good, but the squirrel was a bit dry, and though it was small and barely a mouthful for him, I tossed it to Hog. He caught it in midair, and the glint of his large teeth flashed in the firelight. As I watched, he crunched into the morsel with delight. Standing guard over me hadn't allowed him any hunting time, and though he never complained, I knew he was hungry and that the squirrel was barely even a snack for him.

I considered giving him the last of the fish but kept them for Kel in hopes of his return and wrapped them up to save. Then pulling the bubbling tea from the fire, I set it aside to cool a bit before attempting a sip. The breeze was building and now caused the overhead branches to sway and move, making unfamiliar noises that brought to mind images of wild animals or approaching patrols, feeding my growing paranoia. Hog's low growl startled me and warned me that we weren't alone. I quickly threw dirt over the fire and snuffed it out, plunging us into the darkness of the night. There we waited for our unwanted intruder to leave, but despite my wishes the sounds of movement through the brush only grew louder.

Hog stood up to guard over me, placing his body between me and the sounds of the approaching danger. I could feel his muscles tense and flex, as he waited, ready for what may come. Without warning, his head lowered as his ears lay back, and then with a roar he dashed into the night, leaving me wondering what nightmare was waiting out there for his attack. I listened for sounds of the battle, but the night was silent except for the resonance of swaying branches overhead caused by the wind.

CHAPTER 16

Time seemed to crawl to a stop as I listened to the now silent night and waited for Hog's return. The crack of a branch nearly stopped my heart, and in hope I softly called to him. Hog materialized where he had left me hiding, in the dim light of a partial moon. I could see his tail wagging and something bloody hanging from his mouth. Outside I could hear the sounds of shuffling start again, something else moving closer, and once more Hog rushed out again to greet it while I continued waiting in the dark, unsure of what to do. I heard him mumbling to whatever was out there but couldn't hear any indications of anger, so I cautiously crawled forward, keeping low to the ground, to chance a peek at what had gotten his attention. All I could see in the hint of moonlight was the shadowy bulk of a hunched-over form, still slowly moving toward me.

"The least you could do is pull a little and quit begging. I already gave you a piece," I heard a voice say, and at the sound of it my heart soared with joy! It was Kel; he had made it back.

Relief overwhelmed me, and my fears abated as I jumped up and rushed to him. I hugged him and then caught in the moment, kissed him. When I realized what I had done, I quickly let go of him, embarrassed and suddenly feeling awkward. Kel stood there his teeth shining in the brightening light of the moon. I could see him smiling from ear to ear at the surprised greeting, obviously quite happy with my display of exuberance. For some reason I found his sense of delight over the moment irritating, and I found myself conflicted between hitting him or kissing him again.

MICHAEL SCOTT

"Maybe I should be late a little more often," Kel said with a smile.

That settled it. My eyes snapped as I punched him, both out of embarrassment from my actions and out of relief of having him back, "Where have you been? I've been worried sick. I thought something had happened to you!"

Kel started to laugh but seeing the fear in my face, he stopped and apologized, then showed me the reason of his delay—a large hide full of meat. He had shot a deer, and hauling it back had taken longer than he thought it would. I wanted to be mad at him but couldn't. I was too overcome with emotions just seeing him back and safe, and I knew we needed the meat to keep going. Working together, we dragged the meat packed hide back to where I had slung the tarp and built the fire ring, and then I sent Kel to wash off as best he could, in the creek. His coat and shirt had blood on them as well, but they would have to wait for another time when we could take the time to dry them. Starting the fire again, I let it build to give some light to see by, and then I started cutting one of the large slabs into smaller cookable portions and setting them to the side. Looking over at Hog, I could see the lines of drool hanging from his mouth, and I knew he was as hungry as the rest of us. So I tossed him a large piece, and he flopped down to enjoy it.

I cut green sticks from what I thought was a spring maple and skewered the chunks of the meat onto them until they were all filled. At first the sight of the blood and slimy mess repulsed me. I had never seen real meat from an animal before, but it didn't take long for my hunger to overcome it. Scrapping some of the coals from the fire to form a grilling area, I propped the stick of meat over them, close enough to cook but not close enough to burn too quickly. Kel returned from the creek a bit cleaner and joined me by the fire to warm up from the cold bath. I could see he was done in and tired. A savory aroma rose from the fire, feeding our growing hunger, and I watched as the flames flickered from the spurts of fat that dripped onto the hot coals. Hog kept a close eye on the cooking meat while he lay next to me, waiting for another hunk. On the ground beneath

THE BOOK OF LETTERS

his wide chin I could see a large pool of drool once again starting to build.

"I was only about a mile or so from here and on my way back when this spike just popped up in front of me, catching me totally unprepared. Happened so fast my first shot missed, but then caught him with the second one through the lungs. I then spent almost an hour looking for the missing arrow, but never did find it. Sorry about that," Kel said, then took a big drink of the tea before going on. "I was going to skin him out there, but then I heard a drone coming, so I quickly dragged him in the brush and lay under him till they passed over. I was hoping the buck's body heat would help throw them off. Guess it worked because they never came back."

"I'm just glad to have you back and safe, but don't ever do that to me again," I replied back. "Next time leave the animal, or I'll hit you harder!"

Kel chuckled. "How about I Just promise to try and not make you worry too much? That work? Besides, I still plan on having that date with you one of these days." His eyes twinkled in the firelight, and I felt another run of ridiculous flutters in my heart. Get a grip, Alice; this was definitely the wrong place and wrong time.

While our dinner cooked, he told me about trying to carry the buck back whole, not wanting to take the time to butcher it, and how it kept getting tangled as he tried to drag it through the undergrowth, attempting to stay out of sight of the drones. When it started getting dark, he finally decided that it was safe enough to take a chance, so he stopped to gut it and cut it up. Once finished, he wrapped all that he could in a piece of the hide, and headed back to find us. He knew he was close, but in the dark, he had a hard time locating exactly where it was that we were hiding. Circling the area and his strength close to giving out, he fell, dropping the bundle of meat.

Using the trunk of a tree, he pulled himself up and on his feet again, but then he found that he couldn't lift the meat back off the ground. He finally resorted to dragging the wrapped bundle, while still trying to locate us. When he had circled downwind of us he smelled smoke, and in the hope that it was us, he followed it the last few hundred yards or so. That was when Hog found him. I could

MICHAEL SCOTT

see the exhaustion in his face, and I admired him for what he had accomplished. He was a man you could depend on not to quit easily.

As I looked at him, I saw that the firelight caught on the ringlets of his wet hair and illuminated the features of his face and growing beard; Susan had been right about his good looks. I thought back to the impromptu kiss I had thrown on him and his reaction; the feeling of his warm lips rose again in my mind. I caught myself and quickly chased away the ebbing tide of emotions; I knew this wasn't the time for such foolishness. We were in a race for our freedom and a fight for our very lives; it certainly wasn't the time or place for romantic thoughts. If things were different, I knew the course my heart would take, but for now, we were simple two people tossed together by the chaos of circumstance, both fighting for our right to simply live.

The smell of the cooking venison pulled at us, and it drove us to eat the succulent pieces while still hot enough to burn our fingers. Its flavor was wonderful. I found it amazing how good simple food tastes when you're truly hungry, and tonight I felt starved. There was more than enough of the meat to feed us for days and for Hog to eat his fill, which he did, then he stretched out on the bed under the tarp and fell into a deep, snoring sleep. It wasn't long till we joined him on the bed as well. And lying between them, I soon heard Kel softly snoring, joining the choir. I thought of all these two had done for me, and felt very fortunate that by some gift of providence, they had chosen to be my traveling companions.

Listening to them and feeling the warmth of their bodies, I had a premonition that we would be together for a long time; it was a thought that warmed my heart and gave me a feeling of comfort. It wasn't long before I relaxed and joined them in slumber. At that moment I felt incredibly safe and protected, and at peace. Later that night, I was startled awake as Kel rolled over in his sleep and he lay his strong arm across me. I saw Hog's head popped up and sniff at Kel's arm, but this time he didn't growl. He just looked at me and then at Kel with his sleepy, bloodshot eyes. Then after a few moments, he decided to let it go and laid his head back down on my hat with only a few faint grumbles before fading back into his snores.

CHAPTER 17

We slept throughout the day then headed out into the night, once again guided by the stars, a map, and my compass. We continued west until we were about a mile east of Buck Mountain. There we stopped and cooked some of the meat over a Dakota hole then filled it in and pushed on. A mile later we ate. It was a trick we had read about in the book, in the section marked evasion and escape. If someone had spotted or smelled our smoke, they still wouldn't find us. By leaving before we ate, all they would find is an empty cook site when they arrived. As tired as we were, time was against us so we risked traveling in the daylight and continued on, constantly on the lookout for drones and patrols. I kept an eye on Hog as he paralleled us. Whenever he would stop to listen or sniff the air, I would pause to watch his actions, then follow suit.

At one such pause, he saved us from being seen by someone driving down Tin Shack Road. We had crossed the road only a few moments before and had only gone about thirty or forty yards when it happened. At the sound of the engine, Hog instantly dropped to the ground. Without hesitation we did the same, and then I watched as he raised his head and tested the air, his ears perked and listening. Ahead of me, Kel had dropped as well, and we both waited and watched for Hog to give the all clear before continuing our hike. When he was sure, he gave us a low woof, and we got up and continued moving farther into the wilderness. Pines and cedars dominated the landscape, while the underbrush continued to thicken near the creeks, making travel laborious.

MICHAEL SCOTT

Checking the map and compass confirmed that we were about two miles from High Butte, so we swung a bit more to the north. A few miles later, we found the north bank of Lost Creek and crossed it. We continued on, following the south bank west, till we caught the faint scent of distant smoke in the air. It was impossible to say how far away its source was, but the breeze let us know the direction, as well as confirming that others were definitely out here and somewhere close. We had no way of knowing if it was our people or a patrol camp, so Kel took the bow and circled toward the source from the right while Hog and I circled around from the left. A quarter mile upstream in a clearing a few yards from the stream, we found the camp; it wasn't the sight we had hoped for.

Hog and I stayed hidden in the undergrowth of ferns and rhododendrons, watching the group; it wasn't long before I spotted Kel on the opposite side of the camp doing the same. The camp consisted of a few tarps, a couple of brush shelters, and one small poorly built smoking fire. Surrounding the fire was what looked to be fifteen or so of the most bedraggled people I had ever seen. It was a mixed group of dirty, unprepared men, women, and children; and from the looks of them, I knew that the last few weeks had been hard on them.

Looking back over to Kel, I saw him wave to me from his hidden position, and then motioning for us to stay put, he then stood up and strolled toward their camp. Hog and I watched from our hiding place as Kel hailed the camp, and saw most of the people scatter at the sound of his voice, while a few of the men stood to confront the unknown intruder. Kel stop and waited at the edge of their camp, and after a bit of hesitation, one of the older men cautiously approached him and began talking with him. I was too far away for me to hear what they were saying, so I watched their body language, alert for any signs of alarm. A few minutes later, Kel walked back to their fire with the men; one by one the others slowly and cautiously came out of hiding to meet the tall stranger.

Next to me, Hog gave a low growl, and I looked in the direction of his attention. After a few moments of scanning the brush, I found a pair of vivid green eyes looking back at me. There were only about forty feet between us, and I was a little surprised that he

THE BOOK OF LETTERS

hadn't spotted them sooner or heard something. Hog got up to investigate and disappeared into the brush, while the unknown eyes never wavered. He reemerged about ten feet from where the eyes continued to watch, then did something unusual. He tested the air with his nose then gave a mumble; he cocked his head and mumbled again in higher tones while watching our unseen guest. The eyes stayed put among the concealment of leaves, but were now shifting back and forth between watching me and the large animal that was attempting to apparently communicate.

Dropping to the ground, Hog continued to crawl forward toward the eyes, and he kept his tail wagging and continued his vocal efforts. It wasn't long till his actions had moved him to the base of where our mystery guest was hiding; fascinated, I watched and waited to see what would happen. At first, I could see a look of irresolution and hesitancy in the eyes, and then they faded into the shadows of the thick brush. I tried to find them again, wondering if they had left, but from Hog's actions I knew better. It wasn't long till I saw a small, dirty hand tentatively reaching out and touching his fur. He lay there, patiently letting the hand explore his thick fur while he persisted in his soft mumbles. I don't know how long I sat there transfixed by the moment, but it was suddenly broken when Hog's head snapped around to another spot and gave a low growl. The hand disappeared as he quickly got up and trotted back over to me. Looking back, I saw that our visitor had dissipated deeper into the shadows of dense undergrowth.

It was Kel coming with one of the men from the group below; we stood out in the open to reveal ourselves as they approached us. I heard Hog growl at his mistrust over the unknown man and step forward to guard me. When the man with Kel saw us, he stopped, uncertain of his own safety, eyeing the big dog as Hog's deep rumble continued from his chest.

"Is that dog safe" he asked, fear tainting his gruff voice.

Kel shrugged his shoulders. "I would just leave him alone. He comes to those he wants to." Then he added with a smile, "Oh, and whatever you do, don't rush or threaten Alice, he's a bit protective of her." He then chuckled and added, "If anyone ever did that, my bets would be on the dog, if you know what I mean."

Despite the man's rough bravado, he had heard the low rumble in Hog's chest and decided to keep his distance. "I don't think anyone would be dumb enough to do that after seeing him. You said your names were Kel and Alice? You got a last name to go with them?"

"Her last name doesn't matter anymore, or mine, so let it go," Kel snapped at the man. Then to me, he softly said, "Alice, let's grab your gear and we'll go meet everyone."

From the man's reaction to Kel, I knew something wasn't right and so did Hog. He stayed pressed against my side as I gathered my things then followed them. The people were terrified as they watched us walk into their camp, and as we drew nearer to them, I could feel every eye on us. My hairy companion's massive size was making an effect, and I watched as the men braced themselves, while mothers pulled their children closer, fear lining their faces. It was obvious that this was going to be a problem, so Hog and I went to the far edge of their camp and started erecting a lean-to shelter for the night. It was a quick covering, but from the people's reactions I wasn't too sure we would be staying long.

Kel stayed at the fire, trying to learn everything he could about what had happened and what their plans were. The tarp was soon up, so I cut ferns for a bed, then went to look for dry leaves or grass to fill and stuff the blanket with; there were plenty of ferns, but not many were dry. Hog and I wandered around a bit to see what the area offered, and I picked a few dried Oregon grapes that I found, then we headed back. The woods seemed calm and peaceful; only the feeling of being watched kept me from enjoying it. Hog seemed unbothered by it, although I did see him stare into the woods and brush from time to time and give one of his low-toned warbles.

Back at the camp, I could see that there was a big discussion going on, and from Kel's look I knew it wasn't one I should join. So I went back to our shelter and built a walled fire ring. Hog and I then headed back into the trees to find dry branches that were off the ground or still in the trees for tonight's firewood. The new bucksaw we had gotten from the case made cutting off the branches easy and

THE BOOK OF LETTERS

without the loud pistol-like pop that came from breaking them. It wasn't long before I had cut enough for the night and, tying them into bundles, started for camp. As we headed back, I decided to set spring traps and snares along the way in hopes of catching something during the night.

Finding several likely spots, I set down the bundles and pulled out my toggle triggers and snare lines. Saplings supplied the springs I needed. Once the lines were ran and the toggles were attached to the bent saplings, the snares were quickly set. Finding some flat rocks, I even set some deadfalls using the toggle switches to fashion Paiute traps. The rattraps I set on a large bare log where I found plenty of chewed pine cones. Along the creek I found a few blackberries and used them to bait the traps.

While I was working, the feeling of being watched continued, and even Hog kept turning from time to time to occasionally mumble back at the woods. I tried scanning the brush without making it obvious, but I could only see the chaotic pattern of branches and thick undergrowth. Back at the shelter, I saw that the meeting was breaking up, so I started a fire to do some cooking, knowing Kel would be hungry. This time I used the ferro rod to save matches. It took a few tries, but adding some magnesium scrapings helped, and soon flames were licking at the kindling. While the fire caught, I set the tin pot near the fire and skewered fist-sized chunks of meat onto sharpened green sticks.

I then stuck butt ends of the sticks in the ground and leaned the meat-ladened ends toward the fire; it wasn't long before the scent of sizzling meat started perfuming the air as it cooked. Pulling the pot closer to the coals of the fire, I filled it with water and dropped in the Oregon grapes that I had found. Sitting there by the fire, I looked over the camp and noticed that I was the only one cooking. I thought back over the short time we had been here; I hadn't seen anyone eat anything, only hollowed eyes and strained faces. I had missed something earlier, but now it was becoming very clear to me. On the day of the Butterfly, all these people had fled; they had left unprepared and with no real understanding of what they were getting themselves into. Now they were starving, unaware of the food that grew and lived around them. Inside the lean-to, I opened our packs and started pulling out what was left of our food supply; it wasn't a lot for such a large group, but it would help. It was Hog's soft tone that alerted me to someone's approach, and a moment later, I heard the crunch of their boots behind me.

CHAPTER

10

"I was just coming back to talk to you about that," Kel said as he returned from the group. "These people haven't eaten much lately and need all the help they can get. From what I've been told, things didn't go as planned."

We sat by the fire while he filled me in on all he had learned from the meeting and talking to different individuals—the news wasn't good. At some point during the escape, they had lost both their guide and what supplies they had, in their flight from the Portland area. The last guys that went for help left a week ago, and so far they hadn't come back. The remaining people continued to wait here, not knowing what else to do; now they were so weak from hunger they didn't have the strength to leave. The group had started with twenty-three souls, but they were now reduced to just fifteen. Some had died, while others just disappeared into the woods, never to be seen again. Now, they were talking of splitting the camp into smaller groups, all traveling in different directions in the hopes that it would help some to avoid the inevitable starvation or capture they were now facing.

I looked at the bundles as did Kel; it was all we had with no guarantee of getting more. We had been fortunate so far and hadn't had to go hungry despite a rough start, but who knows what tomorrow may bring? Kel held up the bow and looked at me. Understanding the gesture, I grinned then held up the satchel of fishing gear and snares. We had the ability and the tools to get more as well as the book of

MICHAEL SCOTT

letters. It would teach us what we needed to survive; these people had nothing, so we decided to give it all.

Kel went back to the group and returned with a woman who looked to be in her late fifties and a wide-eyed young woman who tagged along behind her. Kel introduced the older woman as June and the younger one as Mable. As we loaded their arms with the bundles of venison, I saw that they were both watching Hog in fear and curiosity. When they turned to go, June promised to return later after they had distributed food to everyone; her tears of joy said enough to confirm that we were doing the right thing.

It wasn't long before we could see people gathering at their fire and start hastily cooking their portion of meat, hunger driving most to eat theirs nearly raw. It was obvious that these people were going to need more, and need it soon. Hog whined behind me, his nose pointed at a spot in the brush that lined the end of the camp. But seeing nothing, I turned back to the fire. I wondered if what had been watching us in the woods was also the owner of the small hand I had seen earlier. Again, I scanned the brush, looking deeper into the maze of leaves and branches. Only this time it was for the eyes I had seen before. Hog got up and whined as he sniffed at the sticks of meat, so I pulled one from the ground for him, and he gently took it from my hand, stick and all.

Looking back at the spot in the brush that he had been watching, he trotted over to the shadowed area and set the stick of meat on the ground close to a rhododendron. Backing away a few feet, Hog lay down and gave a mumble to the shadow, then plopped his head down and waited. I watched in curiosity; this was another new trick that I hadn't seen him do before. I elbowed Kel and pointed to Hog. We both sat there watching and wondered what might be the cause of his odd behavior. It wasn't long before we had our answer and a few new questions as well.

A small figure that couldn't have been over four and a half feet tall emerged at the edge of the dark concealment of the bush. They lingered for a moment, unsure of the dog, but their hunger was too much and they soon overcame fear. Hog raised his head and gave another mumble to the figure while wagged his tail and trying to

132

THE BOOK OF LETTERS

look as friendly as he could. Our guest froze, trying to understand his actions, but the sight of food drove them forward. Fully exposed now, we could see that it was a young child, one that was dressed in a ragged and dirty orange jumpsuit of an illegal. Slowly the child picked up the stick and scanned the area, then sat down and tore at the meal while watching Hog. He kept up his mumbling like he was having a conversation, his tones rising and lowering, trying to sooth the child. All the while, he slowly kept inching forward.

As best as I could make out through the dirt and mud that seemed to cake the child's hair and hide portions of their face, they looked to be somewhere around twelve or fourteen years of age, but boy or girl I couldn't tell. Their close-cropped hair showed hints of black where it stuck out of the filth, and as they moved you could see the slightly stocky body of someone used for hard labor.

By the time the meat was gone, Hog had worked himself up to the child and now was only an arm's length away, his tail swooshing back and forth. Hog and the child sat there watching each other as we watched them, fascinated by what was unfolding. The child's hand reached out and touched the scars on Hog's muzzle and face; their fingers traced the white lines, while his soft mumble continued. I wondered where this child had come from, as all the other children that I had seen in camp had been with someone. From this child's clothes and fear of people, it was pretty clear they were on their own and not well received by the rest of the camp.

Hog gave the child a lick on their cheek, smearing bits of the grime, and then trotted over to me as the kid watched on. He then gave me a whine for more, food so I handed him another stick of the venison. He took it, and he again turned to the child. Then going back, he held it out to the child and waited. The child looked back at me and then back at Hog. The child then imitated one of Hog's quiet warble noises as they took the gift of food from him. Hog was excited at making a new friend, so while the kid ate the second round, he pranced and rolled, making quite a spectacle of himself and setting Kel and I to laughing.

The kid got up and petted him in appreciation but kept their eyes on us as well as the big dog between us, while watching to see what we would do. Hog tried to lead the child to our fire but, sensing resistance, stopped short of it and continued to visit with his new friend from a safe distance. I took another stick of meat, this time not waiting for Hog's prompting, and set it on the ground only eight or nine feet from us. Staying behind Hog, the kid watched me and waited. Smiling at the nearly hidden form, I then placed a cup of water alongside the stick of meat and went back to where I had been sitting. With Hog's encouragement, the child cautiously advanced and plucked up the stick, then hurried back to sit next to the big guy again, this time sharing pieces of the savory prize with him.

At the sound of June's voice announcing her arrival, the child retreated even farther behind Hog and looked ready to flee, but stopped when Hog mumbled then stood up to guard them.

"Hello again," June said as she walked up to our fire, her eyes looking around to place Hog's whereabouts, and then noting the dog and child in the shadows. "I want to say thank you again from all of us here."

"Please join us," I said and motioned to a place next to me. "We have some Oregon grape tea if you would like any and you don't mind sharing a group cup."

"Oh, that would be lovely," she replied with a smile and sat next to me. "This is good!" she said after a couple sips. "You guys must be really good in the woods. Personally, it's my first time, but I'm not too old to learn."

Kel and I both laughed at the comment, and then at June's questioning looks Kel explained.

"No, we've just been lucky, I guess you could say. Other than Alice's leg, we've haven't had it too bad," he said, and then with a wink to me added, "could say we had help along the way."

I gave her a brief summary of our escape thus far, but I left out details of the case and my mom's death. I saw her look at the repeating bow lying just inside the shelter, and at Hog then the child. Her curiosity was certainly understandable. She told us about her and her husband's escape from one of the many camps and bits of life they shared. She had been a secretary, and her husband had worked as a bookkeeper. Because of something that she wouldn't go into, they had been sent to a reeducation center. When the explosions knocked out the power and tore holes in the fences, they ran with the rest of the people, and they ran into a bloodbath.

June's tears fell freely as she told us about that day and the loss of her husband. I reached out and put my arms around her; I knew her pain all too well. Butterfly would be a day none of us would ever forget, if we lived long enough to survive our escape. I looked back over to Hog and noticed that the child had gone to sleep lying next to him, fingers entwined in his fur.

"Do you know anything about the kid?" I asked June as I pointed to the sleeping form.

June shook her head. "Nobody does really. We were here a week before anyone even noticed the little one. Everyone here took to calling her Chipmunk or just Monk for short."

"You said *her*?" I asked. "How do you know?"

"Well, I don't for sure," June said then pointed back to the sleeping girl. "You see those three strips on the one leg? That is a girl's jumpsuit."

So our mystery guest was a girl named Monk, which no one knows anything about. There was something about the girl that had drawn Hog to her, and I trusted his judgment. As she and Hog slept, we went on taking turns sipping the tea and talking, learning more about the people of the camp and their ideas of what to do.

June looked back at the girl's sleeping form. "You guys are the first couple that she has gotten this close to. She sure has taken to your dog, even as frightful as he is."

I blushed at the mention of *couple* and was hoping the failing light covered it. Were we a couple? The thought that was ridiculous; we were in a fight for survival. Now wasn't the time for romance and such things, right? I looked over at Kel and felt a familiar flutter again in my heart. Who was I kidding? I looked away as I felt the warmth of another blush begin to climb. Then glancing back at him, I saw him grinning at me and my awkwardness, so I punched him, sending him into chuckles.

As the hour grew late, June excused herself and left us to the quiet of the night. From the glow of the coals left, I could see that

MICHAEL SCOTT

Hog had moved into the shelter, and Monk was no longer in sight. We doused the coals with the last of the tea and joined Hog on the bed in our usual places, with me once again protected in the middle. We slept the night in peaceful slumber, and with the beginnings of morning light I found where Monk had gone to in the night.

CHAPTER 19

When I saw the slender fingers of our mystery girl still twisted in Hog's hair, I patted Kel on the leg to wake him, and as he did I nodded to our unexpected guest. We lay there together, not sure what to do, so not wanting to frighten her, we waited to see what would happen when she woke up. It wasn't too long till Monk started to stir and rub her eyes open. Once opened, her eyes flared wide, and I again saw their intense green. We had only Hog between us, and I could see her trying to decide what course of action to take.

"Good morning, Monk," I said in a soft voice with a smile. "If you don't mind me calling you that. It's nice to meet you." Then I slowly reached up and scratched Hog's head. "Good morning to you too, Hog."

He returned the affection with a warm tongue to my face; Monk watched me for a moment then reached out and scratched at Hog's big head as well, to which he replied with a lick to her the face.

"Want to go check our traps and see if they hold any breakfast?" I asked Hog, to which he promptly jumped up, dumping Monk and me, which caused us to tumble into each other.

I could feel her little body stiffen as we touched, and I quickly pulled back, not wanting to frighten her. Hog started prancing as if he thought he had done a clever trick, then stepped forward and gave us both another big swipe of his tongue. That not being enough to suit his mood, he started rolling and twisting around on the bed until he had both me and Kel laughing while Monk watched us all with a big smile. After he was done with his antics I bid Kel goodbye, motioned to Monk to follow, and headed out with Hog.

At first Monk either followed behind with Hog, or she walked with her fingers buried in his thick fur, but as we went from trap to trap her confidence grew. The spring traps seem to fascinate her, so as I reset the snares I took time to show her how they worked. The traps had given us six rabbits, not much, but it was better than nothing. On our way back we veered closer to Lost Creek, and I set new traps and snares along the way as we traveled.

In a small section of slow water along the bank of the creek, I spotted the stocks of cattails and remembered all that my great-grandfather had said about them. Taking off my boots and rolling up my pants I waded into the icy water and started digging down into the mud till I found the cattail roots and wrestled them loose. I continued digging them up and tossing the muddy lumps to the shore until I had a fair-sized pile that I knew would help fill people better than just the rabbits. Once they were washed and packed, we headed back to the camp and the hungry people.

The rabbits and cattail roots were handed out, and people set to work cooking their portions as did I. The men of the camp were again in deep discussions, punctuated now and then with raised disagreements. Kel was among them, and I could tell he was upset over their conversation. Monk stayed with me and Hog at our shelter while I cooked our meal. She trusted Hog, and slowly with Hog's help, I was gaining her trust as well.

The meeting broke up as the smell of cooking filled the air, and Kel joined us by the small fire. I could tell he wasn't happy but he said nothing, so I waited, knowing he would talk when he was ready to. The rabbit cooked quickly, but the cattail root need to roast a while to soften it, so I left it in the fire and doled out the hot pieces of meat. As we ate I told Kel about finding the cattails and how Monk had helped me with bringing it all back. From behind Hog, I could see a slight grin on Monk's half-hidden face from hearing the praise.

"If anyone asks you what your last name is, use mine," Kel spoke at last.

"What's going on?" I asked at the odd statement.

THE BOOK OF LETTERS

Kel looked at me, his eyes still showing signs of anger, and it worried me. He then looked around the camp, and seeing no one near, he started talking in a low voice.

"Listen, I don't know from where or how, but someone told these guys about a bounty that's been put out." His voice was almost a whisper. "It was put out on you."

I sat there not knowing what to say. Why would they put one out on me? What had I done other than run?

"All they know is that it is a girl, traveling possibly with a large dog. No real physical description other than height, hair color, and full name." Kel looked back to the fire. "They claim you are the leader of the terrorist group that led and planned the attacks in Portland, and that you orchestrated the same kind of attacks in other cities as well."

"But I didn't do any of those things!" I said, not believing what I was hearing.

"They made a positive ID from your backpack found at a hospital bombing that claimed three hundred lives," Kel replied.

"That's a lie! There weren't even three hundred people there!" I snapped back. "Only a few guards, Mom, me, and a taxi driver. We had been set up, and they were waiting for us."

Tears started welling up at the memory of that day and flowed down my cheek. Kel put his arm around me and pulled me close, trying to comfort me.

"It's okay, Alice, I know it wasn't you. They're just using you to put a face to their unseen enemy." Kel's breath was warm as he whispered into my ear, "I will protect you and so will Hog. People here are so frightened of him, I don't think anyone will try anything. Just stay close to me or Hog."

Turning back to the fire, I tried to calm myself while fishing the cattail root out of the coals and poked it to see if it softened a bit. Our breakfast of rabbit and root filled us for the moment, but Kel and I both knew there was a need for more, so he headed out hunting with the bow, and I went to look for more wild edibles. Hog and Monk tagged along with me, but at the edge of camp I was stopped by a couple of the women and boys.

MICHAEL SCOTT

"Miss, could we bother you for a moment?" one of the women asked.

I looked the group over; Hog and Monk stood by my side, so I nodded yes.

"We know nothing of how to catch or find any food, and our boys want to learn." The woman looked back at the boys, and then back to me. "I know it's asking a lot, but could you teach them a few things that you know? That is if it's safe with your dog and all."

I looked over at the ragged group and eyed the three boys, and a quote I remembered from one of my great-grandfather's letter came to me: "Knowledge ain't worth spit if it isn't used or taught."

"You boys want to learn?" I asked as the boys stood there, deer eyed. They gave me a nod but didn't speak. "Are there any girls that want to learn?" I asked, not seeing any present.

One of the women from the back of the group suddenly stepped forward. "My daughter will go with you!" Then she looked back at the other women. "I don't care if it isn't ladylike, nether is starving. Billy, go get your sister." With that Bill ran off and soon returned with a girl a bit taller than him.

I took the motley group into the woods with me, while Hog kept Monk off to one side, flanking me. First, I taught them how to make the snares and traps I used, as well as gouge hooks for fishing, and then they learned where to set them and how to bait them. Next, I taught them the few plants I knew, and as we walked we gathered all we could, not that there was much around this time of year. We did find some more cattails, some dried Oregon grape, and blackberries. Though most were out of season, we gathered them up anyway to use for tea or stewing. As the sun began to lower toward the west, I turned toward my snare to check them on the way back to camp.

My small class felt good about bringing back food to the others, and the knowledge they had learned today I hoped would give them an advantage in their survival in the days to come. We brought back various berries, two squirrels, and eight trout, and each student was the proud owner of two toggle-trigger setups. I was sitting with Hog and Monk back at our shelter, and I enjoyed watching the kids showing others what they had learned and done during our time in

THE BOOK OF LETTERS

the woods. Kel returned a few hours later, carrying another deer hide full of meat. Tonight, the camp would be well fed, and I beamed with pride knowing that we had helped by supplying food and giving them an education on how to do it for themselves.

As fires were being built and I was teaching how to clean fish to the kids, Kel and the others had another meeting. The meeting didn't last long, and he soon joined my little class while I finished expounding on stick cookery. The kids then headed to the main fire with fish skewered on sticks to cook, leaving our little group to talk privately.

Kel pointed his thumb toward the group gathered at the main fire. "They have decided to break up and head out in two days. They're sticking to groups of five or six and heading out in different directions that we've been told not to share outside of our groups. It's to avoid any group reporting on another."

"Do you know who they want to send with us?" I asked Kel. The plan had been on being saved, but by a strange twist of fate, we had now become the saviors.

Kel shook his head. "I don't know yet, because of Hog most are afraid to travel with us. I told them that anyone that goes with us must be accepted by our whole group." Kel then looked at Monk and added, "That includes you too, Monk, you are part of us if you want to be."

Hog thumped his tail in agreement while Monk looked at Kel and me, thinking. When she finally understood, her face broke into a wide smile, and she gave us a nod while Hog received a big hug. I couldn't have been happier. Our little family was growing, and the thought of it warmed my heart. After we had all eaten, we continued to linger by the fire, sharing some blackberry tea and just enjoying the moment. I saw June heading our way in a quick-step fashion and knew she had something on her mind.

June called out as she drew closer. "Hello again, would you mind if I join you for a minute?"

Kel waved her on in and handed her the cup of tea when she was settled.

"The kids have been going on and on about what you taught them today," she said then took a long sip of the blackberry tea, and then added, "has anyone asked to travel with you yet? Because if you have room and will let me, I would like to travel with you guys."

I could see her looking at each of us as she waited for an answer. I looked to Kel, and he gave me a slight nod, then to Monk who gave me a grin. Hog got up and walked over to June. We could see a tinge of fear in her face as he looked her over. Leaning in, he sniffed her over while June waited, not knowing what to do or if she would survive the inspection. Then having made up his mind, she then got a wet tongue to the face, and it was settled. June, though happy to be accepted and not eaten, looked a little pale and unsettled; I tried hard to muffle my giggle when she gave a weak smile.

"Welcome to the group!" Kel said. "If you want you can grab your gear and join us. Might as well get used to it now before we hit the trail."

I could see tears in June's eyes as she hugged me and Kel. "Thank you so much, I won't let you guys down. I may be getting old, but I'm resilient."

"You lived through Hog's inspection, which proves you're certainly not faint of heart." I choked out, unable to stop my building laughter. At first I thought I had offended June, but then her face broke into a smile, and soon we were all laughing over it.

While June headed off to gather her belongings, I went into the shelter to make more room for our new guest. It would be tight, but that would just help to keep us warm in the cold of night. When she returned, it was about dusk so we stashed what few things she had and added her blanket to our growing bed. June and I then went and gathered more firewood, joined by Hog and Monk. Soon we had all we could carry, and even Hog and Monk, dragged a branch back to camp.

Sitting around the fire that night, I looked at my companions and felt good about our growing group. Monk was coming out of her shell, and I knew she would learn quickly. Kel had proven himself many times in our journey thus far, and I had no doubts about him. June seemed like a determined lady and having watched her help others around the camp, I knew she didn't shirk from things that needed to be done.

It wasn't until the following evening that we gained our next members, and it was with mixed feelings. It was a young man named Jack and an older blond woman who he called Angel; from their actions I got the feeling that they had become a couple after meeting here in camp at her suggestion. He seemed friendly, but the woman I had doubts about; maybe it was the age difference, or it might have been the way she carried herself. She seemed to think that she was a little better than those around her; I didn't like the way she looked at Monk, and there was just something about her that made me cautious, but I couldn't quit put my finger on what.

They joined to a mixed vote, we all agreed on him, but only two agreed on her. The votes for her I was sure were simply because they didn't want to punish the young man for being with her, so despite the lack of votes for her at first, we finally decided to add them to the group. We asked them to join us at our shelter, but she chose to stay where they were instead until we were ready to head out the following morning.

CHAPTER 20

The sun was just starting to glow on the horizon when Kel woke us up. June and I quickly packed our gear to leave, while Kel went to get Jack and Angel. Monk and I then went out and gathered all our snares and traps, along with a couple of rabbits and a few trout. We cleaned them quickly and packed them away to eat later. Back at camp we loaded our gear onto our backs, and then we headed out before most of the camp was even awake. This time I left the crutches behind and just used a walking stick to steady my limp.

Kel took the lead and headed west till we were about a half mile out of camp, then at a tributary of Lost Creek we turned south. He hadn't said where we were going because of the possibility of someone leaking our direction to others in camp. We knew some of those that we had left back at the camp believed I was the one that security had a warrant for, and had wanted to turn me in for the bounty that was now on my head. Kel was doing all he could to hide our tracks and confuse any would-be followers. Hog, like usual, walked flanking me and was ready to alert us to any dangers, this time with Monk by his side.

We only covered three more miles before signs of weariness started showing on our newest additions, so after we crossed Cook Creek, road we started keeping our eyes open for a place to stop. A mile and a half later we found a fallen tree close to McKenny Creek and made our home for the night under it. Monk and I set some snares, then with the approaching night to hide our smoke trail, I started a small fire and with June's help cooked the rabbits

THE BOOK OF LETTERS

and fish. Kel went and checked our back trail to be sure we weren't being followed, while Jack tended to Angel's constantly growing list of discomforts.

Hog had slipped off to the woods to do a bit of night hunting and with him Monk. I worried about her getting lost in the dark woods but knew that Hog would watch over her; it wasn't like I could stop her anyway. The two had become almost inseparable in the short time they had known each other, and he was as protective of her as he was me. She still hadn't spoken a single word, but when she curled up with Hog, I could hear her make soft little sounds, almost like his mumbling.

When Kel returned we ate, setting some aside for Monk and Hog when they returned from their hunting. Jack and Angel took their portions and went to their bed to eat, leaving just June, Kel, and me at the fire.

"So any ideas on where we should head to?" Kel asked, then opened a map, holding it up for us to see in the feeble light of the fire.

June looked at the map. "I don't vote for north. Winter can be tough, depending on how far north we go." Looking over at Jack and Angel, she added, "I don't think some other members of our group could handle that either."

Watching Jack try to pamper Angel made it pretty obvious that she was going to be a problem anywhere, but I agreed with June— being confined through a winter with them wasn't my first choice. We couldn't go east either, so that left west, which would mean a wet winter or south, which would hopefully be warmer. We all agreed that south was our only real choice; now we just needed a location.

"What about this place by Powder Creek?" I asked while pointing to it. "If it doesn't work out, we can just keep heading farther south from there."

Kel marked off the distance. "If we can keep everyone moving, it would only take five days to get there. Maybe six days, if we stop to hunt a bit. We'll be needing food by then."

June looked at the trail Kel had marked, then knowing she was the oldest person in our party, she said, "I'll make it, don't you worry about me any."

"It's settled then," Kel said and got a nod of agreement from me and June. With our plan set he got up and, map in hand, headed to show Jack and Angel our plan.

June went to bed while I waited for Kel and our night hunters to return. I poked more wood into the fire, keeping it fed but small. Alone, my mind turned to him and all that we had been through so far. I knew how I felt about him, and from his actions it was obvious how he felt about me. I had never felt like this, lost and found at the same time, but not knowing what to do about it. I was startled out of my thoughts when Kel returned to the fire, and upon seeing him I looked deep into his eyes and knew. "I love you, Kel," I said softly and started to pull him close.

We were interrupted by a giggle and a low growl—Hog and Monk had returned from hunting. In embarrassment of getting caught, Kel started to laugh while I died. Hog came over, relieved himself of a muskrat, and then checked me over while giving Kel the evil eye. Once he was sure I was okay, he took his meal and retreated to the edge of the firelight to enjoy his meal. Monk sat next to me, and I handed her the dinner we had saved for them. That night I felt Kel's arm lay across my waist and heard him whisper, "I love you too, Butterfly."

The next day we started toward Powder creek; it was a long and rough day. We covered a little over six miles; they were miles of up-and-down terrain, and several water crossings including North Fork Kilchis River and the south fork before stopping for the night. Before night set in, Monk and I went out and set trout lines and spring traps, while Kel again went hunting with the bow. Hog had gone out on his own this time to hunt as well, leaving Jack in camp to tend to more of Angel's wants.

June had gathered firewood and even found a few berries that we could add to our tea by the time Monk and I returned. I showed both June and Monk how to build a fire ring to hide the light and then how to start the fire using the ferro rod. It wasn't long before we had a nice, warm flames going, and putting the pot over the fire I added water and the berries to heat.

THE BOOK OF LETTERS

Around two hours later, Kel stepped into the firelight; he had gotten lucky and shot a porcupine. While he carefully skinned it out, I set green sticks over the fire to roast it on. I wasn't long before the smell of food brought Angel and Jack to the fire wanting their share.

"I don't think we can keep traveling like this without more rest," Jack said flatly. "Angel's feet just can't take this kind of punishment, and we are totally unprepared for this kind of walking."

I looked over at her while she sat there, trying to looking helpless; the sight of it made me mad. Looking at the others, I could see I wasn't the only one that felt this way. We had all suffered, but the only one whimpering about it was Angel. My anger at Jack was simply for being dumb enough to put up with Angel's whims.

It was June that finally spoke. "You two don't get it, do you? We are being hunted, we're not on a pleasure hike. We are now criminals, outlaws, and terrorists, and there is no going back! If you guys want to survive this, you are going to have to grow up and pitch in. None of us are here to babysit you guys, so either suck it up and help or shut up and leave on your own!" Her eyes were snapping when she looked at Angel. "And you aren't a princess or a delicate flower to be tended to constantly, so take care of your own self, and let Jack help out instead of wasting his time chasing your wants."

I tried to hide my grin as Angel sat there with her mouth open in shock from June's words. She stood up, her back stiff with anger, and looked at Jack.

"I want to go to bed. I seem to have lost my appetite. You can stay here with these people or join me, your choice." Angel waited a moment for Jack's answer, and then before he could say anything she stormed off to their bed.

It wasn't long before he left to join her, not waiting to eat; in some ways I felt sorry for him.

June shook her head as she watched him go. "He is in for a world of hurt if he keeps pandering to that woman. She will never be satisfied. She is just using him, but he's too young and enamored with her to see it."

I knew she was right. I guess that was why I felt sorry for him. I moved closer to Kel, and he put his arm around me. It felt good. I couldn't understand people like Angel; they annoyed me with their parasitic ways. Even though I was reserved about it, I knew that I wanted to be Kel's partner, his equal, not some victim to be saved. Though this lifestyle was new to me, I had already learned that it was going to take a partnership to survive.

The porcupine tasted a lot like the pork patties we ate back in Portland, only better. We packed about half of it away for tomorrow's travel, and then headed for our bed. Morning came early, and we were on the trail before I was fully awake. Monk and June had gathered the snares and trout lines, but they were all empty this time. We continued south and traveled hard for three days, covering twentysomething miles, then took a break between High Peak and Hardscrabble Mountain.

There I went hunting with the bow for the first time, while Kel ran out the trap-line snares. June tried her hand at fishing in one of Moon Creek's offshoots and caught a few hand-sized trout. Monk and Hog were off again in the woods, and I wondered what all she was learning from our big friend. I could see that Monk's time with him was helping build her confidence, and day by day you could see the difference. Jack and Angel had become very distant to the rest of us since June had snapped at them, still unwilling to help but always ready to eat their portions of whatever we brought in.

I found a well-used deer trail then found a place to hide and wait in hopes that one might pass by. It was almost dark when a fork-horned buck came down the trail and gave me my chance. The bow proved its value once again, and in the last of the light I dove into butchering as much as I could. It wasn't long before I had as much as I could carry bundled up and was headed back to camp, happy with what I had accomplished. Back at camp, I set my bundle down by the fire, and June went to work cooking some of it while I went to wash off. Back in camp Kel's face beamed with pride in the firelight, and though I shied from it, his warm hug and kiss on the cheek was all I needed to know that I had done well.

The morning sun found us heading west again for nearly a mile before we turned south. It made our hike a bit longer but put us between Moon Creek Road and Borba Road, which meant we only

THE BOOK OF LETTERS

had to cross Upper Nestucca Road just west of a place called Blaine. We crossed where the Nestucca River passed under the road, which saved us from getting wet until we crossed limestone creek. A mile and a half later, we reached Powder Creek and found a place to stay and rest a while.

CHAPTER 21

At sunset everyone worked to erect shelters and beds against the coming cold night. Angel and Jack chose once again to build their own shelter away from ours, while June, Monk, Hog, Kel, and I continued to stay together. We were becoming a family and a well-working team, each of us finding which jobs best suited us and where we could help each other. As I watched my new family, I knew that somehow, together, we would survive despite the odds. June had taken over the camp chores of cooking and shelter tending, and with my sewing kit she even found time to keep up with the constant job of patching our failing clothes. While Kel took on firewood and hunting, Monk and I continued to run our fish traps and snare lines. Monk had become very adept at setting snares and spring traps, and she seemed to always know the best spots to set them. She was learning the art of hunting and tracking from Hog, and it showed; I often wondered what secrets he showed her on their night hunts.

We continued to build our fires only at night for fear of someone seeing our smoke and kept a constant ear listening for drones or ATVs. I knew we weren't out of trouble yet, and in time we would be on the move again, but for now this place gave us a chance to relax, restock, and rest, and for now that was enough. Since hunting had been banned years ago, the woods were now teaming with game, making hunting and trapping easy, and it wasn't long before we had all we could handle. At night we dried and smoked the meat over the fire, then packed it away to save for leaner times.

THE BOOK OF LETTERS

The hides we scraped and dried over the smoke of the fire, when time permitted. When they were dry, we rubbed the stiffened hides over a rock or tree branch till it softened a bit, making it flexible. We stayed there for two weeks before the sounds of ATVs from the direction Burnt Ridge reminded us of our precarious existence. That night we pulled out our map and had a meeting as to where to head next, and even Jack and Angel joined us in our discussion. We needed to find a place without so many roads, and that proved to not be as easy to find as I had hoped, but in time we all agreed to head toward a place called Laurel Mountain.

It would be another long five- or six-day walk, but the area offered good hunting and few back roads. I was surprised to not hear any complaints from Angel and hoped it was because she had finally understood our situation. We were well stocked with food, so we wouldn't need to hunt along the way, making traveling a bit quicker. We chose not to follow a straight line, in case our back trail was discovered. With a zigzag trail they still wouldn't know our general intended direction, which would prevent patrols from springing any surprise traps on us.

On the third day of traveling, we were almost caught because Angel decided to lag behind while crossing the Three Rivers Highway about a mile west of Midway. Luckily, the day being late and the sun low, the driver of the westward-bound patrol car was blinded enough that he wasn't able to see her clearly as she lay in the ditch along the side of the road. The close call kept us moving deep into the night till we crossed the Salmon River Highway east of Boyer and were a two miles past Murphy Road and nearing Jackass Creek. When it started to rain, we looked for a sheltered place to camp. When we found it, we huddled together under our tarp, cold and wet, waiting for the light of morning.

Tired from lack of sleep, we continued south, and at some point the rain turned to snow and with it the temperature dropped. The falling snow hid our tracks but made the ground slick and travel slow, so we needed to find a place to wait out the storm and find it soon. One look at our group was enough to tell me that they were at their limit; Kel noticed it too and called for a break under a group of snow-ladened pines. Then while we waited under the tarp, he went ahead to find some form of shelter in the now heavily falling snow.

After what seemed like hours, Hog alerted me to Kel's return.

"I found a place about a mile from here," he said. "I know we're all tired, but it will be worth the effort."

The cold air snatched what little warmth I had from me as we headed again into the deepening snow. We followed the shadowy form of Kel as he led us on, the cold stiffening my healing leg, leaving it feeling numb and dead again. I was almost to my breaking point when he stopped and pointed down. In a gorge, Kel had found a logjam of fallen trees that had been buried under years of debris, forming a sort of cave beneath it. Crawling in, I wondered if it had been some large animal's den, and from Hog's sniffs and low growl on entering, I was pretty sure I was right.

The den floor was deep in leaves, so I pushed them all to one side to make our bed on, while Kel started a fire outside, trusting the falling snow to hide the smoke. He soon had a pot of water simmering, and then added chunks of the dried meat to it to boil and soften. June found a few stones in among the logs and set them close to the fire as well; later we would add them to our bed for added heat. Monk went with Hog, and together they dragged branches for firewood. As tired as we were, everyone worked.

Jack and Angel separated themselves again. Once Jack found another hole on the other side of the logjam, he busied himself making it ready while she sat bundled up, waiting. I worried at how distant they had become, and I knew that she was the cause of it; we had all heard her bickering in the night. At times I wondered why she had even left the city; she never talked about her life before all this, and I wondered why. While watching them, it dawned on me that I had never seen Angel without her coat or sweater on, even when they were wet.

Was it to hide the scar we all had from removing our chips? Could she really be that vain? I already knew the answer to that—a big yes. From Monk's scar it was apparent that she had used her teeth to tear her chip out. What had happened in this child's life that would drive her to do that, we would probably never know. I looked

THE BOOK OF LETTERS

up at Monk as they brought in another branch and set it with the growing pile of firewood. Kel, gave her a thumbs-up, and she flashed a smile at the gesture. She certainly wasn't like the girl we first met, but then again, we had all changed since the day of the Butterfly and our flights for freedom.

With the warmth from the stewed jerky in our stomachs and the heated stones in our bed, we slept the night through in comfort, and knowing that the falling snow had hidden our passing, we felt a bit of momentary peace. The next morning, we woke to a thick layer of snow that covered the logs, making our new home almost impossible to see. The snow still continued to fall, but lightly, so Kel and I took a walk around the area to see if we couldn't figure out where exactly we were. We had lost our bearings during the snowstorm and only knew the direction we had gone, but we had no idea of how far.

Two hours of hiking and the use of the telescope led us to believe that we were close to Boulder Creek, where its tributaries came together and about four miles north of Rooster Rock. On our way back we saw the numerous game trails and knew the hunting and trapping would be good, and with the creeks I could put out fish traps as well. Back at camp we talked it over with the others and got a surprisingly unanimous agreement to stay for a while. As long as we kept our outside activities to a minimum and our fires only at night, we would be hard to find, being as hidden we were.

CHAPTER 22

The next morning Kel, Monk, and I went out to set traps, hunt, and see what the local fauna offered, while June busied herself back at camp, adding to our shelter and mending what she could of our clothes. I hadn't seen Angel or Jack before we left, so I had no idea what they were up to, but I had also gotten to the point that I didn't really care. By the time we came back to camp, nearly thirty spring traps and snares had been set. We even caught a string of trout and had gotten a good idea of which game trails offered the best chance of bigger game. That night after dinner the five of us retired to our shelter, and for the first time I showed June and Monk the book of letters.

By candlelight, we read bits of the book, and June was as amazed as I had been over the diversity of information the book held. After a bit I let her and Monk continue to flip through the book, while I helped Kel work on assembling the crystal radio set we had found in the case. Two hours later Kel sat carefully, trying to find a channel he could pick up. When he did, it was a government station out of Lincoln City. I watched his face as he listened through the earbud, and saw both looks of anger followed by looks of confusion, followed by more adjustment to the radio.

"Alice, listen to this and tell me what you hear," Kel said. Then as he handed me the earbud, he added, "Pay attention to the background noise."

I put the bud in my ear and could hear a government broadcast giving the new numbers of people arrested and terrorists found. They

THE BOOK OF LETTERS

were posting rewards for any information that helped them in tracking down fugitives; my name along with others were mentioned, along with updated rewards for our capture. As I listened, I too could hear something in the background static, a sort of rhythmic tapping that the longer I listened to, the more convinced I became of what it was.

At my request June handed me the book of letters, and I went to the section on communications. There I found the page; it was on Morse code and its applications. On the dirt floor I started marking the clicks I was hearing in the static, while June used the book to decipher the code. Soon the message started to make sense. It was town names that were listed as hot or cold and ending with the phrase "Fly free, Butterfly, we are with you." Then the message began to repeat its self, so I set the earbud to the side and looked over the message with the others. We just had to decide now if it was from friends or foes.

Laying out the map and checking the towns marked hot, the message made sense. Towns and cities along I-5 were all marked hot, as were several towns along 101 and a few other scattered highways. Looking at the map made it clear that if the message were true, we were nearly twenty miles from the closest hot spot, confirming the wisdom of our decision to stop. I went back to the radio, but the background static had gone silent, leaving just the government broadcast repeating its propaganda.

Over the course of several weeks, the hidden static messages filled us in on how and where security forces were deployed and their general movements, as well as drone activity. During that time, we worked at preparing for the day we would have to leave as none of us had any fantasies of our settling here for long, but we would enjoy it while we could. The hunting had been good; both Kel and I had shot several deer and one young elk, and along with Monk's handling of the trap lines, we had filled our packs with all the dry meat we could carry. It had also supplied us with numerous hides and furs that, with help from the book, we learned to cure beyond just drying them over our smoking racks. Soon we hopefully would be able to replace our worn clothes with ones we made.

MICHAEL SCOTT

June proved herself more adept at sewing than the rest of us, so she devoted her time to making what she could while we kept the firewood pile stacked and our food larder full. There were three solid days of rain and snow that week, keeping us indoors to stay dry, and even Hog preferred the dried meat to going out in the nasty weather. During that time, out of curiosity, I showed Monk the string game but this time I decided to just write on the ground instead of using a string to hopefully make it easier for her to grasp the concept.

On the ground in front of me I drew a big smiley face, and then with Monk watching me, I pointed to the ground then to my face and made a big smile. Monk looked at the ground then back at me; all I could see in her face was confusion. June, catching on to what I was trying to do, drew on the ground in front of her then pointed to it like I had. Monk looked at the ground where June had written the letters *JUN*, then back in June.

"June," she said as she pointed to herself, she then pointed back at the letters. "June," she repeated, going through the actions several times. Kel then did the same, writing the letters *KL* then repeating June's actions. Next was my turn to try again, and I likewise followed June's example. Then writing an *M* on the ground I repeated the action with her. There was a flash of sudden understanding in her eyes, she looked again at the letters on the ground, taking them all in.

Monk looked over at Hog, and I thought she wanted to know his name so I bent down and wrote the letters *HG* then pointed at him and repeated his name. She looked down at the letters and shook her head, then knelt and using her knuckles and fingers, she formed an impression in the dirt, one I had seen before.

Kel looked down at it. "Is that what I think it is?"

Hearing his question, I looked up. "Yep, Hog's footprint."

Monk then pointed back at Hog and did almost a prefect imitation of his mumbling, even doing his sad-eye routine, sending us all into bouts of laughter. Hog sat up and cocked his big head, trying to figure out our antics, but he was not sure what all the noise was about. He gave one of his deep mumbles at us then rolled over and went back to sleep. We finished the evening as had become our habit with listening for a message over the radio and reading from the book

THE BOOK OF LETTERS

of letters. Tonight, we found a few pages on improvised weapons, and I noted Kel's interest over one of the images with the words *staff sling* written under it.

Kel's actions reminded me of something I had completely forgotten about; Christmas would soon be coming. The radio broadcast had said the date was now December 8; it was hard to believe we had been on the run so long. I looked over our ragged group and wondered how much longer they would be able to keep going. If we could just hold out till spring, things would get a lot easier, if the patrols didn't get more plentiful with the nicer weather.

The thoughts of patrols had us on the trail again two days later; behind we left a packet of dried meat in our shelter as a backup if things went bad. We had pushed our luck staying as long as we had, so our ragged band headed again, this time east toward Laurel Mountain. Following Boulder Creek for around four miles to Boulder Springs, we came upon an old trail where we found some worn and faded tire tracks of an ATV. It was enough to push us on another three miles, till we finally stopped at one of Cedar Creek's tributaries northeast of the mountain. There we bivouacked for the night with hopes of finding more permanent shelter in the morning.

The darkening skies dimmed the sunrise and told us that we didn't have long to find a place. Kel and I headed upstream while Hog and Monk headed downstream, while the others packed up our gear and prepared to head out on our return. Three hours later, Kel and I returned back to camp without finding anything promising. When we got back, though, it was clear from Hog's prancing and Monk's smile that their luck had been better than ours. Half a mile downstream, they had indeed found a place to call home, in the form of a large pine. It was twenty or thirty feet up the bank from the creek and had been uprooted in some bygone day; now its decaying trunk and branches formed a sort of cave under it.

The branches formed a bird's nestlike structure that over the years had filled in with vines and leaves, making it more or less watertight and dry inside. Using rocks and scattered limbs, we blocked off the wide opening, leaving just a small door to conserve heat. It wasn't long before our new home was ready for us and our gear. Jack built a debris shelter for him and Angel; they were still choosing to be alone. Jack had now become the go-between for them because Angel had stopped talking to us altogether. And while it was worrisome, we didn't miss her bickering any.

Jack had started helping with gathering firewood once in a while, but other than that we didn't see much of him. Some nights when we had the radio going, he would stop by and listen for a while, but he never stayed long, always saying Angel was waiting on him. It started raining a few days after we were set up and continued into the night before turning to snow; we woke to a cold white world. The snow fell heavily through the next few days, and we utilized the time to finish gifts for the coming holiday, reading, and taking turns listening to the radio.

We kept busy with hunting, projects, and the constant need of firewood as the weeks passed, and before we knew it Christmas day had arrived. June had worked to explain what Christmas was to Monk, who had never had one before, in the end she settled on a day of gifts. Though she never spoke, I knew she understood some of what we said in a rudimentary way by her actions and responses. Monk's silent life was still a mostly a mystery to us, but when we had bathed in the cold creek I had seen the scars that covered large portions of her body, and they told of the brutality she had already bore in her young age.

Angel and Jack joined us that morning for the festivities, and we greeted them with Christmas cheer; June even lead us in a carol with Hog and Monk howling along with her. Their singing soon had us all laughing and in high spirits; it was a good feeling to see everyone enjoying themselves. Once we had eaten our Christmas breakfast, Monk became impatient, and I knew what was on her mind. She had been told that there would be gifts. From my pack I pulled out a pair of high-top moccasins that June had helped me with and handed them to her.

Her eyes grew big at the sight of them, and she quickly tossed off the remains of her shoes, and then slipped on the moccasins. Her squeal of delight told me she liked them, and her hugs confirmed it. Next, I gave June half of my sewing kit and to Jack a fishing kit.

THE BOOK OF LETTERS

To Angel I gave a raccoon-fur lap blanket, and to Kel I gave a copy I made of the blueprints for the repeating bow and the magnetized needle. To Hog I gave a whole deer liver that had been saved for just him, and in typical fashion he dove into it.

Everyone seemed pleased with their gifts, and then June took a turn to hand out hers. To Kel she gave a game bag, and to Monk and me she gave fur shawls. To Angel she gave a fur hat and to Jack a pair of fur mittens; to Hog she gave a braided collar, but Monk growled when June tried to put it on him. From the scar around her neck it wasn't hard to guess why. June just put the collar back in her bag, and we moved on to Kel's gifts.

To me he gave a whistle on a leather thong; on the side of it he had scrimshawed the words, "May you always know the sound of my heart." He then showed me the matching one he had made for himself that now hung from his neck. I slipped mine on, with the intention of never taking it off, and then I thanked him with a light kiss to the cheek. To June he gave a birchbark parfleche for her sewing kit, and to Jack and Angel he gave one of our softened blanket hides.

"Now, Monk, I think it's time for your gift," Kel said as he reached under our sleeping mat. "I'll show you how to use it later today."

He then handed her a staff sling that he had made; it was a carved staff about five feet long, with designs that spiraled around it and topped with a braided leather sling. Monk's hand felt along the carvings and examined the sling hanging from the top, and everyone was a bit surprised when she jumped up and gave him a hug of thanks as well. Next came Monk's gifts. To June she gave a large handful of dried blackberries wrapped in a squirrel skin. To Hog she gave a large leg bone, and to Kel and I she gave a pillow.

The pillow was actually two pillows tied together and stuffed with leaves; she then did something that left no need for explanation. She reached out and placed Kel's hand over mine, then placed them on the pillow—the message was clear. We both hugged her, and I even noticed June wiping a tear from her eyes, while Jack and Angel seemed unsure of what was going on. I laid my hand over Monk's heart then over mine; she seemed to understand my meaning and hugged me again tighter than ever before.

CHAPTER 29

After our short festivities Angel and Jack retired to their abode, and Kel went outside with Monk to show her how to use her new staff sling. June and I sat in the doorway and watched them, laughing from time to time at their erratic attempts and successes at hitting their intended targets.

"Did I ever tell you about how I met my husband?" June suddenly asked as we sat there. Then without waiting for an answer, she continued on. "I was having a really bad week, nothing seemed to be going right, and it had been one thing after another. It had been raining hard that day, and the elevator was broken again, so I rushed up the stairs already running late. I was in such a hurry that as I ran up the stairs, I didn't see him coming down, and I plowed into him at full speed." June giggled at the memory. "The stairs were a bit wet, so when I ran into him we both lost our footing and ended up tumbling down to the landing at the bottom. The ambulance took us to the hospital where he was treated for a broken arm, and I had my leg put into a cast. Needless to say, it wasn't the best way to meet someone!" June looked back out to Kel and Monk. "I felt bad for what had happened, but Martin seemed to think it was all pretty funny; I always loved his sense of humor. I tried to repay him somehow, but all he said he wanted was dinner with me. I must say we were quite a pair that night. Him with his arm in a sling and me hobbling along on crutches. Needless to say, we got some strange looks at the restaurant. I cut up his food for him because of his arm, while he watched with a

THE BOOK OF LETTERS

big smile that left me blushing. That night started the best thirty-five years of my life."

June looked back over to me. "Just remember, it doesn't matter how or where love starts. Only that it stays true and from the heart. The rest will work itself out. He's a good man, Alice, don't let fear or circumstance stop you from loving someone. There is no perfect time, only the present with no tomorrows promised, so use your time wisely."

With that she got up and went outside to join Kel and Monk, leaving me alone with my thoughts. I knew she was right; everyone knew how I felt about him, and even Monk had let us know that she accepted it. I thought of Susan and how shocked she would be to see Kel and me together. I don't think she would believe it or the life we were all living now.

Watching Monk, I could see that she was getting a knack for her new staff sling; she was hitting smaller and smaller pieces of bark that had been stood up as targets in the snow. Joining the group, I along with June were soon cheering on Monk, as she continued to hit targets that Kel had missed. In retaliation, Kel threw a snowball at me, which caused a snowball fight that ended with us all in a dog pile, wrestling with each other while peals of laughter rolled across the snow-covered hills. Lying there in the snow next to Kel, exhausted from our tussle, I thought of what June had said and knew she was right—there is no right time, only here and now.

I rolled over to lie on top of Kel and looked into his eyes. "I love you, Kel, I am yours as you are mine. And I want my heart to always know the sound of yours." Then I kissed him; it was long and full of unrestrained emotion. It was a Christmas none of us would ever forget.

Things changed a bit after that day. For one, Kel and I no longer felt the need to hide our feelings, and I found myself hugging and kissing him often, frequently punctuated with giggles from Monk. Even she seemed to have become more comfortable with Kel, but I still caught her growling from time to time when she saw Jack or Angel. Monk practiced every day with her sling, and it didn't take her long before she was hitting her targets with consistency. She seemed to be a natural when it came to living in the wild and acquired skills quickly; what she had lost in speech, she made up many times over in adaptability.

We all knew that we would need to move again soon, so that night we pulled out the map and looked it over by the light of our sap candle. South would be our direction, but we needed to plot a designation; that was the tricky part. Was there really a place that would be safe, or were we destined to live out the rest of our lives running? It was a question I had no answer for. That night, we also learned three things from our radio: the security patrols were building up east of us and were staging from the Dallas area as well as at a place called Grand Ronde. The second thing we learned was that the reward for reporting a terrorist now included amnesty, and third, that there was a large storm building in our area.

If we timed things right, the storm would cover our movements and obliterate evidence of our passage. As hard as traveling in weather like that was, it would still be the safest time to move out. With Jack and Angel joining us as we plotted a course, we broke the trip into five- and six-mile days. Our destination, much to Angel's protests, was the Rogue River-Siskiyou Forest area. It would take quite a while to get there, but it looked to hold our best possibilities of avoiding patrols in its wide-open spaces.

Later after Jack and Angel had left, we got out the book of letters once more, knowing it would be quite a while before we would have the time to read it again. The four of us were sitting there reading, while Hog softly snored in the corner. It gave me a sense of peace— we had become a very close family and one I treasured. On one of the pages, we found drawings of a house that was built underground, and the words finally got her finished, written under it.

"Your great-grandfather must have had quite a vision, if this was the kind of things he built on his place," June said. "It would be a wonderful thing to see."

"If it hadn't been for the bomb, his plans were to make it all self-sustaining," I commented as we looked over a page that showed Savonius wheels, along with pumps and generators that could be

THE BOOK OF LETTERS

hooked to it. "He had big dreams of some of his designs possibly changing the world. Now I guess we'll never know."

"In one of his letters he said he would send back proof that he was right and the bomb was a hoax, but so far I haven't found any," I added. "Besides that, all I know is that it was hidden, somewhere east of the town of Prineville."

"Well, it was a nice dream," June replied. Then giving me a hug, she added, "Someday, soon, I know we'll find a place for us as well."

I could only hope; after all, being hunted for crimes we were never guilty of wasn't a life any of us wanted. How long would it be before we would find our safe haven? None of us knew, but I could tell from their countenance that they were still far from giving up on our search. This may not have been the way things were supposed to have gone, but I was sure Mom would have approved of those now with me. That night in Kel's arms I slept peacefully, lulled to sleep by the sounds of his beating heart and warmth of his body.

The next day we started packing; we wanted to be ready to leave before the storm built up too much in its fury. Jack left camp to try out his hand at fishing, while Kel and Monk went to gather up all our traps and snares. June and I packed dried meat and supplies into each pack in case we were ever separated for any reason. Traveling the way we were, it was always best to plan for the unexpected. It was around noon that I saw Hog's head pop up and start looking around. A moment later I heard it, the distinct sounds of a distant drone, and it was coming our way fast.

June and I quickly huddled with Hog and pulled what was left of the Mylar blanket over us, hoping to at least confuse our heat signatures when it passed directly over us. Lying there, we worried about the others but pinned down as we were, there was no way of helping them without being exposed. It made two passes about fifteen minutes apart, and then continued on over the forest, heading back to the east. We lingered, waiting for it to come back. Then finally convinced it wasn't, we crawled to the door and looked out, expecting to see patrols swarming in.

There was no one in sight, and sending Hog out to check the area confirmed we were still alone, for the moment. Fearing we had

MICHAEL SCOTT

possibly been spotted, June and I moved our packed bags to the south of camp, the direction we had planned to leave by. I climbed to a higher point and scanned the area with the telescope, but there was nothing to be seen. Kel and Monk had left a slight trail leading into the woods when they had left, but there was still no sign of them coming back. I could see Jack's trail as well, but nothing past where it faded into the snow-ladened trees.

Hog gave me one of his looks, and I nodded to him. He darted off into the forest, low to the ground and on the hunt. We went back to camp to check on Angel as neither of us had seen her during the entire event. To our disgust we found her still hiding in her bed and their bags tossed to the side, still unpacked.

"I didn't know what to do, so I just stayed here and hid in our bed," Angel said, giving us her doe eyes.

June rolled her eyes back at her. "You're as useless as a fish with aquaphobia." That got a snort of anger from her and a muffled laugh from me. "Get your gear packed, we'll be heading out as soon as the others return!" she snapped, and with that we went back to get the rest of our gear.

June and I were just coming back from stashing the last of our gear, when we found Kel and Monk circling the outskirts of camp with Hog.

Kel greeted me in his arms, and then told us what happened. "We heard the drone, so we burrowed into a snowbank and buried ourselves. It was Monk's idea." He gave her hair a stroke while she hugged his leg. "After that we waited and listened for more drones, but not hearing anything we started back. It took a little time, but we tried not to leave too much of a trail leading back here." He looked down at the girl. "This girl has learned a lot from Hog here; she has even taught me a few new tricks."

Monk beamed with pride at Kel's praise as I bent down to hug her.

"Thank you for keeping him safe." Then I kissed her on the cheek and felt her arms tighten around me.

"Is everyone ready to go?" Kel asked, and June shook her head.

"Jack isn't back yet," I said. "And Angel is just starting to pack."

THE BOOK OF LETTERS

I could see the anger rising in him and his mind spin with ideas of what to do. We couldn't just leave them, and yet we didn't know how long we had before any patrols might show up, or even if any had been sent. June and I led the group back to where we had been watching the camp, and then settled in to wait and watch. Slowly the day passed, and the sun settled into the west, still with no signs of Jack.

CHAPTER 24

Our hidden vantage point was sheltered by the trees and overhanging branches, so we settled in for the night instead of running the chance of being caught in our shelter below. Even the rising winds weren't enough to make us move, but the building black wall of heavy snow clouds did give us hope of getting out unseen. I have no idea when Jack got back, only that it was Hog and Monk that sensed him first. With the telescope I watched him as he went to their shelter and crawled in, and then turned to scan the woods from where he had come—nothing.

We waited, our eyes and ears trying to seek out any possible enemies. There was nothing but the sound of the rising wind. Finally, Kel took a chance and slipped down to their shelter while the rest of us watched for any possible intruders, ready to give warning. My heart beat heavily with fear as we waited for Kel to reemerge with Angel, Jack, and their gear. Then I felt the cold bite of a snowflake hit my cheek and knew the storm was on its way. Soon the falling snow began to obscure our vision, making the shelters below us hazy and the trees nearly invisible.

Only one shadowy form appeared from the blur of snow, and thankfully it was Kel.

"They want to wait out the storm before they travel," he said above the wind. "Jack says he doesn't believe that they would send any patrols out in this kind of weather." Then looked at me. "He may be right. What do you think? It would be easier to travel with a little light."

We all knew Kel was right about having some light, but none of us felt safe going back, so we huddled together under an elk hide and waited for the tendrils of morning light to sneak in through the storm. We didn't have long to wait and soon were gathering our stashed packs like shadows in the now heavily falling snow. I heard Hog growl then heard the whine of an ATV coming from somewhere out of the wall of snow that now seemed to surround us. We grabbed our packs, then slipped them on and listened to the storm, hoping to pinpoint where the sound had come from.

We weren't far outside of the camp and now could hear the distinctive whines coming from both sides of us. Kel turned and handed me the bow and his pack,

> "I've got to warn them!" he said. "Stay here and I'll go get them. If something happens, I'll meet up with you at one of our planned sites. Don't worry, we still have that date you promised me. I'm still holding you to it."

He then kissed me, and before I could say anything to stop him, he disappeared into the howling white storm. From our hiding place we could hear more and more ATVs coming, the building sounds circling around us through the storm. The minutes seemed to hang like hours, and I could feel my fear rise with every passing moment. It was the sound of gunfire coming from the direction of camp that caused me to bolt upright, and June that kept me from running to find Kel. The sounds of the ATVs seem to converge in the direction of the machine-gun bark.

"You can't save him by running into an ambush!" June yelled into my ear. "He'll find us at the next site but not if we get caught before we get there!"

I knew she was right but couldn't bring myself to leave yet, so we waited a little longer with hope. The sounds of Angel's screams and Jack's pleading for their promised rewards slipped through the white nightmare we were now in. Another zipperlike explosion then silence, the sudden quietness fueling our fears for Kel. A few moments later, there was a shout to the west of us, then the sounds of more gunfire spitting from several directions.

"We got to go now!" June yelled at me, and I felt her and Monk push me forward and into the raging storm.

I had to leave Kel's pack and hoped that, if he was alive, he would be able to find it. The bow I now kept at the ready in case of attack, while hot tears streamed down my face at the thought of possibly losing him. I kept telling myself that he will find us, repeating it over and over in hopes of it being true. I used my compass to keep us heading in the right direction, and we pushed on through the deepening snow, away from our enemies and away from my love.

We were lucky that the high winds prevented the use of drones and the snow limited visibility to just a few yards; even then we had to wait out several passing patrols. I kept us heading toward Riley Peak while changing direction from time to time to avoid being tracked. Three miles later we came to our crossing point by Silver Falls, two miles northeast of Riley Peak. There we found another patrol already waiting for us on the south side of the creek as if they knew we would come this way. There were only two of them, so we waited in hope for our chance that they might move farther downstream; they didn't.

It was then that Hog headed away from us downstream. A short time later, we heard his barks and saw the patrol officers run in his direction. We took the opportunity, and I was the first to head across, with June behind me while Monk brought up the tail, spacing ourselves out to draw less attention. I was helping June up the bank, when Hog came prancing back, happy with his little trick. When I looked back to Monk, I saw that she was halfway across the creek. All seemed well, then I saw her face change, and she gave a primordial scream like some raging wildcat as she brought her sling up to fire. Out of the corner of my eye, I saw a patrol step out of the brush with his gun raised at Hog.

Monk's arms blurred as she whipped her staff forward, and I saw the side of the officer's helmet collapse under the impact of the river stone. Then another officer ran into the fray, pointing his gun at Hog's protector, preparing to fire. The fletching from one my short

THE BOOK OF LETTERS

arrows appeared in his throat, and a look of confusion crossed his face. As he turned to face me, another sprouted from his chest, a stone from Monk's sling ended the standoff. I stood there in shock; I couldn't even remember firing the bow. I watched as Monk ran forward and swung her staff down again and again on the heads of her enemies. Then when she was sure of their demise, she raised her head and gave a blood-chilling howl into the raging storm, soon joined by the voice of Hog. Dark and evil things had happened to this child in her past, and I knew that from this night on, she would never be anyone's victim again.

It was June who brought me back to the moment and had the presence of mind to strip the dead men of anything useful; their clothes, boots, and gear were now our bounty. The gruesome task done, we headed out and crossed an old trail where the patrol officers had driven in their quads we found but left, knowing they would be too easy to track. Our planned site was where Lost Creek separated from the Little Luckiamite River, but with the use of the telescope on Riley Peak, it was clear that our plans would have to change. Even at almost two miles away, you could make out the temporary camp of the security forces through the slackening snowfall.

Someone had told them our plans and sold us out. I had my guesses as to who it was, but it no longer mattered; they were dead. Finding a place under some boulder and trees, we waited for the safety of night before moving on. Heading west in the dark, we swung past the end of Riley Peak Road, and we then turned a bit south and continued toward Rooster Rock. Crossing Cadillac Avenue at Short Creek, and with twilight of morning growing, we went another mile then found a place to rest and to wait again for the darkness of night.

Our next meeting site was Camp Walker, at a fork in the Yaquina River, a mile west of Little Grass Mountain. That night, from Chandler Mountain, the lights of ATVs, drones, and patrol vehicles told us in advance that the area around Camp Walker was already overrun. We headed southwest and holed up again southeast of Diamond Peak near the north fork of Mill creek. It was becoming very clear that all our meeting sites might now be corrupted and now guarded in hopes of us blundering into their hands.

My fingers went to the whistle around my neck as I thought of Kel and wondered if he had survived the raid. Was he alive somewhere out there, in the snowy wilderness, looking for us? How would he ever be able to find me? The question hung in my mind as tears again flooded my eyes. June tried to sooth me, as I quietly wept as loss and fear overwhelmed me.

"If there is a way, I know he will find you," she whispered to me. "There's not much quit in him when it comes to you. He'll find a way."

Monk curled up with me, and it wasn't long before I felt the wetness of her tears on my sleeve as we all fell into a restless sleep. I woke up early enough to string out the crystal radio and to see if I could hear any updates. The Morse code hidden in the static was fading in and out, but it was enough to know that the area that we had planned on traveling through was now saturated with patrols, and we were left with few choices. The government broadcasts bragged about killing numerous terrorists found in their camp near Laurel Mountain, and then mourned the loss of twelve officers killed at what they called the Silver Falls ambush.

It was all lies, but only those that were there knew that. The only truth in the broadcast was that we were now all wanted dead or alive for murder. We turned west that night, trying to put some distance between us and the building search forces. Three miles north of Big Tip, we crossed again over Cadillac Avenue then pushed on for another four or five mile. There we found another hole to wait out the day in, about a mile or so east of Euchre Mountain.

From that point, each night we headed south, our hopes were that maybe Kel would have the same idea since that had been our original plan. We would be well north of our goal and a bit west, but it was the only chance we could come up with. My heart yearned for Kel, and many times I strained my ears in hope of hearing his whistle call to me, but the days and miles passed, and none came. Being closer to the coast meant we traded snow for rain, and at times I wondered if I would ever feel dry again.

There were few places where we spent more than the day before traveling on in the dark of night, and we could feel and hear the net of the search tightening around us in its stranglehold. We zigzagged and backtracked our trail to confuse our pursuers, but we knew it was only buying us time. Eventually they would figure out where we were headed. The days and night blurred together as we kept on the constant move. June never complained, but I could see the strain that showed in her face and the loss of weight. Only Monk and Hog seemed unbothered by it; instead it seemed to sharpen their senses and refine their skills. Both were like ghosts in the woods and could seem to vanish before your eyes.

One night, under the light of a half moon, we found what we took to be an old derelict fishing cabin at the east end of Mill Creek Reservoir. Hog and Monk scouted the area and gave no signs of warning, so I went in to check it out. The place was covered in dust and obviously had housed no guests other than rodents for years. We took the chance and decided to stay under a real roof. That day we listened to the rain bouncing on its tin covering.

Its calming effect soon had the others sleeping, while I kept watch at a window. Looking out into the rain, my thoughts turned again to Mom and Kel. Mom I would never see again, I knew that, but with Kel there was still hope. I knew in my heart that somewhere out there Kel was alive and looking for me. Somehow he would know where to find me; I only had to survive till he did.

The rain poured down for three days, and from what we heard on the radio several of the local roads were flooded, so we stayed on, taking the chance at night to build a fire in on old wood stove to try and dry our things out a little. While our clothes hung drying, we heated water and bathed. June had even found a cake of soap in one of the cabinets to wash with. It felt like heaven to finally feel warm and clean again, even if it was only for the day. Soon we would be on the move again and back to being wet and muddy.

When I dressed again in my now dry clothes, I found June by the window, looking at my amulet that I had lain on the table while bathing. She held her reading glasses close to it as she studied the worn etching, then saw me watching her and apologized.

"I'm sorry, I should have asked first," June said as she handed it back to me. "In the light of the window the etchings caught my eye, and curiosity took over."

"I couldn't make them out when I looked," I replied, and then asked, "did you figure them out?"

Her face broke into a smile. "I think so, they're numbers."

She held out her reading glasses. "Use these and in the light you can make them out."

The glasses magnified the etchings, and they were indeed numbers. One string of numbers ran down one side of the amulet, and a different set ran down the other.

"What do they mean, though?" I asked as I looked back again through the glasses.

"I have an idea," June replied, then started digging through our packs. She pulled out one of the maps that Kel and I had found in the case, and she spread it out on the table.

"Look here, along the edge," she said as she pointed. "I remembered how strange it seemed when you first showed me this map, but now it all makes sense."

Two edges of the map had numbers marked at spaced intervals; I had seen them before but didn't know their meaning and, under the circumstances, hadn't given them much thought, till now.

"Read off the numbers," June said and I again held the amulet up and focused the glasses on it.

"On the left side it says 44 then a dot, followed by the numbers 221683," I replied and watched as June made a mark on the left side of the map. Then continuing, I read out the rest of the engraving, "On the right side it says -120 then a dot, followed by 696689."

June marked a spot on the bottom edge of the map, then using her fingers she traced from the marks in straight lines till they intersected. It was east of Prineville; we had found it, my great-grandfather's farm. While June and I were excited over our discovery, we also knew it did us no good; his farm was still in the dead zone. Figuring out one of his secrets made me feel a little closer connected to him, but in the end it only offered a false hope and no place of refuge. We had stayed long enough to push our luck, so as night approached, we packed our bags and prepared for another long night hike. At least the rain had stopped.

CHAPTER 25

Two nights later, we entered the Drift Creek wilderness area and found a place to land for a few days. We were only a mile and a half from north Bayview road, so we kept our ears and eyes open for possible patrols or drones. The last report we got from our static messenger, before we were out of range, said that most of the search activity was still to the east of us, but moving this way. If we didn't figure a way out of this area soon, we might not make it out at all.

Our food was running low, and fires were out of the question here. So we moved on again, traveling by moonlight when visible in the overcast skies. The monotony of our life went on till I lost track of the days and weeks of hiding, running, and the constant struggle for food and shelter from the nearly constant rains of Oregon's coastal winters. We had been spotted by a drone once and by a fisherman another time, and both led to quick changes in direction and long runs to stay ahead of the patrols. At times I wondered if this was all my life would ever be, but it seemed that our only other option was surrender and death; I wasn't ready for that yet.

The south end of the state was now filling with security forces, so we headed east, figuring it would be the last place they would expect us to go. North of Grass Mountain, I shot a young elk doe, so we took what we could carry and continued on. A few hours before daylight, we built a small fire, and then we cooked some of the meat before moving on for a few miles. After finding a hideout, we then ate before sleeping most of the day away. Hog or Monk would always scout the area throughout the day and alert us of any danger.

Monk had even learned enough writing from playing the game we had taught her, that she would leave us messages along the trail or at the shelters, to let us know where she was. A letter here and a symbol there was all she wrote; they were simple markings but enough for us to understand. Northeast of Flat Top Mountain and near Gleason Creek, we found a nice place to hole up again, dry and well hidden. Hog mumbled as he entered and sniffed of the place. From the musky scent, I wondered if it had been a bear den recently occupied.

We took advantage of the hidden location and decided to stay a few days. June and I needed the rest. While Monk and Hog went to scout around, June and I unloaded the packs to see what was still dry and what needed drying. I was thankful that the tarp wrapped around the book of letters had kept it dry; the history book hadn't fared so well, but I still couldn't bring myself to part with it, so I set it out to dry a bit. Next, I set out the crystal radio set, hoping later to catch a signal. It would be helpful to know what was happening out there before we moved on again.

Monk and Hog returned a few hours later and brought two geese with them, both proudly displaying the rewards of their hunting skills. Our mouths watered at the thought of roasted goose, while we waited for the cover of night to hide our cooking. Later, while the others slept, I went out and found some spring green that were starting to pop up with the warming weather. Dandelion greens, burdock, and even horsetail were added to my haul. It felt strange being out in the daylight, but I kept to the wooded areas and kept my ears open.

I wasn't as skilled as Monk at being silent or invisible, and I often envied her talents. She had taken to this life, and I often wondered if maybe it wasn't for the best; she could never go back, yet the way ahead held only uncertainty and hardship. I considered what kind of woman Monk might become in the years ahead, and I wondered if I would be around to see it. My thoughts were turning as dark as the falling night sky, and I remembered the line from the book of letters that I had read so many times: when all hope is lost, faith will carry you forward.

THE BOOK OF LETTERS

My hope was almost at an end, but I had no idea of what to put my faith in. I had put my faith in Mom, and now she was dead. I put it in Kel and had lost him as well. What else did I have left but what I carried in my pack and my waning hope of Kel's safe return? Neither inspired faith in my dark mood, so I turned myself to the task of building a fire to pull myself out of my despair.

Our plentiful meal of goose and greens brightened all our spirits a bit and helped us turn our memories to better and happier times. While Hog and Monk slipped off to do some night hunting, June and I lingered by the dying fire and sipped hot tea. I could tell that June had something on her mind, but she remained silent. Maybe we all were having doubts tonight. With the fire out, we went back to our shelter, and I sat to listen to the radio while June went to bed. I knew this lifestyle had all been hardest on her.

The radio broadcast contained the same load of propaganda about the efforts of the security patrols and of my apparently growing numbers of killings. They needed a boogeyman, and with my backpack and phone left at the hospital during my escape, they had all the info they needed to make me the face of their new war. In the background I heard the static begin to click again, tapping out another message. The broadcast was coming out of Eugene, so I knew the interrupt signal must be somewhere between us, but where would be anyone's guess.

I woke June up and with her help we translated the message of hot and cold areas, and then it repeated the last area three times before signing off with "Fly free, Butterfly, we are with you." The repeated part of the message started a spark of hope anew in me; it had given the name Laurel Mountain followed by cold. It was the first time I had heard an area repeated like that. Maybe it wasn't for me, but my heart told me that Kel was somehow reaching out for me. Walking away from our camp, I did a reckless thing, but I couldn't stop myself—from a ridge I blew on my whistle, letting the night carry the sound.

"Hear the sound of my heart, Kel, I hear yours," I said softly into the night, and then turned back to camp.

CHAPTER 26

Monk and Hog had heard the sounds of my whistle and soon appeared in the bush to walk back with me. I knew that Monk had been missing Kel as well; I had caught her at times when she was sleeping, holding the staff sling close to her chest and making a whimpering sound. June was awake and smiled when we came in; she had heard the whistle as well, and I think maybe it gave her hope too. That night I dreamed of Kel. I called to him, but no matter how I tried he was always just out of reach.

The next day we pulled out the maps and marked the cold and hot spots, so we could plan our next move. With the spring rains melting the last of the snows, there was now a security push through the wilderness areas to try and find the last of those that had fled the day of the Butterfly. They knew as well as we did that there were only so many places to hide or find food; their plan was to either hunt us down or drive us to starvation. We all knew they would never stop; they couldn't let us live if they wanted to save face. Our evasion was an embarrassment that they couldn't allow to continue if they were going to keep control of other would-be societal rebels.

We decided on going north, not that we had much choice, and like so many times before we repacked our gear for another run. I saw June pick up the worn history book and start thumbing through the pages. As she reached the back of the book, an odd look came over her face, and she called me over to see what she had found. The back cover had started to separate from being wet then drying, and just inside the gap you could make out what seemed to be the edge

THE BOOK OF LETTERS

of an old photo. Carefully I peeled back the covers inside liner, and in doing so, I exposed several more photographs and a hidden note.

June looked over the pictures while I read the note; it was in my great-grandfather's handwriting.

> Hello again Cricket I finally have the proof I promised you and I hope it didn't take you to long to remember this old trick. The pictures are of the town and were taken just before I sent the case to you through a good friend. If you can look up EMPs, then you'll know how they did it. Hopefully this is enough to convince your father as well and my prayer is that I will be seeing you again soon. May the case help you on your journey and I pray for your safe travel.
>
> GP

As I finished the note, I handed it to June and looked at the photographs. They were pictures of buildings and houses empty, but intact and unharmed as if frozen in time. In several of the photos, deer could be seen walking down the abandoned streets, looking healthy and well fed. The camera had posted the date on each photo, but it had to be a mistake; they were all dated from the year 2031. That wasn't possible; everyone knew it wasn't! I looked to June and saw her sitting with tears running down her face; she looked old and worn down.

"Alice, they're never going to stop till we're dead. You and I both know that," she said then held out the note. "This is where I'm headed. Live or die, at least it's a chance. I'm too old to do this much longer, and I know I won't make it through another winter. I'm taking a leap of faith and am going to believe that this proof is all real." She looked at me. "I know it has to be true, it was my husband's inquiries into EMP weapons that sent us to the reeducation camp. Now I know why."

Could it really be true? Could it have all been a hoax to drive the people out of the area? What was the purpose behind all of it?

I looked again at the photographs and knew in my heart they were real; only fear was restraining me. It was my fear of never seeing Kel again. I had no way of telling him what we had found, and I knew without being able to tell him that he would never travel to the east side of the mountains.

When Monk returned with the catch from her snares, she saw the photos and looked them over.

"What do you think, Monk?" June asked her. "They're pictures of Prineville, it wasn't blown up."

From Monk's unimpressed expression, I knew she hadn't been told of the bomb or the dead zone, and then I remembered that illegals were denied education by the system. It would be up to June and me to make the decision, and we both knew there wasn't a lot of other offers available to us.

"Let's do it," I finally said out loud and saw June's face fill with hope.

Knowing my fear of losing Kel, she hugged me, "He'll find us, someway he'll find us."

With Monk, we went back to the maps and plotted our new course, heading into the dead zone. Our first problem would be getting east of I-5 and across or around the Willamette River. South would take us around but also into the bounty of security patrols, and north wasn't looking too good either. It was June who remembered an easy place to cross the river at a place called Buena Vista; years ago, when she was just a young girl, it had been a ferry crossing. Now it was no longer used.

It would also allow us to pass between Salem and Albany, and with luck, through security patrols. The area was listed as cold for now, with most of their patrols looking to the west and south, making it a good time to make our gamble. Plans made, we packed the maps and the last of our gear and waited for the cover of night once again. I admit I shed a lot of tears while we waited. I just couldn't see how Kel would ever find us now, and the thought tore at my heart.

That night the sliver of a new moon rose to cast its weak illumination to help guide us to our new destination. As I shrugged on my pack and weapons, I saw Monk tie Hog's collar around his thick

THE BOOK OF LETTERS

neck, and from it hung a small pouch. She mumbled to Hog, and he mumbled back as if they were having a private conversation, then kissing him on the head she walked over to us and slipped into her pack. She then raised her hand and waved to Hog as he turned south and headed into the woods away from us.

"He's going the wrong way," I said to Monk, to which she shook her head. "Well then, where is he going?" I asked.

Monk stooped, and on the ground she wrote the letters *KL*. My heart stopped, and I felt June grip my hand.

"What did you tell Hog to do?" June asked Monk.

She again wrote on the ground, and in the dim light her message filled me with hope. There in the dirt she had drawn a crude butterfly followed by a circle that looked like a clock pointing to three o'clock, then with a stick-figure house that had a *GP* in it. Alongside of it was added a smiley face and ending with *KL KOM*. If the message made it to Kel, I had no doubt he would understand it.

"Thank you" was all I could say, as her actions caused a flood of hope and gratitude to fill my heart; it was a gift I could never thank her enough for.

June looked at the message, and I saw her boot point at the butterfly. "She must have gotten that from the radio, only reason I can think of." She gave me a wink, and then dragged her foot across the message, obliterating it. "No sense telling anyone else our secrets."

My feet were now lightened with the knowledge that Hog was out to find Kel and would lead him back to me. Turning northeast, we headed into the night, three women with a new hope, a new dream, and a new destination that would guide us into the mystery of the dead zone and perhaps a chance at a life of freedom. We only had to survive the journey ahead.

The End

THE PRINCIPLES OF SURVIVAL

(General truths or methods to adopt as the basis for action in the act of surviving or living beyond a life-threatening event)

> It would take reams of paper to explain every aspect of wilderness survival, but I can show you the principles that work in each field. The following are simply notes and lessons life has taught me along the way. I hope they help you on your journey. I've used many of these things myself while in the hills, and they've proven to be quite handy.
>
> P.S. Good luck, Cricket. Safe travels, and never forget that when times are tough and hope is lost, faith will carry you forward.
>
> GP

Knowledge is your most important resource, but practice makes practical application possible. With practice, you build muscle memory and understanding that will assist you with your skills in stressful and non-ideal situations. Starting a fire at home with a match is far different than lighting that same fire in the wind and rain. Practice will teach you the tricks to making fires in all kinds of weather, and understanding the principles of fire will help know how to start and maintain one with a wide variety of items. This works for all aspects of survival and life, no matter where you live or the situations you may encounter. The added benefit is that as you learn your skills, you will find that your need for gear becomes reduced, allowing you greater mobility, speed, and calorie conservation.

Keep a clear mind by using your mind and not your emotions or shock. Ask the important questions and act on them. Am I safe? If not, can I move? If yes, move to safer location. Once safe, am I injured? Treat injuries. What happened? Are you able to assist other? If so, go and help where you can. Stay aware to your surroundings both for dangers and resources that may be available in the immediate area.

Basic rules to remember:

- Three minutes without air
- Three hours of harsh exposure
- Three days without water
- Three weeks without food

People have survived many times past these limits, but they can be used as a simple time guide of your basic needs.

Mental Mindset

In survival situations, people are often defeated before they've even begun. Shock, fear, and indecision will cause most to fail. However, this can be overcome through mental preparedness, practice, determination, and adaptability, all of which you can learn. Mental preparedness is simply gained through learning as much as you can for as many situations as you can. There's a game I played as a kid growing up, which helped me learn which areas were lacking in my studies.

The game begins by naming a place or a scenario. Once called out, you are allowed only five items to use to survive. Anything outside of those five items you must be able to fabricate from the natural environment. It was a fun game for an adventuresome boy and led me to learn a lot of different things along the way, all of them useful. That leads us to the next item—practice.

There are two areas of practice that I want to mention, mental and physical. Playing the game above is one way to practice your mental preparation, as is studying to fill in your knowledge. They both help you build a mental plan of action and give you some idea of what to expect or how to overcome potential barriers.

Physical practice gives you both practical knowledge and muscle memory. These two things will lead to better performance from you and a high degree of survivability when things go bad.

The last is determination and adaptability; these are two of your most important building blocks to your survival arsenal. Both are gained through self-experiences already learned and self-talk. Self-experience helps you know what you're capable of doing, and self-talk builds positively on that. A good example of this can be best described like this: I know that I can walk a mile because I've done it many times, but I've never walked twenty. Instead of focusing on a task I've never done, I'll focus on what I know. So I will just walk one mile, but I'll just repeat it twenty times. I've crossed miles and miles of wilderness using this method, sometimes at just ten feet at a time. Other times it was used to fight off pain, one minute at a time.

It takes time to study, learn, and practice these things but once you do you will be able to do more and survive more than you may ever imagine.

First Aid

My best advice is to study, study, study! There are many good books out there, so read as many as you can; take a class if possible. This is one of the most important areas of study as most survival situations involve injuries. As you learn, build yourself several first aid kits both small and large. That way you're likely to have one with you if ever needed. I find that my basic kit is made up of three items: superglue, gauze pad, and medical tape. This kit is small enough to fit in my pocket and is enough to deal with a good share of injuries with some ingenuity. I'll leave you with a trick I learned from a doctor; it's a good thing to know when dealing with cuts.

1a: Shown here is a typical cut.

1b: Clean wound then lay gauze over it and apply a strip of superglue through the gauze about a quarter of an inch from the edge of the wound. Let dry then pull on the free end of the gauze to pull the wound closed.

1c: With the wound pulled close, put a strip of superglue through the gauze as you did on the other side, again a quarter inch from the wound. Let dry then trim gauze as needed. This little trick has helped me numerous times and can save your life when your miles from help. I also added a simple chart of pressure points to slow blood loss.

1. Armpit and inside of biceps, blocks blood flow to arm.
2. Inside of elbow blocks blood flow to forearm and hand.
3. Wrist blocks blood flow to hand.
4. Inside of thigh or groin, blocks blood flow to leg.
5. Back of the knee, blocks blood flow to calf and foot.

Remember that the longer you stop blood flow, the bigger the chance you have of creating new problems so use only as needed.

One last recommendation I would make is to learn the useful plants in your area. There are many with medicinal properties that may come in handy should medical help not be available or soon coming.

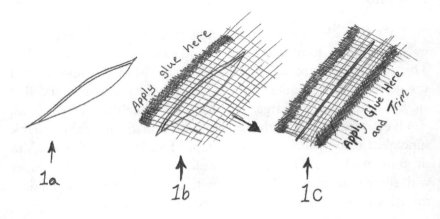

THE BOOK OF LETTERS

Shelters

Simply put, shelters are your insulation from the elements of wind, water, temperature, and sun. Anything that slows the transference of heat and air movement can work as insulation. While anything that can direct water away from the interior of the shelter can be used as roofing. Open-faced shelters can be heated with reflective fires but cool quickly and only stay warm while the fire is going. Brush shelters are easy to warm but highly flammable and for that reason should only be heated with hot stones or body heat. When building a shelter, consider what do you really need and not what you want. Smaller is always better as it saves on labor, materials, and is easier to keep warm. Always remember to insulate or raise your body from the ground whenever possible. The insulation under you is as important as the insulation over you. Below I drew out a few of the shelters I've used over the years.

A brush shelter like figure 2a and 3b have been made for thousands of years. The interior structure as indicated at point 2b and 3b is made of branches that are interwoven or tied together. It must be strong enough to support the load of your covering and any possible load that might be gained from rain or snow. The exterior section of your shelter as seen in 2c and 3c can be covered in a multitude of items, depending on your needs and local offerings. I find that ferns and long grass work really well and when layered as seen in figure 3c sheds rain

MICHAEL SCOTT

quite readily. In high wind areas, lay additional branches on top of your structure to keep your covering from blowing away or being destroyed. Remember, these structures are highly flammable so no fires.

The snowball igloo as seen in 4a can be made even when there are only a few inches of snow. Each snowball starts with a hand-sized snowball that is then rolled around in the snow till it's as big as you need, usually around Twenty-four to thirty-six inches tall. In 4b and 4c, you are shown how the snowballs are stacked, four on the bottom and one on the top. In 4d it shows where you need to pack snow into voids and round out your structure. Start digging into your igloo and throw the removed snow on top and add to the front to create an entrance tunnel. Remember to leave your sleeping bench raised, or you may wake up to cold, wet bedding. Melting snow may make the floor wet, so always keep yourself and your gear off the floor. As 4g indicates, always add insulation under you. It's amazing how much body heat you can lose by lying down without it. And 4h points to an air hole; this is very important if you block the tunnel entrance. As you warm the interior of your igloo, a thin sheet of ice will form on the snowy walls, sealing the snow and blocking air flow, so always add a small air hole.

Shelters can also be made with trenches that are covered over, like in desert regions or on sandy beaches. There are many ways to build shelters, but all follow a few basic rules. Drainage is a very important thing to keep in mind when choosing where to build; no one wants to find out that their floor is a pond. Better to overbuild your roof than underbuild it; snow has crushed many a weak roof and never at a good time. Make sure you always give yourself plenty of time to build your shelter. Trying to build in the dark is a lot harder than you would think and a good way to get injured. Never build on or next to a game trail or local water hole; it scares some animals away from needed water and also exposes you to predators on the hunt.

My last bit of advice is, if possible, add large garbage bags or contractor bags to your outdoors kits. They have a multitude of uses, and a few are shown on figure 5a. Using a bag, you can make an Oregon raincoat as seen indicated by 5b. A few slits for your arms and head, then slip it on. These work really well and are amazingly warm;

stuff with grass or crumpled newspaper for extra warmth if needed. Have wet feet? Try wrapping your feet in plastic like figure 5c; this has helped me many times during spring thaw. If you need a sleeping pad or blanket, fill a garbage bag with grass, rags, leaves, or anything that will work for padding and tie it off as seen by 5d. With a little string or rope, you can even string a few of them together into a tent like 5e.

Other uses include water gathering, boiling water, animal traps, fishing lures, bandages, twine, heating stones, and many others. Needless to say, having a few around is always a good idea when possible.

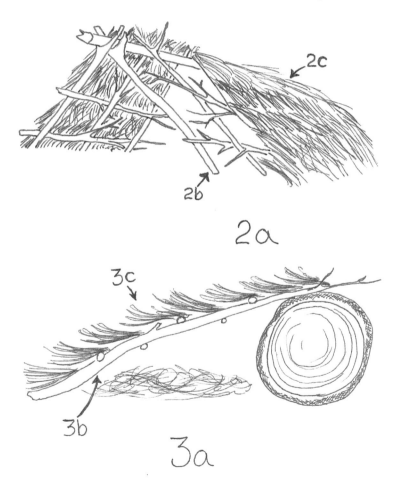

MICHAEL SCOTT

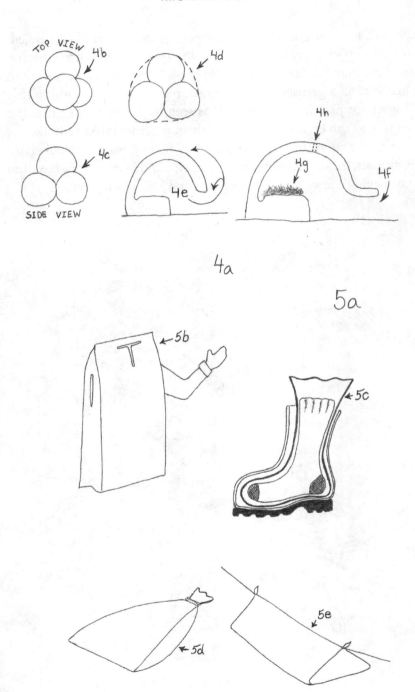

THE BOOK OF LETTERS

Fire

The most basic of fire methods is friction fires. Rather than trying to teach all the different ways to do it, I will share the principles all of them use. Friction fires all require four basic parts.

6a: Friction source, this is the moving part that creates the heat forming friction.

6b: Friction point, also call the fire board, this is the surface that the friction source will use to create both heat and carbon.

6c: Carbon catch, this is one of the most important parts to making a friction fire. Without the proper carbon catch, you won't be able to form an ember.

6d: Tinder bundle—the finest, most flammable tinder should be placed in the center of the bundle. Finely ground charcoal, fuzz from cotton, or scraped dry inner bark work well.

6e and 6f are different grades of tinder working outward from the finest to the coarsest. Grass, moss, shredded bark, or paper, all these things will work but they must be dry.

6g: Once you have formed an ember, you place it with all of your gathered carbon into the center of your tinder bundle. Pull the sides of the bundle up and around your ember to cradle it, and then gently blow into the bundle to feed it oxygen. Go slowly and let the ember slowly build in size. As it does, increase the air you're feeding your bundle. As you blow faster and faster, the ember will grow in such intensity that it will cause the bundle to burst into flames.

Below are several examples of friction fires; each work on the same principles but use different methods. All require well-dried materials, patience, and practice for guaranteed success. Here are the basic steps to using a friction fire.

Step 1: Place your fire board (6b) where you can pin it down to prevent it from moving and place a piece of bark or a leaf under the carbon catch (6c). This will aid later in transferring the ember to your tinder bundle. Take your friction source and place it in the prepared divot of the fireboard (6b). Now move your friction source (6a) in the direction of the arrows. Start slowly, approximately one to

MICHAEL SCOTT

two strokes per second; this will start warming the board and should be done for up to a minute.

Step 2: At that point, begin to increase the speed and the downward force of your friction source (6a). You should soon start to see two things begin to happen: carbon building up in your carbon catch (6c) and smoke. Keep going and push yourself. The longer you push, the more likely you are of success, so give it your all. When you have a plentiful, steady stream of smoke going, carefully remove your friction source (6a) and place it aside.

Step 3: Watch your carbon catch (6c) for signs of smoke, and if there is, prepare to place the ember into the tinder bundle (6d). Now just follow the directions given above to turn your tinder bundle into a flaming fire and add to kindling.

The examples found here (7a, 8a, 9a,) are all friction sources. In 7b, 8b, and 9b, you are shown fire boards. And 7 is a trough fire, 8 is a bamboo fire saw, and 9 is a bow drill. All are very similar, with a few differences necessitated by their function. The addition of 9e and 9d aid in the ability and ease in building up the speed needed to create the heat required. Meanwhile, you can see that 8e is simply a stick to hold your tinder bundle against the carbon catch. Other fire methods and means can also be found if you know where to look, such as 10a, a magnifying glass. These can be found or made from reading glasses, binoculars, cameras, clear bottles, or even plastic bags. Just focus the pinpoint of light on your tinder bundle until you have a good-sized ember.

If you have a car battery handy, you can use 10b, which requires jumper cables and a pencil that has been shaved down to the graphite on one side. Attach the cables to the pencil and place into flammable material, and then attach the other end of the cables to the battery. When the pencil catches fire, disconnect the cables from the battery and pull the other end from fire.

If you only have a small battery, you can do about the same thing using steel wool or a gum wrapper as shown in 10c.

You can also use spark producers such as ferro rods, and in the case of 10d we have a magnesium bar with a built-in ferro rod. The important thing to remember about using either of these items is to keep your knife at a ninety-degree angle to the rod or bar. The idea is to scrape, not to shave or whittle; the fine particles produced are much more flammable than chunks.

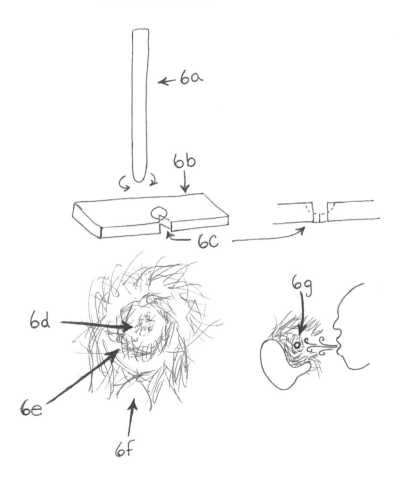

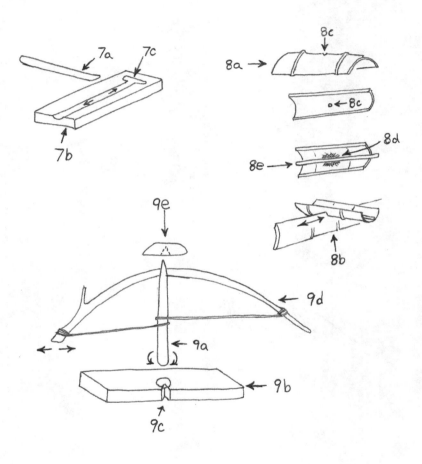

THE BOOK OF LETTERS

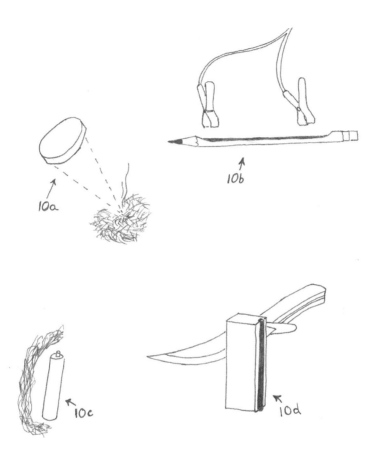

Fire starters can be made from wax and paper or in the wild using sap and grass or moss. Cattail heads, when dry, also work well and can make a fine torch. Birchbark and cedar bark are also useful fire starters as well as having many other uses. The driest firewood and kindling will be dead branches still hanging in the lower sections of trees and brush. You can also find it inside of deadwood by splitting it to the dry interior and cutting away the wet exterior.

Having a fire means you need some place to put it, so here are a few of the fire pits and rings I've used over the years.

The Dakota hole as seen in 11a is a good fire pit for high wind areas but not well suited to rocky or soaked soil. In 11b, it shows the

MICHAEL SCOTT

overhead view of your Dakota hole. In reality this is an earth-formed rocket stove. Air and fuel are fed into one hole, and the flames and heat rise from the other. Be sure to place stones under pot, or you will kill your fire with the trapped smoke. When you dig, save the sod and soil. When done, replace back into your hole topped off with the sod. In this manner, you will leave almost no trace of your fire.

A trench pit like 11c can also be handy in high winds. Just be sure to have the wind hit it widthwise instead of lengthwise. If you keep the trench narrow you can place pots and pans bridging over the open space. If you angle the bottom of the trench from deep to shallow, you can use it for boiling with flames on one end and grilling with coals on the other. When no longer needed, fill again with removed soil and sod, as with the Dakota hole.

In areas of standing water or snow, a raised or insulated platform like 11d is recommended. In this case we have a raised platform with a reflective back. The basic platform is built on stakes with cross pieces holding up the greenwood and soil, the soil being the insulator under the fire, so don't skimp on the soil. In snow you can also create a base or platform for your fire by just using layers of greenwood and branches under your fire. They will eventually burn through, but it takes quite a while.

Fire rings can be easy or complex to construct, depending on your needs and overall size. For long-term camps, a well-designed fire ring like 12a can help a lot with cooking and staying warm. As you build the sides, stones can be added that protrude into the fire ring as indicated by 12b. They provide baking and warming shelves, while a low area as seen in 12c gives you an area for grilling over coals. The high-backed wall demonstrated in 12d are helpful in blocking wind but also provide you with a place to use a cross piece to hold up a pot, blocks a lot of visible light, and at night you can add the upper stones to your bed to help you stay warm for hours. In prairie-type areas sod can be used to replace the stone as seen in 12e. One really important thing to remember: never use wet stones or stones that have been lying in water. The water that is inside of the stone will expand as steam when the stone is heated, causing it to explode, sometimes very violently and with enough force to cause injury.

THE BOOK OF LETTERS

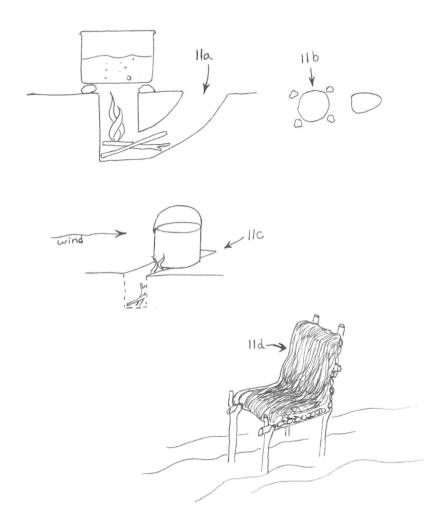

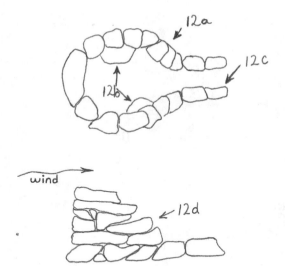

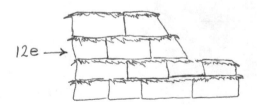

Water

There are three sources of water:

Aspirated water—Fog, water vapor, and your breath are all ways of seeing examples of this in action. You will see 13a demonstrating this: simply tie a plastic bag over a live branch or vegetation. As the day passes, you will see water droplets form on the interior of the bag as drinkable water. Adding a small stone as seen in 13b will help keep one corner down. And 14a shows another method of doing the same type of action. Start by digging a hole about two feet deep or deeper but small enough around that your plastic can fully cover the top of the hole. As 14c indicates, vegetation is placed inside the hole, but

THE BOOK OF LETTERS

almost anything containing water can be. In saltwater or polluted water areas, you can put containers of the bad water in place of the plant matter. In the center of the pit, you place your catch cup as shown in 14b. Ehen the plastic is over the pit, this is where the water droplets will fall. You can also do this using a bottle of dirty water inside the bag and catching the evaporation on the interior walls of the bag.

Once the hole is set up and ready, plastic sheeting is spread over the top, and the soil that was removed from the hole is piled in a ring, sealing the edge of the plastic at the edge of your hole as seen in 14e. In the center of the plastic, you set a small stone or weight directly over your catch cup as indicated by 14f. These are best opened at night after temperatures have cooled to prevent the loss of water vapors, or if available, add a drinking tube.

Stored or static water—Ponds, holding tanks, trapped pools, and seeps are good examples. When looking for water, watch for game trail and the landscape. Animals need water as much as you do, and game trail often leads to water sooner or later. Landscape will tell you likely places to look and what areas will shed water or dry out quicker. Water always follows the path of least resistance and gravity, so look with these things in mind. If you can't find visible water, seeps are your next option. Seeps can be chancy because you'll lose both sweat and energy in digging, but in the right location it can produce a lot of water. Here are a few standard suggestions. In 15a, you see the inside of a creek bed with living vegetation on its banks; green leaves are a good sign of water. As you see in 15b, at the base of a cliff or steep hill, this works especially well if there are clay layers in the soil. When at a body of saltwater, 15c shows to dig after the first set of sand dunes or one hundred yards from where the sand begins to dry. Dig only till you hit freshwater; digging deeper will only allow saltwater to infiltrate the seep. Another type of seep is done by tapping trees like the birch or maple as well as vines like grape. However, know your tree and vines to be sure of what you're drinking.

Flowing water—Rivers, streams, and rain are a few examples. No matter how good the water looks, it's always best to purify before you drink. If the water is salty or contaminated, it can be distilled using two bottles as seen in 16a, or a variation can be made utilizing the same principles. 16b shows where the two bottles can be connected using foil, bark, or mud, don't make it airtight, as seen in 16c, or a bottle may bust. The longer the distance is between the two bottles, the better the condensation that produces the drinkable water. The dirty water is placed on the 16d side, and low heat is applied. Heat can be from any source, even solar. The bottle as indicated by 16e is cooled either in water or with wet rags. The cool sides of the bottle allow the water vapor to collect and drip to the bottom as drinkable water. There are numerous types of these distillers all using the same principle, so use your imagination and improvise.

Remember that all water should be purified by boiling before drinking and, if at all possible, by boiling for at least ten minutes. If the water is suspected to have toxins, salts, or heavy metals it must be distilled.

Boiling without a pot can be accomplished in many ways, especially when heated stones are employed. In 17a is an animal skin that is hooked over four stakes flesh side in. You can see in 17b green birchbark with the folded corners held with split pins. In 17c is a simple felt hat; some canvas hats work for this as well. And 17d is a hole that has been lined as shown in 17e, with plastic or water-retaining fabric. A piece of cloth, bark, or sticks are laid at 17f to keep the hot stones from melting the plastic. Using forked sticks as shown in 17g allows you to move the heated stones to the water easily. As the stones cool, replace them with the hot ones and continue until your water has boiled a sufficient time to kill any bugs.

THE BOOK OF LETTERS

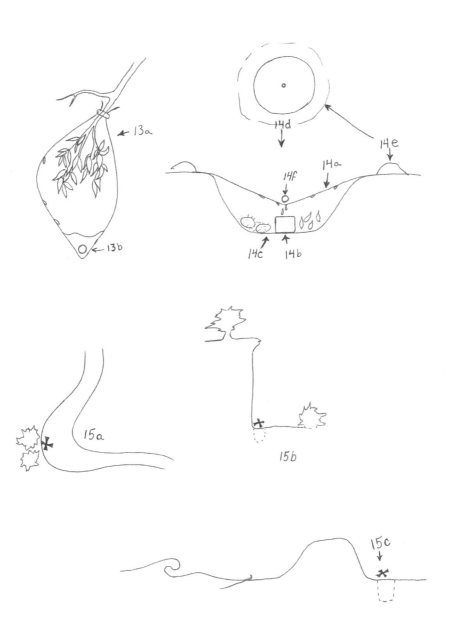

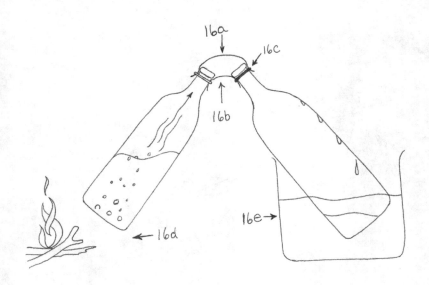
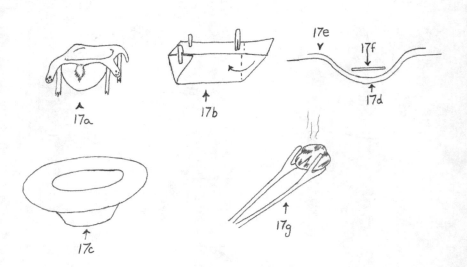

THE BOOK OF LETTERS

Traps and Snares

Traps are usually spring action or weight driven and are, in most cases, designed to kill when triggered. While there are many traps and many designs, there are some common types of triggers or releases. I have found that one of the most common ones is the toggle trigger, although I've also heard it called many names. The basic setup requires five parts: 18a is the spring action from an overhead branch or a counter weight, 18b is the toggle, 18c is the bait stick or trigger, 18d is your fulcrum point, and 18e is your trigger point. In figure 19, all the letters correspond with the parts as shown in figure 18. In the field there are many ways to use this setup; figure 19 shows two possible arrangements. The top image is a spring snare using the toggle trigger, while the spring tension is coming from an overhead branch. In 19e, it shows how the snares are set in place; this forces the animal to put their head through the snare to reach the bait. And 19g points to the distance between the snare and the trigger stick; it should be no less than the length of the head and neck of your intended game, with a bit more added for the animal's reflexes. These are best used on game trails and with brush or stakes blocking the sides of your snares to guide the animal in.

The lower trap is a foot trap and is basically the same snare as above, only set horizontally and a platform placed on the trigger stick. These can be useful in catching larger game to detain them till you can arrive to dispatch them.

In figure 20, you can see another variation in the use of the toggle, but using the same principles, this type of trap is known as a deadfall. In this case, the downward force of the stone (20f) gives pressure to (20a) which supplies the spring necessary to put the trigger under tension. It (20a) must be long enough to allow the stone to clear (20d) when it falls, and a center notch can help when seating in on top of 20d. It (20e) is simply a point on the stone that you can make your trigger stick hook to. If the stone is too smooth, you can use another stone to chip or scratch a place that's suitable.

Another deadfall can be found in figure 21, this one using only sticks to form a figure-four trap. Touching the bait on 21c dislodges it from the notch on 21d, allowing 21a to move and releases 21f. This in turn, hopefully, kills the animal, leaving you with needed food.

Snares for the most part simply entangle your prey or restrain them till you can dispatch them. They are useful in areas where small game is plentiful, and there are plenty of brushy areas with game trails. Once you have found your potential spot, rig up your snare as seen in 22a. If the sides of the trail are too open, they can be blocked as shown in 22b with stakes, brush, or rocks. You can see in 22c an overhead view of a typical snare layout and a good one for rabbits and small pigs, as well as several other animals. Snares can also be placed on, over, or around bait as well, with good results.

A simple addition to the snare as seen in 23a is the slip trigger, and 23b is a stake with a notch set to accept 23a and a spring pole or overhead branch. When the animal struggles against the snare, it dislodges the trigger, activating the spring. It's a pretty easy and self-explanatory, so I think you can figure it out.

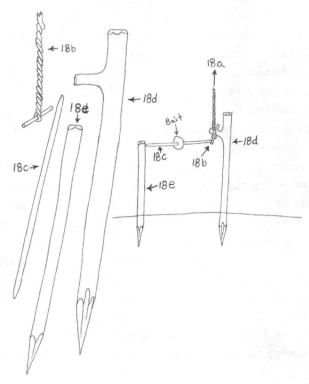

THE BOOK OF LETTERS

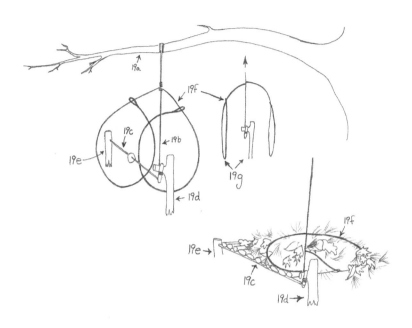

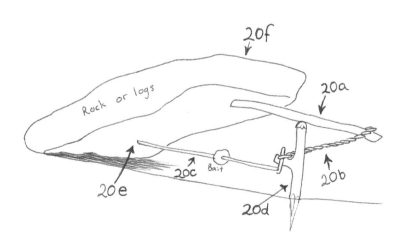

MICHAEL SCOTT

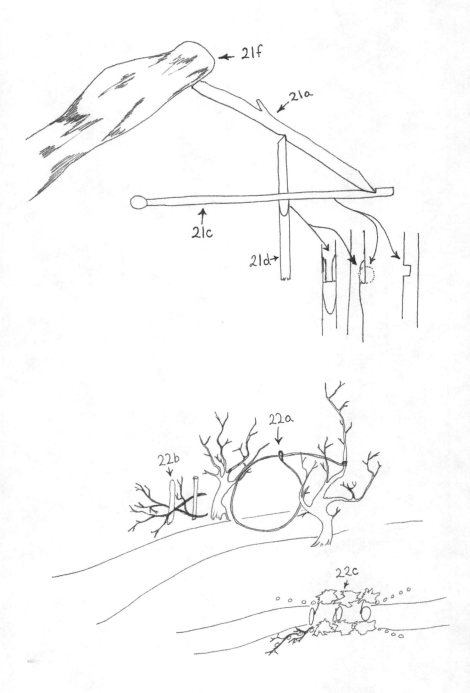

THE BOOK OF LETTERS

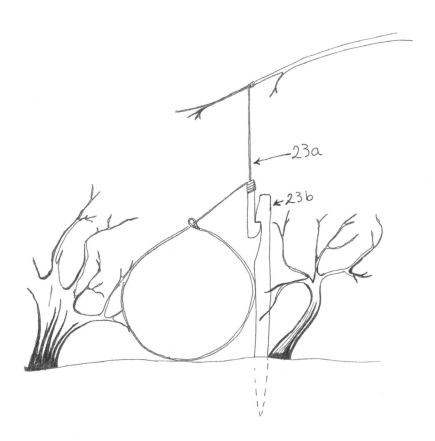

Wilderness Fishing

In a survival situation, fishing can be an easy way to glean food from the local waterways. Traps like the ones shown in figure 24 are, by far, the easiest way to procure fish while leaving you free to tend to other needs. In 24a, you are shown how the body of the trap is constructed using branches or reeds, and then grass, vines, or reeds are weaved in, making a tube-shaped basket. The cap is made the same way as seen by 24b and then attached at the top. And 24c shows how it fits together and how the opening needs to correspond to the size of your intended catch. Finally, 24d shows how it is placed into a stream and how rocks or brush can be used to direct the fish toward your trap.

A variation of this trap can be seen in 24e, where the stream itself is turned into the trap. By adding a back wall (24f) to a funneled front, you can trap fish in small creeks, streams, and tidal flows.

A simple fishhook called a gouge hook as seen in 25a can be easily made from bone, wood, or metal. In 25b, it shows how it is typically baited and when it is swallowed it lodges in the fish's throat as shown in 25c. Other fishhooks can be made from wire, bent bamboo or bone, thorns, or a variety of other materials—just use your imagination. Bait can also be anything from bugs and worms to bits of cloth, jewelry, or feathers.

When cordage isn't available, fish spears are a good option if the location permits. Two things to remember with fish spears: one is the water creates an optical illusion and bends your point of aim, so it is best to have a little of your spear in the water to help your vision correct this. The other is that multiple barbed points on a fish spear helps both in hitting the fish as well as retaining it. When possible, push your spear down till you hit the bottom of the creek to set the spear into the fish before trying to lift it out of the water.

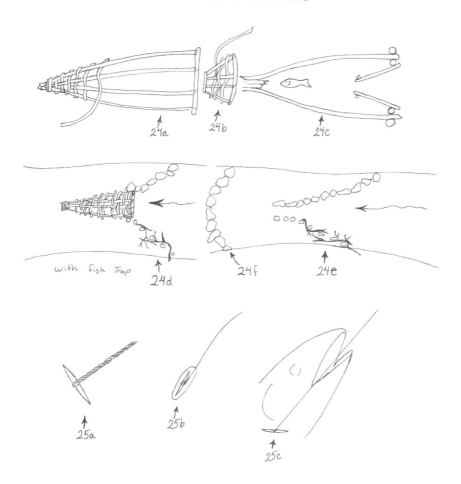

Hunting and Protection Weapons

Man has been producing weapons since the dawn of time, from thrown rocks to nuclear bombs. For this reason, I won't cover to many examples but rather share some basic designs and principles.

Hunting with a simple thrust spear will work but is usually best utilized from a raised position such as a tree stand. Placing your bait under the tree stand will bring your game within reach. Hunting this way will work in the right settings but greatly limits your range. If you plan to throw it, there are a couple of guidelines. The spear tip should always be heavier than the butt. A spear with a light tip

MICHAEL SCOTT

will veer upward when thrown, and if it's too heavy it will nosedive and often flip on impact. A well-balanced spear should be slightly tip-heavy when held at the center point. Wooden tips can be fire hardened by lightly toasting it over coals then sharpened.

Thrown or launched projectiles increases your range and your hunting capabilities. Throwing with just your arm limits your distance and power to only that which can be obtained by the length of your arm. By adding a lever or sling, however, you can double this length and thus the power plus velocity. The staff sling as seen in 26a is a good example of this; the staff is five or more feet long with a sling attached to its top end as shown in 26b. One end of the sling is bound to the staff, while the other end has a slip loop that fits over a finger at the top end of the staff (26a). Below the staff sling is how to use it. In 26c, it shows us the carrying position with end of the sling and stone held in place by hand. And 26d shows the firing position: as you move your upper body forward, your arms snap the sling end up and over, while your other hand pulls down and back. As the staff descends toward your line of sight to the target, you should appear as in figure 26e, releasing the sling and propelling the stone. Your release timing can be adjusted by trimming or shortening the finger.

This type of leverage can also be applied as shown in 27a to long arrows or spears. And 27b shows the lever and how it is held and mounted to the end of your throwing arrow. As with the staff sling, it is best used with an overhead throwing style.

Throwing sticks are quite handy in areas with high rabbit counts but are useful for other small-to-medium game as well as personal protection. Lashing two sharpened sticks together as in 28a can produce a deadly weapon for both hunting and protecting. Throwing sticks like 28b are easy to make and use both for hunting and close-quarters combat. Sticks like this are best carved with the head heavier than the handle, to promote spin. They don't need to be heavy as that only slows the throw and shortens range, so make them only as heavy as needed for your game.

When hunting, always try to be downwind, or your prey can smell you before you get a chance to see them. If you find a well-used game trail, it is usually better it find a place to sit and watch the trail

THE BOOK OF LETTERS

from a hidden position rather than to try stalking, especially if you're not used to the woods.

If you choose to stalk, you must try to learn to be invisible or blend in with your environment. Remember that movement out of place or time draws attention. Move when the surroundings do, such as when the wind blows or others animals move. Wear colors that blend into the natural landscape and cover anything shiny. Adding bits of plants to your clothing will help you to blend in even more, and the closer you get to the ambient nature of your surroundings, the harder you will be to see. Adaptability is important when you learn the art of hunting.

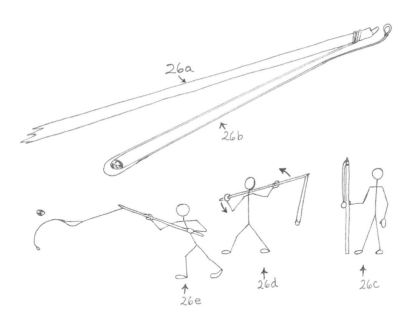

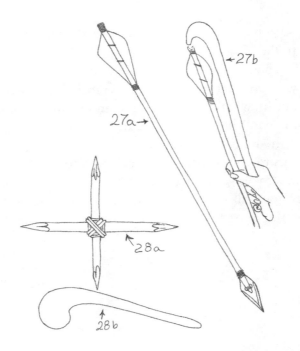

Wild Edibles

The gleaning of wild edibles by someone uneducated is a dangerous endeavor, but there are many plants that are easy to identify and memorize. Study the plants in your area and learn from educated sources. Many plants can be found nationwide while others will only grow in small areas. Avoid mushrooms unless you are experienced. Stress and hunger can cloud your judgment, so unless you know it positively, it's better to go without. Two easy-to-identify plants here in North America are the aggregate berry as seen in 29a and 29b. Aggregate berries include such berries as blackberries, raspberries, salmon berries, loganberries, and mulberries to name a few.

The other plant is the cattail plant, one of the most useful plants you can learn and find nationwide by ponds, streams, swamps, and drainage ditches. When green the inner stalk can be eaten and are quite tasty, and the green top can be roasted or boiled to eat, while the roots can be eaten year-round. When the heads pollinate, the pollen can be stripped off and used like flour for baking. The leaves can be woven together to make mats, hats, or baskets. It's a good plant to know and is so widely spread that it's rare to not find some within your area.

As you learn plant identification, you'll be able to find food in places that might surprise you, like your local parks, woods, and canals. Things like rose hips, huckleberries, miner's lettuce, Indian potatoes, and more can often be found. Remember, you can go three weeks without food and survive, so better to go hungry than to eat something you don't know and risk poisoning yourself. One thing I always recommend to people who are just learning survival is to go three days without food. Do it on a weekend or whenever you have the time to experiment. The reason for this is to teach yourself that you can survive going hungry and help yourself learn the feeling and how to cope with it. Lessons like this will help you build knowledge about yourself and your abilities, adding to your mental preparedness.

Survival Kits

In any survival situation, your survival gear will be what you have with and what you might be able to obtain from your location. For this reason, building your survival kits in layers is important. Big kits with everything in them are great but rarely with you when a

MICHAEL SCOTT

crisis occurs. Your first layer will be your knowledge and experience from practice; next will be the items in your pockets. Start with small kits then build in size, with the larger kits including food and water. The more kits you have stashed in your vehicle, office, home, day pack, and elsewhere, the better your chances are of having one close when you need it. In 30a you can see a survival kit I have made many of over the years; the body of the kit is an empty Zippo lighter. With it are the contents and how it's put together; 30b shows how to cut your magnesium block and ferro rod. The numbers show where certain items are while the others are all contained in the lighter body.

- Medical tape
- Electrical tape
- Braided fishing line, along with fishing leader
- Duct tape
- Rubber bands (these also help hold the lid closed and the fishing line in place)
- Magnesium/ferro rod as seen in 30b
- Birthday candle or fire starter made with wax and tissue paper
- A few waterproof, strike-anywhere matches, glue, and a striker strip inside the lid if desired
- Fishhooks of small and medium size, a lure, and a few flies
- Needle and thread
- Razor blade or X-Acto blade
- Balloon or condom
- Bouillon cube or salt packet
- Piece of hot glue stick
- Steel wool, small piece
- Stiff wire or paperclip

If there is any room left, fill it with anything you can fit in that may be useful. Remember not to make it too bulky, or you'll soon find yourself leaving it at home.

THE BOOK OF LETTERS

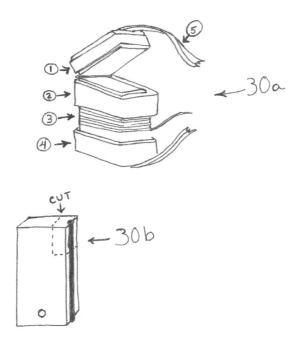

Direction

Having a compass and a map of your area is always the best way to go, but things don't always go as planned, so here are a few other helpful tips.

Most people know how to find the Big Dipper as seen in figure 31a. The last two stars in the cup of the dipper as indicated by 31b point to the North Star.

A magnetized steel needle or wire will always point north and south. To use, you float it on water, place a leaf or piece of paper on the water to float, then place the needle on it as seen in 32a.

As simple as this may sound, it is often forgotten that the sun travels east to west. A ninety-degree angle from that is north or south; just be sure of your sunrise and sunset locations.

If you are near flowing water, you can follow it down stream. Cricks turn into creeks and then into streams. Streams run into rivers, and rivers run past towns and cities. The only problem with following streams in some wilderness areas is that travel can be complicated because of waterfalls, steep canyon walls, and brush.

When you discover that you are lost or confused by your surroundings, stop. Take a few moments to get past the moment of panic and clear your head. When ready, stand still and look around you to see if there is anything that brings back any memories. You're looking for a trail or markers of some kind. If there isn't, move to the next search. Look at the landscape and mountains to see if there are any indicators that might give you clues to where you might be. If not, move to step three. This step is best done in daylight, and trying to do it in the dark rarely proves successful. From where you are standing, start to search the ground for telltale signs of your passage. Footprints or scuff marks, overturned leaves, torn moss, broken spiderwebs, broken branches, and bent grass are all things that can reveal your passing. If all these fail to help you locate yourself, then in most cases it is better for you to remain where you are and help others find you. Yelling, banging on trees or logs, using a whistle, and a smoky fire are all good ways of helping searchers find you.

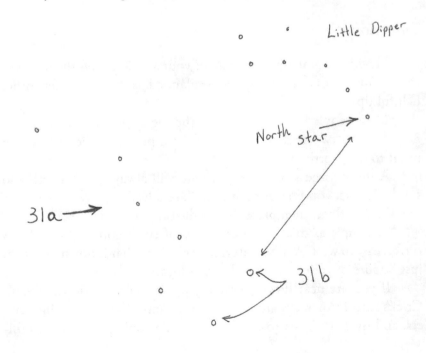

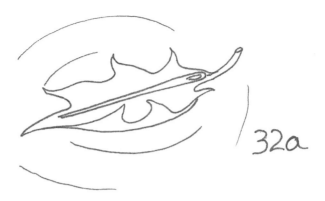

Hey, Cricket,

I just sketched up a couple projects I'm starting to work on, one's a telescope and the other is a repeating bow. This bow has an eight-shot cylinder, but I may make it smaller and more streamlined. It looks like it would be pretty simple to operate and aim for a novice shooter as well as being just plain fun. Once I give this thing a try, I'll have to figure out how to get one to you. Take care, Cricket. Study hard, practice what I've taught you, and prepare. Now it's back to the workshop for me, I've things to build and designs to play with. Come see me soon, I'll be waiting.

GP

MICHAEL SCOTT

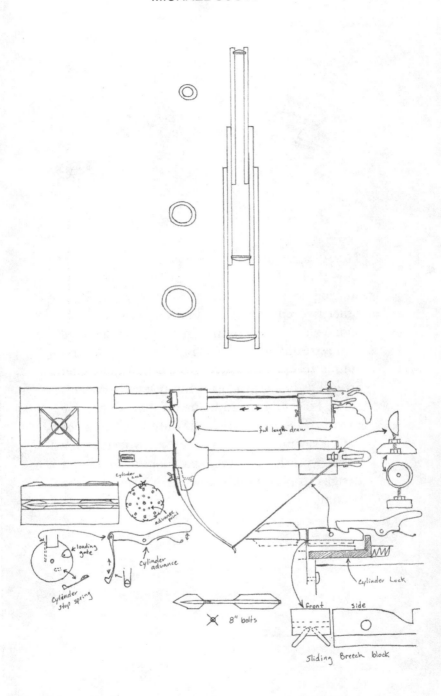

ABOUT THE AUTHOR

Mr. Scott has done private art internationally and written numerous children's stories, plays, and articles; however, this is his first full-length novel. While residing high in the hills of Central Oregon, he lives quietly on his farm, seen here with his beloved companions Karma, Hog, and DD. He prefers the woods and hills to the hustle and noise of cities or towns.

Combining his years of teaching outdoor skills with those of storytelling, he has created a world that captures the imagination and makes us question the possible path of our future. When not sharing his knowledge or talents, he can be found roaming the hills or working on another soon-to-be-published book.

CPSIA information can be obtained
at www.ICGtesting.com
Printed in the USA
FSHW012352041121
85921FS